# THE DARK REALM

## FEYLAND BOOK 1

## ANTHEA SHARP

FIDDLEHEAD PRESS

# DEDICATION

*For all the readers in my family – but most especially, for Brynn.*

## PROLOGUE

Jennet faced the Dark Queen, her mage staff at the ready. Excitement fizzed through her blood like it was carbonated. This was it. She'd completed the quests, mastered each level of the game, and made it here. The final boss fight.

"Fair Jennet." The queen's voice was laced with stars and shadow. "You think to best me in battle?" A faint smile crossed her pitiless, beautiful face. Her dress swirled around her like tatters of midnight mist.

"I plan on it," Jennet said. She tucked a strand of blond hair behind her ear, then shook off the sudden anxiety that settled on her shoulders, cold as snow.

She had no idea what this particular fight held. Feyland was the hardest sim she'd ever played, full of weird twists and turns. She thought about it all the time. The game filtered into her dreams, shaded the edge of her days. Sometimes the computer-generated world felt more real than her ordinary life.

"Very well," the queen said. "I accept your challenge."

Jennet couldn't see any weapons on her opponent, and that dress was no substitute for armor. Safe bet that this was going to be a magical duel, spell-caster against spell-caster. Jennet flexed her fingers around the smooth wood of her staff. Anticipation spiked through her, tightening her breath.

Fantastical creatures watched from the edges of the clearing: feral-faced women with gossamer wings, dark riders with red-eyed hounds at their heels. The sound of drums and pipes wove through the shadows. Overhead, a sliver of moon tangled in the black branches of the trees. Then, between one heartbeat and the next, silence fell.

A dark figure stepped forward, forbidding in midnight armor and a wicked helm, and Jennet's stomach clenched. The Black Knight. She'd barely beaten him in an earlier quest. If he got involved in this fight, she was in severe trouble.

He held his gauntleted fist high and grated out a single word. "Begin."

It echoed eerily through the glade, and the fey-folk let out a rough cheer. There was no one to cheer for Jennet.

Without hesitation, she tipped her staff and shot a bolt of fiery white light at the queen. A sphere of shadow appeared, blocking her attack and swallowing the fire into its dark depths. More spheres materialized and began floating toward her, called by the Dark Queen. Jennet ducked and wove, avoiding their deadly touch.

Lightning crackled from her staff, illuminating the clearing with shocking white light, but the queen evaded her bolts. Still, Jennet kept pressing the attack. The dark spheres were multiplying now, bobbing in the air on all sides. A low, menacing hum surrounded her as she tried to find a clear shot.

She couldn't afford any mistakes - but the fight was pushing her to her limits. Worry started to nibble at the edges of her concentration. She just had to watch for an opening... there. She took aim and sent another bolt crackling through the air.

White fire sizzled and Jennet heard the queen gasp. Yes! She could do it. She could beat this game. The first player ever to claim victory over Feyland.

A dark sphere brushed against her shoulder. Ice stabbed into her skin, sent numbness down her arm until she could barely hold onto her staff. She stumbled back, trying to regain the rhythm of the battle. Keep breathing. Keep fighting. But where was the queen? The place where her opponent had stood was now filled with twisting shadows.

Everything rippled, as though the clearing was made of cloth billowing in a sudden gust. Jennet heard high, chiming laughter as she fell backward...

And landed in an ornate chair set before a feasting table. *What?* She jumped up, heart racing, and knocked the edge of the table. A goblet sitting in front of her shook, sending a drop of deep red liquid to stain the white tablecloth.

"Sit down, Fair Jennet," the queen said from her place across the table. "This is the next stage of our battle."

Pale candles in thorny candelabra illuminated the feast. Their silver flames reflected in the queen's fathomless eyes.

"You changed the rules! You can't do that." Jennet's legs felt shaky as she edged back into her chair. She was so not prepared for this.

The queen laughed. It was the sound of ice shattering on a black lake. "Of course I can. This is my court. My realm. You are but a visitor. Please - drink." She waved one delicate hand at the goblet.

"No thanks."

Jennet's mouth said the words, but her hand reached out anyway and lifted the heavy silver goblet. A sweet, thick smell drifted from the cup. Roses and burnt sugar. The edge of metal touched her lips.

No. She was not going to do this. The queen might try to control their battle, but she could still fight back. Fingers trembling from effort, Jennet forced the goblet away. The air around her was sticky and nearly solid, like dough. She pushed against it, her breath coming in gasps, until at last the cup touched the table.

"Very well." The queen's voice was edged with frost. "If you disdain my hospitality, then you must answer a riddle."

That seemed safer than drinking whatever was in the goblet. And the game wasn't giving her a lot of other options. "A riddle? All right."

The candles flared and the queen's eyes glowed. "Listen then, and listen well, the answer to this riddle tell, or forfeit of thyself will be, and never more wilt thou be free."

Jennet shivered. The queen's voice was ominous, her

words intoned with deep meaning. Whatever happened, it was clear that failing to answer the riddle carried a price. Jennet curled her fingers tightly into her palms and tried not to show the fear flickering through her.

"Ask me your riddle," she said.

"As soon as it begins, it is ending. Without form, still it moves. When it is gone, it yet remains." The queen smiled, sharp as a blade. "You have three guesses."

"Ah..." Jennet's mouth was dry. Her mind beat against the riddle like a bird trapped behind glass. Without taste or form. Something powerful, but insubstantial. "Is it the wind?"

A low sighing went through the branches of the dark trees. The candle nearest her snuffed out, as though some invisible hand had abruptly doused the flame.

The queen shook her head. "One chance gone."

A circle of watchers had formed around the table. Lithe women with gossamer wings gathered beside the queen. Gnarled brown creatures with sharp teeth and fingers that were too long for their hands swayed next to them. Red-capped goblins and capering sprites - they all watched her with avid, gleaming eyes.

Freaky. This whole battle had turned beyond strange. Jennet pulled in a deep breath, though her chest felt tight, and gave another answer. "Music?"

The second she said the word, she knew it was wrong. She shivered as a second candle flame went out. The watchers surrounding her tittered, and the low breeze rustled the branches.

Jennet squeezed her eyes closed, blocking out the shadowy glade, the fantastical figures, the wicked curve of the Dark Queen's smile. Her heart thumped loudly in her chest, and she tasted the metal edge of fear on her tongue. Think. She had to figure this out.

"Your time has run, Fair Jennet. Speak your final answer."

She opened her eyes, to see that the Dark Queen had risen to her feet. A single candle burned between them.

"I..."

Panic banged through her, like a hundred doors slamming shut. The watching creatures grew still and silent. Even the wind quieted, waiting. She had to answer.

"Is it... a dream?" The words floated from her mouth and hovered there, just beyond her lips.

In the silence that followed, Jennet felt shadows gathering closer. Dread crawled through her, carrying the awful sensation of failure.

The last candle died. A high, wailing music started up, the keening cry of pipes swirling through the air. Slowly, the queen shook her head. Diamonds sparkled like frost in her dark hair.

"No," she said. "You have lost. Now, mortal girl, I take my due."

The queen held up a hollow crystal sphere in one hand. With the other, she scribed strange gestures in the air. Her fingers left glowing streaks of silver against the darkness. Then she pointed straight at Jennet.

"Ahh!" A sharp pain speared through Jennet, as though

the queen had stabbed her in the chest. She doubled over, gasping, while agony iced her blood. Oh god. It hurt.

"Behold, Fair Jennet," the queen said. "The answer is Life. Your essence is captured here. It will serve us well."

Jennet looked up, tears clouding her vision. The queen held the sphere aloft. It wasn't empty any more. Inside was a bright swirl of color, like rainbow flames. They pulsed and danced, trapped inside their crystal prison. Wavering, calling to her.

"How," Jennet forced the words out through lips tight with pain, "how do I get that back?"

Every game had a second chance, a third. You kept fighting the last battle until you finally won. Failure wasn't permanent. Not like in real life.

The queen laughed, and the sound carried a bitter chill. "You cannot. Without a champion, you are lost. Now go. Go! I send thee, defeated, from the Dark Realm."

Pain wrenched through Jennet and she screamed. Golden light blinded her senses and she swirled through a sickening vertigo. Blackness waited, merciful and dark, on the other side. She opened her arms to it, and fell.

JENNET WOKE, aching, in the sim chair. Her fingers were stiff inside the gaming gloves, and when she sat forward, fire exploded in her shoulder. She could barely lift her arm, but it was impossible to take off the helmet one-handed. Trying not to whimper, she gritted her teeth against the agony and pulled off her gear.

She had lost.

Feyland was more than just a sim game. The clues had been there all along, but she hadn't paid enough attention until now. Now, when it was too late. And she'd done worse than lose the game.

There was an icy hollow in the middle of her chest. The Dark Queen had taken something from her - something she feared she couldn't live without. Bright flames trapped inside a magical sphere. Her *mortal essence*, the queen had said.

She had to get it back.

# CHAPTER 1

Jennet leaned her forehead against the tinted window of the grav-car and watched as the unfamiliar neighborhoods went from decent to tattered. So much had changed in the last few weeks. She couldn't believe she was here, friendless and alone, starting a new school.

And no closer to winning back what the Dark Queen had stolen.

She sighed, and her breath left a mist on the window glass, obscuring the boarded-up windows and graffiti-festooned buildings along Crestview's main street. From what she'd seen so far, this decaying town in the middle of the country's flatlands was barely wired. Did the kids here even know what a good sim-system looked like?

Dad had offered to pay for her to stay as a boarding student at Middland Prep, back in their old town, when the company transferred him here. He thought she had a choice, but she didn't. Not with part of her soul trapped inside a computer game. She couldn't get it back without going into Feyland, and the only system that could even run the game was Dad's prototype Full-D. Which no way was he leaving behind. So here she was, too.

The car slid to a stop outside a blocky gray building with *Crestview High* stamped in concrete over the front doors. Students funneled into the school, trampling the thin grass out front.

"Here we are, Miss Carter," said George, her dad's chauffeur.

"Great," she said.

She wanted to make George turn the car around. Wanted to crawl back into bed and pull the covers over her head. Or power-up her system and lose herself in an easy game - some fluffy simulated world where the goals were catching butter-flies and collecting candies. Something pretty and safe.

But virtual worlds weren't safe. She'd learned that the hard way.

She still had nightmares about that final battle. Some-times, in the deepest hours, she woke in a cold sweat with the Dark Queen's laughter cutting through her. A computer game shouldn't be able to affect the real world. But it did. Jennet pressed her lips together so hard she could feel the edges of her teeth.

"Whenever you're ready, Miss Carter." George swiveled in the front seat to look at her. "I would like to be able to inform your father you weren't late for your first day."

Her stomach clenched, as though she'd eaten rocks for breakfast instead of toast. She squeezed her eyes shut, then blinked them open. Staying in the back seat wasn't going to solve her problems. She *had* to find a gamer here - someone who was even more skilled than herself. Someone adept at wielding a virtual sword. Someone who could help her win free of Feyland. Permanently.

*Without a champion, you are lost.* The Dark Queen's words echoed in her mind.

"Miss Carter?" The car door slid open.

"All right, I'm going."

Forcing her fingers to unclench, Jennet grabbed her satchel and stepped out. Late fall air lay clammy on her skin, and a wave of dizziness made her cling to the door.

Breathe. Don't let George see her weakness. She caught her balance and moved onto the sidewalk. The grav-car skimmed silently away, and she turned to face the school.

A metallic beeping from the building made the few stragglers scramble for the doors. She swallowed back the dry fear lodged in her throat, and followed.

Inside, it smelled like schools always smelled - a mix of cleaning products, sour lunch, and faintly, old-fashioned books. A security checkpoint loomed just inside the front doors. Her steps slowed. This was nothing like Middland Prep. Were the students here really that dangerous? Nervousness squeezed her lungs as the big guard waved her through the scanners.

No alarms went off, and she began breathing again. When she asked where the office was, the guard pointed to the first door down the hall.

The secretary, a thin, dark-haired man, peered at her through his glasses. "Can I help you?"

"I'm a new sophomore. Jennet Carter."

"One of the VirtuMax kids?" He said the company name like it left a bad taste in his mouth.

"Right. Um, my dad has been in contact with the school?"

The secretary poked the screen in front of him. "Ah yes, Carter. I'm transferring some additional forms over. Make sure you fill them out in full. The school will issue you a tablet so you can access your account."

He pulled a battered tablet out of a drawer and set it in front of her. It was an old Epox, outdated beyond belief. Her hopes slipped another notch. This place was a technological wasteland. How was she going to find someone here who could help her?

The secretary pushed a piece of paper toward her. "If you'll sign here—"

"I have my own." She pulled out her brand-new tablet and watched the secretary's eyebrows lift as if pulled up by strings. She scrolled through the menu until she found the red and blue *Crestview High* icon, and then tilted the screen toward him. "This it?"

"Yes. And you'll want to be careful with that tablet. Make sure you don't leave it unattended. The school takes no responsibility for lost or missing items." He dropped the battered Epox back into the drawer, then glanced at his own screen, his eyebrows settling. "You have twenty-four seconds to get to class. Early World History with Ms. Lewis. End of the building, room 114. No running."

Great. Like she needed to be late on her first day. She slung her satchel over her shoulder and pushed herself to move faster down the hall. A boy wearing a blue jacket dashed past, and a brown-haired girl disappeared into a nearby room. Other than that, the halls were deserted.

There - room 114. Worry skittered up her spine as she pulled the door open.

The plump, red-haired teacher standing by the desk glanced up as she entered. "Miss Carter?"

Jennet nodded, her skin prickling as she felt the attention in the room shift. All the kids were looking at her. Sizing her up: her hair, her clothes, the way she stood. Her heart thumped against her ribs, but she forced her breathing to stay slow. She lifted one hand to smooth her hair back and heard a murmur as they caught sight of her wrist implant.

A quick scan of the room confirmed there were only two other kids with wrist-chips. They met her gaze with serious relief. The rest either turned their heads away or narrowed their eyes, giving her you-don't-belong-here-we-hate-you looks.

"Your desk is at the end of the row." The teacher pointed. "Welcome to Crestview."

Welcome. Sure. Jennet slid into her seat just as the second bell blared through the room.

"Class," Ms. Lewis said, "please access file 73 in your history doc."

Jennet pulled out her tablet and tried to ignore the whispers that followed. Maybe she should have taken the old Epox - but she shouldn't have to be embarrassed that her gear was cutting-edge.

She straightened her shoulders and scanned the room. The two VirtuMax kids smiled at her. One was a girl with dark hair, the other, a mousy-looking boy. Like herself, they held shiny, newer-model tablets. The rest of the class though.... Despair crawled through her.

Almost none of the Crestview students had their own tablets. The clunky school-issued Epoxes were the standard. How could any of these kids be 'leet players if they didn't even have the most basic tech? This was like being transported back to the Middle Ages.

Still, she *had* to consider the possibilities. For all she knew, that brown-haired boy in the back row was a flawless gamer. She thought he was watching her, his green eyes hostile behind the swag of hair in front of his face.

If not him, what about the blond guy sitting two seats over? Seeing her looking, he winked and blew her a kiss.

On second thought, no. Neither of them could be the sim hero she needed.

Half of her wanted to put her head down on the desk and cry. The other half smoldered, ready to jump up and start yelling curses at the universe. Instead, she stared at the schedule glowing on her screen. Six classes. Six chances to find someone to help her.

If she didn't get to the Dark Queen soon, she was dead.

# CHAPTER 2

Tam watched the new girl. Sure, it looked like he was taking notes while Ms. Lewis droned on about ancient civilizations, but under cover of his moving hand, under the hair he never bothered brushing out of his eyes, he was watching.

He always watched. Everything. Never said much, but that was okay. It kept him invisible and out of trouble.

So, the new girl. Jennet Carter. Everything about her screamed 'elite.' Elitist, too. She tucked a strand of pale hair behind one ear, and the chip implant in her wrist glinted. More proof that she didn't belong here.

"Welcome to Crestview High," Ms. Lewis said.

Jennet only nodded. She didn't look too happy to be there, and for a moment, unwilling sympathy moved through him. Everyone was staring at her. It couldn't be easy, coming into a new school after the year started - even if you were one of the privileged. Which, here in Crestview, made you a severe outsider.

She sat down and pulled a shiny new-model tablet out of her bag. Clearly the school ones weren't good enough for her. Though, to be honest, some of those tablets barely worked. If he had the option, he'd bring his own gear, too.

She obviously lived in The View, the compound VirtuMax was building for their company employees. He'd heard the houses there were huge, that they were putting in specialty stores, a g-board park. Probably money falling off the bushes, too. All you needed to get in was a wrist-chip.

What would that be like? Wave your arm and have the gates of paradise open. Instant access to a safe and sanitary little world, full of the best tech money could buy. A fat credit account, probably kept full-up by a doting daddykins. Strings fully attached. He grimaced and rubbed his own wrist.

No thanks. Better to be under the radar, far as he was concerned. Not that the VirtuMax kids would know anything about being chewed up and spit out by the authorities. Even the regular townies thought they lived in the real world, but they were dreaming. Nothing was grittier and more real than the Exe. Even the locals tried to avoid his part of Crestview.

But despite his dislike of the new girl, he couldn't stop sneaking looks. There was something about Jennet Carter. Something more than her long pale-gold hair and the high curve of her cheekbones. She seemed fragile. Mysterious.

He shook his head. The last thing Crestview High

needed was another VirtuMax entitlement diva walking the halls.

At lunch, he and his friend Marny claimed a table near the back of the cafeteria. He'd known Marny for years - she lived on the outskirts of the Exe. But where he was lean and agile, she was easily as large as the big guys on the football team. Most kids avoided her, like being fat was a contagious disease. But she didn't care.

Marny was who she was and the rest of the world could go blink. She was unapologetic to the point of rudeness, and he liked that, how actual she was. Plus, she noticed stuff. Not as much as him, but enough to make it worthwhile to hang with her. Sometimes. There were plenty of days he wanted to be alone, when he was all edges and sharpness. But not today.

"Look at her," Marny said, pointing with her chin across the cafeteria. She made her eyes narrow and took a long, slurping drink of her cola, as if to show she wasn't impressed.

"Who?"

He knew though. Jennet Carter was pretty hard to miss. He'd been aware of her from the moment she walked into the cafeteria. It was like an itch. Maybe if he ignored it, it would just go away. Uncomfortable, yeah, but scratching always made it worse. So he tried not to stare at Jennet's sky-blue eyes, or notice the way she moved. Though now that Marny was pointing her out, he had to.

"That new girl, the rich bitch. She's one of *them*." Her voice was scornful, but he could hear the jealousy underneath.

Could taste it in his own mouth.

Them. The VirtuMax kids. They'd started showing up this summer, with their money and grav-cars and g-boards. Their privilege and arrogance. He pulled his battered brown coat tighter around his shoulders. He wanted nothing to do with them.

Marny took another gulp of her drink, then wadded up her napkin. "Are you done yet? Come on." She grabbed her tray and stood.

"Where?" He looked down at his half-eaten lunch. It would be better if he finished it, since breakfast had been scarce and dinner was never a guarantee, but the grey meat and congealed white sauce was too unappealing. He pushed the tray away.

"The library. I have to see about graphics mods."

"I guess." He dumped his lunch and followed Marny out of the cafeteria.

The library smelled good. The scent of old paper filled up his nostrils, though there were fewer books every year. He went past the meager shelves and straight to the netscreens. Maybe he could find more info on the new simulators VirtuMax was working on.

The corporation had shouldered into town, but he could almost forgive them. After all, they were one of the few companies working on a full-sim.

Full sensory simulation. Total immersion in the virtual world.

His nerves tingled at the thought. What if that world - the world of pixels and programming - could feel as real as this one? Sometimes when he was simming he almost felt it, like he was *there*, inside the game. But the feeling never lasted. It was impossible to completely escape his reality.

He leaned back in his chair, one leg propped out in front of him. Maybe the people who said there couldn't ever be a perfect interface were right, that the tech couldn't ever get to the level of complexity that matched a human brain.

VirtuMax had been developing their full-sim for years, but the release was always delayed. Tam skimmed the articles, but he'd read all of them. The most recent one was a couple weeks old, about how the lead game developer's death had brought the project to a stop.

Marny paused beside his screen, her taped-together reader glowing in her hand. "Anything interesting?"

"No. What are you looking up?"

She cocked a shoulder. "3-D meshes. I can't get my avatar fat enough in Freelife. I don't want to look like somebody's idea of the perfect woman. I want to look like me."

"Good luck with that. I hear Freelife's a hard world to modify."

"That's why I chose it. Have you *seen* the avs in there?" She gave a snort of disgust. "If you saw someone who looked like that in RL, you'd think they were a genetically mutated freak. All legs and skinny and boobular."

He hadn't really noticed. In fact, he'd always been fine with the standard avatars in virtual reality. The females were usually cute and sexy. The guys were handsome and brawny, or fearsomely monstrous and warlike.

The point was, he *didn't* want to be himself. All the options from there were good with him. Marny wanted to make a statement. She wanted to bust the parameters wide open. Him? He just wanted out.

"How's your system?" she asked. "Still having issues?"

He shrugged. "It's ok. I mean, it works. I can play, there's just a weird thing with the imaging."

And the sound card was going, and sometimes he lost connection altogether, but he didn't want to say it out loud, in case it completely jinxed his system.

"That's the problem with over-clocked gear." Marny shook her head. "You'd think it would last more than a year, huh. My uncle Zeg might have some spare parts around. Or you could go back to playing at his simcafe."

Back to the rental-quality systems. The thought left a sour taste in his mouth. For years he'd helped around the cafe in exchange for system time. Marny's uncle didn't mind the extra help - or the way people would come in to watch Tam play, after he got good.

Good enough that he won last year's tri-state simming tournament. He'd scored his system out of it - plus a chance to compete at nationals. And he could have won there, too, if only...

His heart twisted at the memory and he yanked himself back to the present - away from the poisonous thoughts of what might have been.

"Ok," he said to Marny. "If your uncle has some parts, that could work. I might end up needing them."

He didn't even want to think about his system failing. The best part of his day was when he could pull on the helmet, slip on the gloves, and go slay some monsters. Be a hero for a little while, someplace where he was the best.

"Why don't you ask him," Marny said, direct as usual.

"Fine then, I will."

Maybe Zeg had something worth scavenging. Tam's little brother could figure out how to wire it in - the only thing the Bug was really good at. His blood-stabilizing meds made the kid so manic he couldn't concentrate on anything unless it was full of fire or electricity.

Tam shook his head and went back to reading. There were no solutions.

Sometimes he was pretty sure his life was on its way to being permanently broken.

# CHAPTER 3

"How's school going, Jennet?" Dad asked after dinner on Thursday. "It can't be much like prep. Are you sure you made the right choice?"

She'd made the only choice. "It's fine, Dad."

If by *fine* you meant bleak.

Whatever the Dark Queen had done to her, it was severe - and getting worse. Every morning, a paler version of Jennet stared out of the mirror. Dizziness swirled around her when she stood up or walked too quickly. She could hide the hollow shakiness filling her up, but eventually Dad would notice she was sick again, the way she'd been right after she lost the battle with the queen. The doctors had no clue. They'd called it 'summer pneumonia' and had kept her in the hospital ten days. But this time, she didn't think hospital meds would help.

Her time was running out.

Dad leaned forward and rubbed the bridge of his nose.

"Are you meeting people? I know it's not an easy transition, but by next summer there should be a lot more families here in the View."

If she made it to next summer. "I've met a couple of the company kids. They seem nice." And tragic, as far as gaming went.

The dark-haired girl shared a lot of her classes, but she was all anti-tech - in full rebellion against the company both her parents worked for. And from Jennet's few conversations with the other Viewer, he didn't seem to be much of a gamer. He claimed to like simming, but he had no idea about any of the new games or systems.

"Glad to hear it." Dad smiled at her, though there was worry in his eyes. "The academics here can't be that challenging for you. Going back to your old school as a boarder is still an option. I wish you'd consider it."

Panic stabbed through her and she shook her head. They had been over this so many times. Wherever the Full-D system was, she had to be. The only way to save herself was to get back to the Dark Court - she knew it in her bones.

The only problem was, she couldn't get there.

She'd tried, over and over, had spent frustrating hours in-game, trying to get past the first level. No matter what she did - rolling new characters, trying all the quest lines - she couldn't get to the Dark Court. Couldn't even get past the starting areas. At least, not by herself. Just as the queen had decreed - she was barred from Feyland.

"A review of the academic subjects isn't going to hurt me,

Dad. I'm staying here, with you. Not changing my mind about that."

She'd tried telling him what had happened. But every time, the words dried up in her mouth. How could she explain? It was pretty unbelievable. If it weren't for the fact that she *felt* what the game was doing to her, she wouldn't believe it herself. And she didn't think he'd listen to her argue about why she should be allowed to play again on the Full-D. He'd just see it as gamer excuses. The system was currently off-limits to her - which just made everything more complicated.

Two years ago, Dad had used his program-manager privilege and brought a version of the new Full-D system home. Always working, that was Dad, but in this case it had been fun for her, too. He'd let her try out the early versions of the games the company was developing. When the next-gen system came out, he'd scored one of those, too, arguing that his daughter was a great tester. It was true.

At first she and Dad had run the proto-sims together. He was a terrible player, but he'd watch how she did things in-game and take the information back to the game designers, the rest of his team. She even played an early version of Feyland, though it was nothing like the world she'd become lost in.

Then Dad's work heated up. His old college friend, Thomas Rimer, joined the company as lead game developer. That had been fun - Thomas was like an uncle to her, and always brought her interesting things to read. Old books, rare ones unavailable in e-format, full of fantastical creatures and odd stories. It was obvious, reading them, where his ideas for Feyland had come from.

Dad had gotten even busier with work and she spent more time by herself on the Full-D, playing through the same old content. Until she'd found the password-protected files. Dad's security was always easy to crack, and she was curious to see what his development team was working on.

What she had found was magic.

Golden light surrounded her, and she was transported to another world. She walked through a meadow of flowers and felt the breeze against her face, smelled the fresh scent of grasses and earth. Pixies fluttered around her, laughing. Odd creatures gave her quests that led to unexpected puzzles. Her first fight in-game had been ferocious - magebolts sizzled from her magical staff and she had slain a black wyvern, receiving a glowing treasure in return.

She'd known that VirtuMax was working on adaptive technology, but this, *this*, was beyond anything. The game was incredible, and the sensory interface felt real. More than real. Everything else fell away and she was *there*, in an enchanted world.

She spent the summer in-game. Sure she ate her meals, slept, hung out with her friends, but her mind was spun about with the silver threads of Feyland.

Until she was defeated by the Dark Queen. And then Thomas died.

His death hit Dad hard, not only because he'd been a co-worker, but a good friend. VirtuMax got paranoid and work on the game stopped. Rumors flew that Thomas's death was some kind of corporate espionage. They cracked down on security, stepped-up transfers to the View - and Dad absolutely forbid her to use the Full-D.

But by then it was too late.

"You're looking tired," Dad said. "Make sure you get to bed on time tonight, all right?"

"I will if you will." She smiled, to show she was teasing, but he didn't look so great himself. There were lines on either side of his mouth that hadn't eased since Thomas died.

"You drive a hard bargain." He smiled back, though there was something distant in his eyes. Probably already thinking about work.

She couldn't take another night of pretending to watch vids while trying to ignore the Full-D systems in the game room. "Right. So, I'm going out to board a little."

"Be careful." He always said that.

There was nothing dangerous here, in the half-built world of The View. The fence was live, and nobody without a chip or a pass was allowed in.

"I am." Besides, she always wore her helmet.

There was still some watery light in the sky as she coasted down the empty streets, the g-board humming under her feet. She didn't have the energy to try any tricks - not that there was much here to work with. No rails or half-pipes or ramps. So she just balanced on her board, moving past houses and landscaping that didn't exist yet, except inside some architect's sim.

Nobody here. Nobody who could help her. Which left Crestview High, with its drastic losers. The sky grew darker, and she shivered. There had to be a reasonable gamer here, somewhere. Even if they didn't live in The View.

She'd seen a flyer earlier that week for the school's Gaming Club. The meeting was tomorrow. Maybe she'd find her champion there.

# CHAPTER 4

Tam headed across the scabby grass outside school. He needed to do something about his system, and soon. Yesterday it had made a horrible grinding vibration when he powered up. The noise finally faded, but it had been bad.

"Tam!" a voice called behind him. His steps slowed.

Not just any voice, but *hers*. Jennet Carter. She had a faint accent. He'd noticed it in class, the way her answers were inflected with a lilt that Crestview didn't have.

"Tam Linn!" she called again. "Hey, could I talk to you?"

He turned around. She was standing on the steps outside the school doors, her pale hair shining in the afternoon sunlight.

"What?" he said. Why would Jennet Carter want to talk to him?

She moved toward him, her expression cautious.

"Hi." She tried a smile. It faded when he didn't smile back. "Right. Well. I hear you're a simmer."

"Yeah."

His tournament win was common knowledge. The fact that his prize system was tapped into the 'net - that was secret. He wasn't about to get all chatty with anyone about his gaming, let alone a Viewer.

"So... you're a pretty good player, right?" she asked.

He narrowed his eyes. "How am I supposed to answer that?"

If he told the truth, he'd come across as bragging. If he didn't, he'd sound like a loser.

"Honestly." She gave him a measuring look and he tried not to notice how having her gaze on him made that restless feeling start up again under his skin.

Okay then. "Yeah, I'm good."

She hitched her bag up on her shoulder. "Best simmer in town?"

"What is this?" Annoyance heated his words. "You have some assignment to interview another student or something?"

"No. I was just... wondering."

Nosy rich girl. Still, a part of him - a stupid, doglike part - was flattered that she was interested. That part was sitting up, wagging its tail and ready to do anything for a word of praise from those soft lips.

So he turned his back on her and started walking away.

"Wait!" She came after him and caught his arm. "Please tell me."

The vulnerability in her expression made him pause. Made him answer, despite himself.

"I'm the best simmer in the tri-states, actually. Happy? Now let go."

She did, and he felt the absence of her touch almost as keenly as he'd felt the warmth of it.

"Could I..." She looked down at her hands, then back up at him. "Could I watch you game sometime?"

He pushed his hair out of his face, so he could see every nuance of her expression. "You've seen people sim before, haven't you?" The high-tech world she was from, she must have.

"Of course!" She looked offended for a second, and it made him smile a little bit inside, to see emotion blazing like that from her eyes. "I play, too, you know."

On equipment that he didn't even want to try and imagine, or jealousy would eat right through him.

"I don't doubt it. Are you trying to ask me out or something?"

She blinked, and he caught the flash of disbelief in her eyes before she spoke. "Ask you out? No. I'm not."

"Good." Relief and disappointment circled in his stomach. He turned to go.

"Hold on a sec." There was an edge of desperation in her voice. "I *do* want to see you game. Just... let me explain."

He folded his arms and waited.

She was silent a minute, and a bubble of stillness dropped down over them. There was a tickle on the back of his neck, like what she was about to say was important. Beyond important.

"All right." She let out a breath. "Here's the thing. My dad's one of the senior managers for VirtuMax. He's been working on their new sim system. Maybe you've heard about it."

"Yeah. I've heard of it."

He tried not to show how her words had sent a jolt of interest through him. Her dad worked on the full simulation project? How much did she know?

"Full-D, they call it. And there's a new game to go with it. Has to be, to show what the system can do. It's like nothing else out there."

"You've, uh, seen this new game?" His heart thudded in his chest like he'd been sprinting down the street, not standing in one place for three minutes.

She nodded. "Yes. In fact, I've been playing it and... well, I need help."

"It's in beta-testing? Why don't you get your dad or one of the other devs to help?"

He thought he knew the answer though, and anticipation sizzled through him, burning away his jealousy, his resentment of the rich kids in the View. Was she going to ask *him* to play?

"Pre-beta, even. Basically..." She bit her lip and glanced to one side. "I can't ask them for help. I'm not even supposed to know that this version of Feyland exists, let alone go in-game. But I can't stop."

He nodded. Games could get inside your skin and

become the most important thing in the world - at least for a little while. It always wore off though. And simming didn't keep his little brother out of trouble, or scavenge food from behind the grocery store, or help his mom when she finally came home after one of her episodes.

But a new game, on a brand-new sim - his fingers tingled at the thought. And Jennet wanted to see what he could do. Check out his cred, like some kind of audition.

"When do you want to watch me play?" He glanced down at his scuffed boots and tried to sound casual. "We could go over to Zeg's simcafe—"

"No. I want to see you play on your own gear."

He wished, for a gut-searing moment, that he didn't have the life he did - that he could wave his hand and call a grav-car and they could drive to his house, a real house, full of good things to eat and shiny equipment.

And they could game. With a legal account, not his 'jacked connection. On a system that wasn't half broken, in a place that wasn't falling down, in a neighborhood that hadn't turned to rot long ago.

"I have to go." He turned and started walking again.

She followed. "But - you do have a sim-system, right? I heard you won a great rig. I want to see you in your home element. At your best."

"I don't think so." He hunched his shoulders. His home was none of her business. "I'll see you around."

It was stupid, to think he could connect with someone like Jennet. They had nothing in common. No matter how attractive her world was, or how much he might want it, he didn't belong there. Just like she didn't belong in his. The thought of taking her into the Exe, showing her where he lived, revealing his secrets... just, no.

"Wait." Something trembled in her voice - hope or tears. It didn't matter.

Tam shoved his hands into his pockets and kept going. He had long-since perfected the art of walking away.

# CHAPTER 5

Jennet watched Tam march off the school grounds, and desperation clawed itself up out of her throat. She *needed* him. Needed to see him play, needed his help.

Now that she'd maybe found the one person in Crestview who could sim, she couldn't let him get away.

So she followed him, keeping a block behind and sticking to the shadows. He didn't look back, not once. Still, it wasn't easy. He zigzagged through smelly alleys, and went over a fence that smeared her white shirt with grime. Sweat prickled on her skin, but she couldn't lose sight of him. She had to see him play.

Maybe he wasn't all that good. But even if he was poor and lived in a bad part of town, at least he wasn't a complete idiot like that guy Fernald. And she was out of options.

The buildings around her were increasingly run-down, and the air smelled like old garbage. Were there rats here?

Tam dodged down an alleyway and she followed, watching where she stepped. When she looked up again, he was gone.

The air felt colder, darker, and a shiver raked across the back of her neck. A rustling noise sounded behind her and she whirled, heartbeat spiking.

Nothing there.

Ok. Relax. She pulled in a breath of rot-flavored air. He'd be around the next corner. Surely he would. The shaky feeling taking over her legs didn't believe her, but she forced herself to move. One step, then another.

The alley intersected a deserted street. There was no sign of Tam. She swallowed. Time to call George. He'd come with the grav-car to get her right away, no matter where she was. There'd be some explaining to do, since she'd told him she was staying after school for a study club - but staying lost in the outskirts of the Exe seemed like a really bad idea.

She backed into an alcove and fished around in her satchel, trying to ignore the things squishing under her feet.

From out of nowhere, a hand grabbed her arm. She shrieked and tried to pull away, punching wildly with her free fist, while fear opened a dark hole under her feet.

"Shh." It was Tam. He grasped her other arm, keeping her from connecting with his face. "Calm down."

She took a gasping breath. "Tam - you scared me!"

"Why'd you follow me? That's a stupid thing to do. Especially here." He kept hold of her arms, but she didn't feel threatened by how close he was. Despite the fear still echoing through her, she felt oddly safe.

"I told you," she said. "I need to see you game - see if you're good enough to play Feyland."

He let go of her and took a step back. "And if I'm not?"

"I think you are."

He had to be. He was the best chance she had. Her last chance to get back in-game and win free of the Dark Queen.

For a long minute they stood there, the smell of garbage wafting around them. Tam stared past her at the crumbling, graffiti-etched wall. Then he shook his head.

"No," he said. "Come on, I'll take you back to school. You don't belong here."

"I'm not going anywhere." She glared at him. "Except your place."

"Damn it, I'm not—" He broke off and held up one hand, his whole body going tense.

His nostrils flared and he cocked his head, listening. To what? Fear shivered through her.

He leaned forward and spoke in a barely audible voice. "We need to get out of here. Now. No questions. Follow close."

"Ok," she whispered. Her skin prickled, like somebody was watching them.

Tam led them down the alley. He moved silently, carefully, like some wild creature used to danger. She stayed right behind him, doing her best to be quiet. But despite her care, her shoe knocked against an old can. It teetered for one tense second, then tipped, clanging and rolling along the cracked pavement.

Calls erupted behind them, yips and crazy laughter. Tam grabbed her arm and hauled her forward. "Run!"

Panic powered her steps and her breath rasped in her throat. She didn't dare look behind them. Tam dodged and turned, leading her through a series of broken-down buildings, cutting through weedy lots. The noise of pursuit faded, and finally he slowed.

"I... have to... rest," she panted. She felt like a knife was stabbing into her side, sliding between her ribs, over and over.

He slanted a look around the dingy street they were on, then led her toward an abandoned building.

"Alright. In here." He ducked beneath a door hanging crookedly by one hinge. "We should be safe - they usually don't go much outside their territory."

"They?" She clasped her hands tightly to make them stop shaking, and concentrated on getting air back into her lungs.

"The Jackals - local gang. Good thing they didn't get a closer look at you, or we'd still be running. There's a black-market demand for wrist chips, and they wouldn't be gentle about taking it out. They have knives."

She pulled her wrist against her body. "That's... horrible." Would the gang really have taken a blade to her flesh and cut her chip out? She shuddered.

"Welcome to the Exe." There was a flash of sympathy in his eyes.

"Nice place."

All told, she preferred the dark places in Feyland. Though with his real-life skills, she had no doubt Tam would be great in-game, too.

"Ready to go?" he asked.

She drew in a deep breath, let it out. Disappointment curled cold in her belly, but he'd made his point. She was in danger here, and it was better for both of them if she left. She'd have to find another way to see him play.

"All right."

Steps dragging, she followed him down the street. At the next intersection, he paused. A low, liquid groaning sound, like something dying, floated down the street. Tam leaned close, his lips almost brushing her ear.

"I'll count on my fingers," he whispered. "When I hit three, run straight across - right for that alley. Don't look back."

The cold in her stomach moved up to her throat. She nodded.

He listened a moment more, then held up his hand. One finger. Two. Three.

They bolted across the street. She got a confused impression of figures clustered around an oil-can fire, and then they were in the alley. Tam put his hand on her back, silently urging her to keep going, though there didn't seem to be any outcry behind them.

What a fool she'd been, to follow him into the Exe. Good thing he'd figured out she was there, or she'd be in severe trouble. But now she was completely lost. Tam had doubled back so many times she had no idea which direction the school was. She just had to trust him, and keep following.

Finally, he stopped. "Here we are."

Jennet blinked. This wasn't Crestview High - they were still in the Exe. Cautious hope unfolded inside her. "Here?"

"Yeah. Home sweet home."

Tam tilted his head to the flat-roofed building in front of them. It looked like an abandoned mechanic shop, with rickety exterior stairs going up the side. On the roof was a smaller box - a little apartment maybe, repaired with old boards and pieces of salvaged metal. At least there were windows, though a blue tarp covered most of the roof.

Jennet blinked. "This is where you live? I thought you didn't want me to—"

"I didn't have much choice. The Jackals were between us and school." Unhappiness edged his voice. He turned to her, his mouth grim. "Do *not* say a word about my place. Ok? Nothing."

She nodded, swallowing back the questions crowding the tip of her tongue. The fact that he'd brought her here at all - that was key. She tried not to glance up at the shack on the roof. It looked like it could fall down in the next big storm.

Ignoring the stairs, he led her around the building and unlocked a big metal door in back. It scraped open across the concrete floor with a low groan. Inside, the single huge room was dim and cold, light straggling in through high, grease-filmed windows. It smelled like old machines.

"I've got an hour til the Bug gets home," he said.

"The Bug?"

"My kid brother."

"All right. I'll call Dad's driver and—"

"No." He frowned, clearly uncomfortable with the idea

of a grav-car skimming up to his front door. "The Jackals will have gone to ground by then. I'll take you back to school and you can get picked up there."

Without waiting for her agreement, he moved to the far wall and waved his hand in front of the light plate. It took three tries before the bank of fluorescents overhead flickered on. The sickly glow illuminated his sim system.

It was a newer-model Zing, though it looked like it had been used hard. The chair had a long rip across the seat, partially hidden by a lumpy pillow. Cables ran like crazed electric worms from the drive to the helmet and gloves, and silvery tape seemed to be holding half the system together.

"This is... I mean, you won this?" she asked.

"Yeah." He dipped his head, letting his hair fall back over his eyes. "Last year's tournament."

"So, you made Nationals? What was it like, playing there? Where did you rank?"

"I didn't go to Nationals." His voice was tight.

"Didn't go? But that's—"

"Something came up." He turned away from her and clicked his system on. "So. You want to see me play. Any game in particular?"

"Um..."

As far as subject changes went, that one had been pretty obvious - like a door slamming shut. All right. What game did she want to see him play?

She had originally thought WorldStar. It was the sim most like Feyland - not that any other game could compete. But now... she glanced around the grimy space that housed

Tam's system. He obviously didn't have the money to buy new expansions of the popular games, or pay the access fees. She bit her lip.

What were the free sim games, anyway? She'd never paid any attention - they were inferior, crammed with ads, and usually the graphics were sub-par. Come on... think. She had to know some games. She fished around for a name, but the grating, low-pitched hum coming from Tam's system made it hard to concentrate.

"Does your drive always make that sound?" The question was out before she could reel it back in, but the noise was truly awful. It sounded like a moaning beast, with the added bonus of a teeth-gritting vibration of metal against the concrete floor.

He scowled at her. "If you don't like it, you can leave."

Heat rushed into her face. Great. She was going to ruin this. Better get to the gaming as soon as possible.

"What games do you have?" There. Nice safe question.

"Anything." He tossed the word out, casual.

"Really? Even WorldStar?"

"Yes, *even* that. And Zombiemecca, and Ruler of Days, and—"

"Okay, okay." She swallowed back her questions. Tam had all the top games, and it was probably better if she didn't ask how he could afford them. "WorldStar is kind of like Feyland. Fantasy-based quests, you know. Battles with monsters." And queens. She shivered.

"WorldStar it is - and you don't have to sound so surprised." Tam slid into the chair and picked up his gaming helmet. "The backbone of the 'net runs through Crestview, and plenty of people know how to use it - at least in the Exe. Anyway, it's why your company is here."

"VirtuMax isn't *my* company."

He shrugged and pulled the keyboard onto his lap, tapping out a few commands. "You'll have to watch second-hand," he said, leaning forward and flicking the battered monitor on. "I only have one helmet."

"Oh. Right." Still, even the flatscreen would give her a decent idea of his game-play.

The screen was dull, with holes in the display where pixels were stuck. There were enough, though, to see the overall picture. She was getting the feeling his whole system was that way - barely enough.

The monitor lit up with the WorldStar background. Then Tam's characters appeared, lined up along the bottom of the screen.

"Do you have a level 200?" she asked.

"A few. Do you want a caster, thief, or tank?"

She blinked. "You have a top level in each class? You must spend a lot of time playing."

"Not all that much." He slid on his worn e-gloves. "I'm efficient. So, who do you want?"

She leaned forward to scan the character portraits. A decked-out Soldier, a Shifter - no, too low level. She needed something that would push Tam to the limit.

"That one." She pointed to the Sorcerer, a tall, green-haired character without any telltale marks of superior gear. No glows hovering around him, or towering shoulder armor, or billowing capes. She didn't want this to be too easy. "Lorne?"

"It's an anagram," he said, not looking at her. He drew the helmet down over his face, and selected the character.

Jennet turned the letters around in her mind. Lorne. Loner. No kidding.

Then the game of WorldStar opened, showing the Sorcerer standing in the street of a small village. Somewhere in Dvelt Province, judging by the grassy plain that spread out beyond the mud-brick buildings.

"Where to?" Tam asked.

An ordinary spell-caster, up against... She tapped her lower lip with her fingers. "Isn't there a Guardian-class encounter near here? Some big kitty in a cave to the east?"

He let out a muffled snort. "That big kitty is called Saberclaw. People don't fight him solo. It usually takes three - *with* a healer."

"Can you do it, or not?"

He turned his head toward her, the visor reflecting the dim light. "My least-decked character, and in a lightweight armor class, too. That's a pretty mismatched fight."

She knew it wasn't fair - but then, life wasn't. And she needed to see what he could do against nearly impossible odds. She couldn't take a complete noob into Feyland with her.

"Yeah, it is mismatched. Maybe Saberclaw needs some reinforcements. Poor kitty." It was a dumb joke, but she saw the side of his mouth twitch up a little.

"Alright then," he said. "Here we go."

Tam guided his character to the mount master, and before long, Lorne was on a gazelle-like creature, galloping east. Purple mountains loomed in the distance, and a flock of black birds swooped up from the plains like a spiral of smoke. Soon, Lorne reached the low hills.

At the edge of one canyon was a gaping shadow edged with rocks that looked like fangs. Saberclaw's cave. Bones littered the ground in front, some old and bleached, others new, with bloody hunks of meat hanging off them, evidence of a recent player's death. Would Lorne's bones join them?

A knot formed in Jennet's stomach. She folded her fingers over the back of Tam's chair and watched as he dismissed his character's mount.

Tam lifted a finger, and his Sorcerer's arms rose. Magical energy gathered in a ball of glowing light between his hands, then spread down over Lorne's figure, encasing him in a layer of invisible armor. Another wave of his hand, and potions appeared, hovering in the air before him. Blood red, glimmering orange, dark purple - without hesitation, the Sorcerer chose two, uncorked the vials, and drank.

Magical preparations complete, Lorne stepped over the litter of bones and walked to the edge of the darkness.

Truth time. Jennet held her breath as the pebble of fear in her stomach turned to a boulder. What if Tam wasn't good enough?

CHAPTER 6

Tam was barely conscious of Jennet hovering behind his chair. Please, don't let his system cut out now. Jennet had set him a drastic challenge. But he *would* win it, impossible odds or no.

He took a deep breath and focused.

There was only the faint hiss of the wind in the plains grasses, the hollow footfalls of his Sorcerer as he approached the cave to confront Saberclaw. Tam made a quick check of his inventory, making sure his oh-crap items were in place - the things he'd need to win this. Extra health potion, blinding dust, one-use spectral shield. A cloth-wearer had to have tricks like this up his sleeve to survive most scrapes. Though a solo encounter with a Guardian-class beast hardly qualified as a *scrape*. More like a severe mutilation.

For a second the graphics wavered, rippling like a heat wave. Tam froze, waiting. Come on, system - hold together. It felt like his heart stopped too, until the image stabilized again. Just in time.

In the darkness of the cave, something growled. A red flash of light showed that Saberclaw had sensed a trespasser in his lair. The attack came without warning as the enormous cat rushed forward, a mass of striped and angry death. His growl turned into a roar as the beast lunged, sharp claws extended to rake the Sorcerer's chest.

Adrenaline pumping through him, Tam waited until the last possible instant, then popped his shield. He cast an instant spell that slowed the cat a precious few milliseconds - enough time to lob a flaming ball of magefire into the cat's face. Saberclaw yowled in fury, his long teeth shining and deadly.

Tam leapt to the side, but didn't quite avoid a furious bite from those teeth. His life energy dipped and his character slowed down. Dimly, in the other world, he heard Jennet gasp. One trick gone. But he and the cat were even.

Using his mage abilities, he tried to keep his distance while still sending spells at his opponent. Not always successfully - the big cat got a few painful bites and swipes in on his character in return.

They were both around half health when Saberclaw's eyes lit with an uncanny green glow. It was the sign he was about to use his special ability - an unavoidable stun that froze his victim in place. As soon as the stun wore off, the cat would pounce and shred his enemy to bits. Tam's heart raced as his fingers gestured the next combo of moves. This had better work. It was the only thing he could think of.

He tossed the blinding powder, the bright flash distracting Saberclaw for an instant. Then... there was no avoiding this next part, no matter how much it hurt. With a pang, he summoned his favorite pet - the battle-hawk companion he'd won in a ferocious duel two years ago. The two of them had shared more adventures than he could count. But he'd have to sacrifice the hawk in order to win this fight.

"Goodbye, Bright," he murmured as he sent his pet forward to certain death.

He yanked Lorne behind one of the jagged rocks at the entrance, getting out of line-of-sight as his golden companion winged straight for Saberclaw. The hawk let out a high, pained cry as the big cat's eyes flared. Saberclaw's evil green gaze pinned Bright to the cave floor.

Tam couldn't just keep Lorne standing there - he had to make Bright's death count. He stepped back into the cave and began his longest incantation. It was his most powerful spell, a fire-lance that would blast a serious hole in his opponent.

The cat ignored Tam and leapt on Bright, yowling with joy as he began to rip the bird to pieces. The hawk let out high, piteous cries as bits of golden feathers swirled in the air. Finally, Bright lay still, his broken body trapped under Saberclaw's wicked paws.

The image blurred in front of Tam's eyes - but this time it wasn't a system problem. He blinked furiously, clearing his vision. The hollow ache in his chest from losing Bright joined all the other sorrows piled up there. Sure, it was just a game, but now he was alone. Again.

Tam swallowed. His spell tingled at his fingertips, the energy building, building...

"Now!" he shouted, flinging deadly fire at Saberclaw.

The beast lifted his snarling face just as Tam's fire-lance hit. The force of it made Saberclaw stagger, and the smell of singed fur scorched Tam's nose. But it wasn't enough. The big cat recovered quickly, too quickly, and gathered himself to leap on the Sorcerer.

:WARNING. SYSTEM OVERLOAD. AUTO-SHUT-DOWN IN TEN SECONDS:

The red letters etched across Tam's vision, overriding the game's graphics.

"No," he breathed. "Not now."

Despite the reactions coursing through him, his hands remained steady in the gloves. Although it wasn't scorched fur he smelled. It was the metallic stench of burning electrical cables.

He had to finish this, and fast.

It was hard to throw incantations while taking serious damage. Every rake of claws and bite of fangs slowed Lorne's spell-casting down, while his life energy continued to drain. If it got to zero, he was dead. Tam managed to shoot another flame-blast, but his Sorcerer was in trouble. Lorne was dying - and when he did, Tam would lose.

He got another instant spell off, then grabbed his health potion. It would buy him a little more life. Enough, if he were lucky, to outlast the big cat.

:WARNING. AUTO-SHUTDOWN IN FIVE SECONDS. SAVE WORK NOW:

Yeah, not likely. Save himself. His Sorcerer popped the potion.

Saberclaw pounced, and Tam drew his dagger. No more time for casting spells. Good thing he had spent time maxing this character's weapon skills - though it went against all common sense to skill-up magic users. He only prayed Lorne would be strong enough.

Jab and rip. Slice and claw. Both Lorne and Saberclaw were almost dead. A sliver of life energy kept the Sorcerer on his feet, while the cat limped after him.

:TWO SECONDS:

Tam judged the timing and pulled his Sorcerer back, just missing a razor-sharp death swipe. Then he lunged in, the dagger piercing Saberclaw's side. With a last yowl, the big cat staggered, then collapsed in a heap of fur and claws. Lorne fell to his knees, but the Sorcerer was still alive. The battle was over.

Victory!

:SHUTDOWN:

The helmet went dark, and Tam slowly pulled it off. His mind was ultra-clear - that gaming high he got whenever he beat impossible odds.

"You did it!"

Jennet had a huge smile on her face, and her blue eyes sparkled. If he hadn't been sitting down he thought she would have thrown a big hug on him. Instead, she gripped his shoulder. Her touch was strong and warm.

"That was amazing," she continued. "I've never seen anyone think so fast on their feet. And with your system going down and everything. Just, wow."

He took a breath and scrubbed a hand through his hair. "Yeah. It was a good fight."

"Good?" Her expression was full of admiration, full of light, like the sun coming out from behind clouds. "You're a prime game-player, Tam Linn."

The praise made something inside him glow, and he didn't know how to respond. It wouldn't do to get used to this feeling.

"I should get you back to school." He stood up, and her hand fell away from him, leaving only cool air behind. "My brother will be home soon, and I have to be here, or he might burn the place down."

Jennet smiled again, as if he were joking. After a few seconds her smile faded. "All right. But Feyland is going to amaze you. You'll be great at it. When can you come over to my place to sim? Tomorrow? Wednesday?"

"Maybe Thursday." If Mom showed up, and he could get her back on her meds, then there might be a chance. He shrugged, though the fierce desire to see the new sim and play Feyland was scorching through him.

"Please, I really need your help." She looked impatient, and worried. "Can't you come any earlier?"

"No." He let the word hang flatly between them.

He'd let her see his place, see him game. That was too much. No way was he going to explain the details of his life -

details that would only horrify her sheltered little world-view.

"Well." A frown gathered on her face. "Let me know as soon as you can. All right?"

"Sure." He turned the still glowing flat-screen off, then shoved his hands in his pockets. When he got back, he'd be doing some major system repair. "Come on. Let's get you back to school."

# CHAPTER 7

THE NEXT DAYS DRAGGED. JENNET VEERED BETWEEN
elation that she'd finally, *finally*, found the gamer she needed,
and frustration that he couldn't play that instant.

She couldn't expect him to understand her urgency - not
when she hadn't explained the problem to him. But the first
step was getting him in-game. With his help, she was sure she
could finally get deeper into Feyland.

During World History class on Thursday she couldn't
help but sneak glances at Tam. His hair was covering his eyes,
as usual, and he didn't look at her. Not once. That wasn't
good. Worry squeezed her lungs tight. When the bell rang,
she took an extra long time packing up her satchel. Tam
lagged behind too, and her breath eased.

"Well?" she asked as he paused by her desk. "Are we on
for today?" *We have to play. Please say yes.*

"No." He hunched his shoulders. "Maybe next week.
See ya."

"What... hey, wait up!" She reached for him as he stepped into the hallway, but he ignored her outstretched hand. He slipped into the crowd, seeming determined to get away. Disappointment raced through her as she scanned the students, trying to see which way he'd gone. How could he just leave like that?

"Don't bother going after him," said a voice at her shoulder.

Jennet turned to see Marny standing beside her. The big girl didn't look friendly - but she didn't look too mean, either.

"Hi, Marny."

The girl waved down the hall to where Tam had disappeared. "Tam's like that. He doesn't explain things, so don't even ask."

Jennet folded her arms. "Why do you think I would ask him something, anyway?"

"Oh please." Marny flicked her gaze up to the ceiling, then back to Jennet. "Obviously you've talked to him. Besides, he told me about you, too."

Surprise jolted through her. "He did? What did he say?"

"Not much." A look of irritation crossed Marny's round face. "Even for Tam, he was remarkably quiet. I hope you're not just messing with him."

"I wouldn't—"

"Good." Marny leaned forward. "The two of us go way back, and if you hurt him, you'll be hurting too."

"Okay." Jennet held up her hands. "Message received. Are the two of you... umm, together?"

"No. Nothing like that. But he's a good guy, and I don't

want to see some rich girl screwing with his head just because she can."

"How do you know he's not screwing with mine?" She was going to be late for her next class, but she didn't care. "How come he can't make plans? What's wrong with him, anyway?"

"Hey." Marny's voice grew softer. "He's got it rough. I bet he didn't tell you about his mom."

"All I know is he has a little brother." And lived in a falling down shack in the worst part of town. And was a flawless gamer.

"Well, it's his life. He can tell you if he wants. But it's complicated."

Like anyone's life was simple. A piece of her soul was trapped in a computer game and it was literally killing her. How was *that* for complicated?

There had to be some way to make this work - some way to break Tam free from his life for at least an afternoon. He had to come over and play Feyland on the Full-D. She had to get back in-game, before it was too late.

She looked at Marny. "Do you ever... babysit?"

"No." Marny's eyes widened. "No way. I am not watching that crazy kid brother of his so the two of you can go mess around together."

Heat rushed into Jennet's cheeks. "I'm not interested in him like that."

"Well, you're interested somehow."

Jennet opened her hands. "There's stuff I can't explain, either."

"Ah. Are you sure you don't have some kind of pervy fixation?" Speculation flashed in Marny's dark brown eyes. "Those questions. About gaming. Why did you ask *me*?"

"I figured you pay attention."

"Really." Marny's expression hardened. "Why's that?"

"For one thing, you seemed like the smartest person in the Gaming Club. And you're different."

Marny's mouth twisted. "Different. That's not quite a compliment."

"Well, it's not an insult, either." Jennet glanced down the hall, where the parade of look-alike students was starting to thin out. "Especially at Crestview."

"Heh." A half-smile ghosted across Marny's face. "I—" The blare of the second bell cut through whatever she had been about to say. She hefted her battered purple backpack onto her shoulder. "Gotta run. See you later, Fancy-girl."

The way she said the words, they weren't quite an insult, either. There had been an undercurrent of approval in the big girl's voice. Maybe, just maybe....

Marny stopped partway down the hall and swung around. She pointed at Jennet. "I'm not making any promises. But - make sure you're free tomorrow after school."

# CHAPTER 8

Tam couldn't believe it. The clamor of the lunchroom faded as he blinked at. Marny. "Really? You'll watch the Bug this afternoon so I can go to Jennet's? That's the nicest—"

"Shut up, or I'll take my offer back. And it's only the once, clear?" She made a face. "If your little brother gets too crazy, I'm calling the cops."

As if the police would come out to the Exe for anything less than murder. Maybe not even then.

"Ok." Tam fished in his pack for the emergency cash he kept tucked away. He held the money out to Marny. "You'll need this."

"I'm not taking your money!" She sounded offended. "Do you think I look like a babysitter? I'm doing this out of friendship."

"I know." He waved the cash. "But you're going to need to get some stuff at the store to keep the Bug occupied.

Sugar Crunchies - the big box. And the new Manza-boy comic."

"That had better work." She took the money. "I have to be home by six, though. So whatever it is you and Miss Fancy-girl are up to, be done by then. And Tam," her expression softened, "be careful, right?"

"Hey. It's not like I'm going to go rob a bank or anything. She's just showing me a new sim-system."

"She says."

"I don't think she's lying." He didn't think Jennet's appreciation for his game-playing had been faked, either.

Marny narrowed her eyes at him. "Something else is going on, Tam. There's something not normal about this."

"What, that one of *them* would want to spend time with me?" That stung, though it wasn't anything he hadn't thought before. Jennet's interest was hard to explain. Except that it had something to do with gaming, the one thing he was really good at. "Don't worry, I can take care of myself."

"I know." Her lips pulled into a frown. "Just - pay attention."

"I always do."

IT WAS HARD NOT to be overwhelmed as he slid into Jennet's chauffeured grav-car after school. The interior smelled like status and money, and the seats were more comfortable than his own bed. Tam glanced over the divider as the chauffeur manipulated the shiny controls on the dash. How would it feel to drive this thing, to glide, frictionless, over the gridded roads?

"Here." Jennet settled beside him and held out a shiny plastic card attached to a clip. "Your visitor's badge. You'll have to wear it in The View, so the sensors don't go off."

"Nice." He took it, the holograph of VirtuMax's company logo shimmering as it caught the light.

Of course, there had to be a system to let the peons in. Cleaning and maintenance people had to have controlled access to the rich people's world, after all. He took a pinch of his shirt and attached the badge. It hung crooked, but he didn't care.

He glanced at Jennet, who looked a bit embarrassed. Maybe it was the first time she'd had to provide one of her 'friends' with an access badge.

"It's good for two weeks," she said. "I got you a long pass, just in case. Although I need to be with you while you're inside the walls, since it's got a low security clearance."

"Yeah. Wouldn't want to set off any alarms." He felt like a sheep. A criminal one.

She cleared her throat and went for an obvious change of subject. "Anyway, I'm glad you could come today. Marny is a pearl."

"I wouldn't call her that. But yeah."

The car was moving so smoothly, Tam felt like they were standing still. He glanced out the window, just to check. The neighborhood they were going through was about a hundred times cleaner than the Exe. No falling-down buildings or trash lining the streets. People here even had green lawns with neatly-trimmed bushes instead of scrappy, bare dirt where not even weeds grew.

"Here we are," Jennet said as the car whished under a gleaming plas-metal arch. The company logo gleamed under the words proudly etched in the arch. *The View*.

"Is there one?" Tam turned to look out the back window as they passed through.

The archway of the View framed the cloudy sky - nothing special. The buildings scrolling past were huge and pristine, but the neighborhood felt eerie. It took a moment for him to identify why. There was no one in sight. No little kids playing on the perfectly groomed lawns. No lanky teens shooting hoops or riding g-boards. Not a single person. It was emptier than a computer game, where at least the NPCs were always there, moving around and making the world look occupied.

"A view?" Jennet asked. "Yes. The houses in the back have one. You'll see." She picked up her satchel and looked out the window in an expectant way.

Tam grabbed his pack as the car slid to a perfect stop and the door hissed open. Even the air in The View seemed different. Cleaner. Fresher. He followed Jennet out of the car, then stuck his head back in.

"Thanks for the ride," he told the chauffeur. The man looked mildly startled, and then gave him a nod.

"Yes, thanks, George," Jennet said, an undertone of excitement in her voice. "Come on, Tam. I can hardly wait to show you the set-up. This way."

As if there could be any other way than the wide stone

path leading to the fanciest house Tam had ever seen. No, not a house. A mansion. The place was four stories high, with balconies that jutted out on the upper levels and dozens of windows. There was even a fountain in the front, a lit-up sparkle and cascade of water. It looked like something from a mall.

Jennet held her wrist up to the front door and it opened with a soft chime. She threw a glance over her shoulder, and Tam hurried to follow her.

*"Welcome home, Jennet,"* a perfectly modulated female voice said as they stepped over the threshold. *"You have brought a visitor. Staff has been notified."*

"Right," Jennet said. "Let Marie know we'll be up in the game-room."

*"Confirmed."*

Tam looked around, trying to be nonchalant. The warmly-lit foyer was empty, except for the two of them. "Is that... your house computer?"

He'd heard of fully-wired houses, but never imagined what it might be like to actually live in one. It was interesting - and creepy. Jennet didn't stand much chance of sneaking out at night, did she?

"Yes," she said. "Dad calls the computer HANA - House Activated Network Assistant." She set her satchel on the floor and started up the wide stairs.

"Who's Marie?" Tam trailed after her. He was afraid to touch anything in this pristine, clean-smelling place. Half-turning, he checked to make sure he wasn't leaving grimy footprints on the pale carpet.

"Marie's the house manager. She makes sure that everything is working smoothly, meals are done on time, that kind of thing."

"How big is your family?" He knew almost nothing about Jennet's life. Then again, she knew almost nothing about his, either, and he was happy to keep it that way.

"It's just me and my dad," Jennet said. "My mom left when I was a kid." Her words rang hollowly in the quiet corridor. All the doors were closed, except the tall double-doors at the end.

Really? A fully-wired house and a 'manager' just for Jennet and her Dad. Good thing she hadn't seen his sorry house - the living room that doubled as bedroom for both him and the Bug, the scrappy furniture, the tiny kitchen. The distance between his house and Jennet's felt like the distance between galaxies. And just as unbridgeable. The only thing that kept him from turning around and going back to the Exe was the enticing promise of the Full-D system.

She led him through, then shut the doors behind them. "Here we are - the gaming room. Complete with Full-D."

Tam's feet stopped moving. He was dimly aware of other sim systems in the room, a bank of screens against the far wall, but all he could do was blink at the simulator right in front of him. Wait - the *two* simulators.

The helmets gleamed silver. The chairs were wide and comfortable, upholstered in something that was probably real leather. The gloves were studded with LEDs that shone like jewels.

"Yeah." The word escaped from between his lips.

"So." Jennet's voice dropped to a whisper and she pushed at the plush carpet with one foot. "Don't tell anybody about this, okay?"

He pulled his gaze from the sim-systems, trying to ignore the stab of hurt lancing through him. Of course she wouldn't want people to know that he'd been invited over. Trash from the Exe sullying her perfect house.

"What, that I came to your house?" The words left a sour taste in his mouth. "I hadn't planned on it."

"No, no. I mean, don't tell anybody about the Full-D system. Nobody except corporate is supposed to see it. And..." she stepped closer to him, "*nobody* is supposed to know about Feyland. Not even me. All right?"

Her blue eyes stared into his, pleading, and his heartbeat was suddenly louder in his ears. "I won't tell."

"Not even Marny."

"Ok. She's not interested in simming anyway."

Jennet nodded and the urgency in her eyes faded. "Then come take a look."

Tam stepped up to the systems. He slid his fingers over the top of one helmet, the plas-metal cool and smooth under his touch. Excitement began shooting through his nerves like crazy firecrackers. He hoped Jennet couldn't tell how sparked he was.

The Full-D system. Here, real, and within his reach.

"See this?" She flipped a switch beside the systems, and a low buzz filled the air.

"What is it?"

"The scrambler. To make sure no corporate spies - or hackbots - can tell what's going on in here."

"That's..." totally insane. But apparently not, since here it was.

Tam picked up one of the gloves. It felt heavy and expensive in his hand. He could hardly wait to see what the game was like. Feyland. The syllables rolled silently down his tongue.

"Miss Jennet?" There was a knock, and then the door to the hallway swung open to reveal a dark-haired woman in a suit. She was holding a tray of food. "I brought you some sandwiches."

"Oh, hi, Marie. Thanks," Jennet said, her voice pitched higher than usual. She gave Tam a look he couldn't decipher.

He put the glove down, and silence settled awkwardly in the spaces between them as Marie put the tray on a nearby table.

She turned and raised her eyebrows at Jennet. "You have brought home a guest?"

"Um, yes," Jennet said. "This is Tam. From school. He likes to game, so I thought I'd give him a peek at the Full-D."

The woman pinned Tam with her gaze. She looked down at his battered boots, then back up, taking in every rip and fray in his secondhand clothing. The suspicion in her eyes only deepened, like she expected him to pull a tab of spray out of his back pocket and start tagging the nearest wall.

"I see." Her voice was clipped, with an accent he couldn't identify. "If he is going to be a regular visitor, we'll need to run a thorough security clearance."

Jennet turned wide eyes to him, as if she feared he had a criminal record just waiting to be discovered. "Oh! Well, I'm sure—"

"No problem." Tam stepped forward. "Do you need fingerprints or something?"

He knew he was clean. Taking care of Mom and the Bug didn't leave much time for getting wild, even if he leaned that way. And yeah, he'd broken the law before, out of necessity - but in the Exe the rules didn't matter. Only survival. And not getting caught. He was good at both.

The house manager flicked her gaze up to his face. "That would be best. Fingerprints."

"How about later," Jennet said, with a too-bright smile. "It can wait til next time, right?"

Marie's eyebrows gathered into a frown, but she nodded. "Very well. I will be downstairs. Tell HANA if there is anything more you need." She stepped into the hallway and gave Tam one last, skeptical look before closing the door behind her.

"Whew." Jennet rolled her eyes. "I didn't expect Marie herself. Usually one of the maids brings up snacks."

One of the maids? He couldn't imagine. "Obviously she wanted to see what kind of spoilage you're bringing home."

As if it wasn't obvious. The Exe clung to him, a grungy cloud there was no escaping. Even if his boots had been clean and his hair neatly cut, he couldn't get away from it, from who he was.

Except in-game. He shot a glance at the Full-D systems, anticipation curling and uncurling through him again.

"You're not spoilage," Jennet said. Then she tilted her head, giving him a long, level look. "I think you're fine how you are."

A tiny flame of a smile warmed him inside, though he tried not to let it show. "Ok, then. Let's play."

She went to the door and turned the lock with a decisive click, then grabbed a couple sandwiches off the tray. "Here. Marie gets mad if her food isn't eaten."

"I'd hate to see what she's like mad." Regular Marie had been bad enough.

He took a big bite of sandwich - real meat, and crisp, fresh lettuce instead of Vegipro. It tasted great, and he never turned down free food.

"Finish that up and grab a brownie," Jennet said. "I'll get us ready. There's a sink in the corner when you're done snacking."

The quiet hum of the Full-D systems vibrated the air. Tam bolted down a brownie, taking a second to savor the rich chocolate on his tongue, then went to wipe his hands. He didn't want to get smears on the shiny equipment, after all.

"Ready." So ready.

He felt like a kid on his birthday, with a million presents waiting, all wrapped in glittery paper. In one minute he was going to tear into them, and each one would be exactly what he'd wanted.

"Come on, then." Jennet settled into one of the chairs. She gave him a smile that trembled at the edges, then slid on her gloves. "Gear up. When you get to the main screen, it's the **F** icon from the menu. I'll see you in there!" The helmet's visor covered her smile, dimming it from bright noon to moonlight.

Tam eased into the chair. It welcomed him with a soft and comfortable embrace. He pulled on the helmet and slipped his hands into the gloves. Excitement filled his lungs, thick and sweet, like honey.

Game time.

# CHAPTER 9

THE GAME HELMET WAS LIKE WEARING AIR - so comfortable, he barely felt it. Tam let out his breath as the main menu lit up in front of his eyes. The resolution was about a hundred times clearer than on his system. No fuzzy graphics, no weird color shifts or lines across his vision. It felt like the images were inside his brain.

The **F** icon glowed, softly golden, looking like it was made of scrolled flame. It took only the slightest flex of his finger to select it. These gloves were prime. Super responsive - nothing like his thrashed-out gear. The menu faded out, replaced with blinking words:

*Feyland: A VirtuMax Production*

*Alpha 1.5.0486*

This was going to be incredible.

The visor-screen went dark. Faint music began playing, mysterious and chiming. Light slowly etched across his vision, a delicate tracery like webs or tree branches. He hoped, rather desperately, that this wasn't one of those girly games. But if Jennet needed his help, he'd do his best - even if it meant defeating sparkly pink dragons.

WELCOME TO FEYLAND

The words unfurled across the screen. The letters glowed a rich gold that deepened to crimson, then faded to grey, as though they had burned down to ash. The music twisted, and the dim letters suddenly whirled up into a flurry of dark-edged leaves. Behind them Tam thought he saw a pair of eyes watching from the shadows, but before he could be sure, the leaves swirled once again. This time, the screen cleared to show something much more familiar: a character-creator interface.

"Have you made your avatar yet?" Jennet's voice came clearly through the headset. It sounded like she was standing right next to him.

"Just about to." He studied the choices, trying to get a feel for the game's design, the various roles people could play. Was Feyland really going to be as different as he hoped?

Spellweaver - no, not another magic user.

Bard - interesting, but obviously not a heavy combat class. He figured Jennet would need a serious warrior-type.

"Got any thoughts on this?" he asked.

"How about a Knight?" she replied, confirming his guess.

Lifting his index finger, he highlighted the choice.

KNIGHT - *Skilled at feats of arms, noble, courageous, and true, the Knight can best almost any enemy in battle. Only magic can bring this hero to his knees - but even then, the Knight's sword may prove of greater power.*

Below the description stood a basic character, ready to be modified to his specifications. He scrolled through the options, adding more detail to the avatar. His Knight would be tall, of course, and strong. But not bulging with too much muscle - quickness could usually beat strength, if there was room to move. Thick dark hair, and, yeah, that heroic-looking chin. Blue eyes, but not quite that close together. With another flick of his finger, he put the final touches on his new self.

The character bounced slightly up and down, and Tam smiled to himself. Now for a name. Roland? No, that seemed too stuffy. He needed another anagram. Wernin? Newrin – yeah.

He double-clicked his thumb and index finger, the universal glove command to bring up the keyboard. Though he preferred voice and finger commands, he could type well enough when he had to. He entered the name, Newrin, then vanished the keyboard interface. Yes, his Knight looked good, clad in shiny silver armor with a huge sword at his side and a grim-looking shield strapped to his back.

*Character complete. Enter game?*

He pulled in a breath, then tipped his thumb up. *Yes.*

A fanfare of trumpets blared as his vision went golden. There was an odd, queasy sensation in the pit of his stomach. The sandwich and brownie weren't sitting too well.

Then all discomfort was forgotten as Tam got his first glimpse of Feyland.

He found himself standing in a clearing surrounded by white-barked trees. The sky was bright blue overhead, the grass a vivid green. Wind moved across the leaves of the trees, leaving flashes of shimmering silver as they rustled in its wake. A bird swooped past him, singing, and he could practically feel the warm air against his face. He glanced around, looking for Jennet, and saw he was in the middle of a circle of pale mushrooms.

Beside him, the air glowed brightly, and Jennet suddenly appeared. She was wearing a green dress that looked like something from the Middle Ages, but fancier. Her hair was intricately braided, and she carried a tall oaken staff with a white glowing crystal set in the end. Other than that she looked almost exactly like herself - her features a touch sharper, her eyes brighter.

"We're in!" She smiled at him. "Welcome to the game, Tam. What do you think?"

"I'm not sure." He took an experimental step forward.

"Careful! Don't crush the fairy ring."

"The - oh." He eyed the mushrooms surrounding them. "Ok. How do you change the camera angle to a different POV? I'm not used to gaming in first person."

An anxious line appeared across her forehead. "I should have explained. You stay in your character - it's part of the immersive experience. The designers decided you should always see through your character's eyes, hear through their ears - and feel," she reached out and brushed her fingers across his cheek, "what your character feels."

"I think I actually felt that." He moved his shoulders. The armor weighed practically nothing, but he could still feel it.

Could feel the wind, too, tickling through his hair. "Those are some serious advances in game tech."

Her gaze dropped to the rich green grass beneath their feet. "Yes. I told you it was different from anything you've ever played. But don't worry. The devs made sure to dial the uncomfortable stuff way back. You won't feel much pain here."

"I just wanted to see myself. Check out my gear and stuff."

"Of course. You can draw your sword and enter combat stance by—" She broke off, laughing, as he found the control movement before she could explain. "Very good." There was admiration in her voice, and something that sounded like hope.

"It's just a pull-back. Easy enough."

He swished the sword through the air a few times, and then re-sheathed it. His shield had immediately appeared, strapped to his left arm, as soon as his weapon was drawn.

She cocked her head and examined him a moment. "Hey, I didn't know you had green eyes. Your hair is always in your face, you know."

"Huh. I thought I chose blue." Hadn't he? He was sure of it.

"Well, the game still has some bugs. You could say it has a mind of its own." She laughed again, but there was a forced edge to it. "Ready to quest? As soon as we step out of the fairy ring, the creatures of the world will be able to interact with us. The starting lands are pretty easy to handle, though. And you'll pick it up quickly, I'm sure."

"Great. Let's go." He took a step forward then, for fun, leaped over the boundary of mushrooms.

This gaming system was really amazing. He no sooner thought of the movement than the sim translated it to his character. There must be some kind of complicated neuro-interface built into the gear. Every other system he'd played had a response-time lag. With his own, he had to rely a lot more on manual commands - specific combinations of hand and finger gestures that sent instructions to the game. This, though, was practically powered by thought alone. It made him giddy.

Jennet stepped out of the ring, her movements graceful, then waved to a mossy path leading between the trees.

"The game begins this way," she said, starting down the path.

Branches rustled behind them, and Tam whirled, sword at the ready. Nobody was visible, but high laughter chimed from between the leaves.

"Who's there?" he called.

"It's just the pixies," Jennet said. "Don't worry about them - they're harmless. Come on."

Tam sheathed his weapon and followed Jennet between the pale tree trunks. Soon the forest thinned and beyond the tree-line he glimpsed a rise of small green hills. At the very edge of the wood was a house, one of those English-cottage looking places with white walls and a thatched roof. Sitting on the doorstep was the ugliest little man Tam had ever seen.

His nose was enormous, a jutting cliff that overshadowed his dark eyes and thin lips. The only things larger than his nose were his two ears, great ugly flaps of skin on either side of his head. He was covered in a pelt of coarse brown hair, his only clothing a tattered cloth tied about his waist. He smelled, too, like moldy earth and old wood-smoke.

Jennet stopped in front of the creature. A clay bowl filled with what looked like milk appeared between her hands, and she knelt and placed it on the weathered step.

"Greetings, Fynnod," she said. Then she leaned toward Tam and spoke softly. "He's a Brownie - they like milk. I'll try and explain the game lore to you as we go along."

Tam nodded. "Right."

"Fair Jennet." The little man's voice was hoarse, as though he were unused to speaking. "You return - with a companion. Will you continue further into the realm?"

"Yes," she said.

Fynnod tilted his head up and looked at Tam. Something murky moved in his eyes. "Knight. Are you brave enough to accept the first quest?"

"Sure," Tam said.

Every game had its beginner quests. Generally they were pretty easy. They started a storyline, and gave you a chance to practice your abilities and get comfortable in your new surroundings.

The brown man remained silent, and Jennet cleared her throat. When Tam turned to look at her, she nodded her head up and down and mouthed the word *yes*. Oh, right - a role-playing script. RP wasn't his favorite, but it looked like "sure" hadn't been coded into Fynnod's list of acceptable replies.

"Yes, I accept your quest," Tam said.

The little man let out a cackle. "Very good." He reached into a lumpy bag beside him. "Take this sieve, and fill it with water from the river. When you return it to me, I will grant you passage to the next level."

Tam took the object from the Brownie. It looked like an old-fashioned strainer. "Fill this with water, huh?"

Well, he'd had odder quests, but he'd hoped this first one would involve fighting. He really wanted to try out his moves.

Suddenly the sieve disappeared and his sword was in his hand, the blade flashing in the sunshine.

"Ack!" Fynnod leaped up from the step, overturning the bowl in his haste. "Take your cold iron and be gone from me!" He shook his fist at Tam, and then scuttled into the cottage.

"Wait. You didn't drink your milk—" Jennet said, but the heavy wooden door slammed shut on her words. "Tam." She turned to him. "You need to be careful. Remember, the game responds to the slightest movements. Were you thinking about battle?"

"Yeah, sorry." He re-sheathed his weapon. "I didn't mean to frighten him."

She frowned. "A lot of the creatures here don't like iron or steel - your sword affects things just by being drawn."

"Got it. Easy on the swordplay." He gestured to the closed door. "Will he be back?"

"No. Not until we return with the quest complete." She bit her lip. "I haven't actually done this one before."

"And the milk?" He glanced at the doorstep. The liquid had seeped into the stone, leaving a dark stain. "Was that bad?"

Jennet didn't look too happy. "We were supposed to get Fynnod's blessing. Without it... I'm not sure what will happen."

She turned to look out over the green hills, and Tam stared at the cottage. He hated feeling like he'd messed things up already. Here he was, usually a prime gamer, and he'd screwed up the first quest. Nice going.

The breeze kicked up, and he turned to look at Jennet. A strand of her pale hair blew against her cheek. From now on he was going to do his best. He wanted to impress her. Wanted her to smile at him again, the way she had when he'd beat Saberclaw, so he could carry the warmth of that inside himself for a little while.

A dark shadow crawled over the landscape, dimming the sunlight. He peered at the hills. Something was coming toward them - fast.

"Tam?" Jennet sounded scared. "We've got company."

# CHAPTER 10

THE THING IN THE SHADOWS BECAME CLEAR AS IT GOT closer - a huge black horse, galloping toward them. On its back was a forbidding-looking knight, wearing armor as dark as his steed. A wicked helm concealed the rider's face.

Pulse quickening, Tam set his hand on the hilt of his sword. "First fight?"

Not a pleasant thought - he would feel better if he'd had at least some experience with combat in the game. Frightening the hairy man with his blade didn't count.

Jennet shifted her grasp on the staff. Her cheeks were pale. "The Black Knight. He... he shouldn't be here. Usually he's much deeper in the game."

"That sounds bad." He squinted at the approaching rider. "What's that, in front of the saddle?"

There was a small figure perched on the horse's neck, seemingly unafraid of either its precarious position or the imposing knight just behind. As they drew close, the creature scrambled forward, using fistfuls of mane to pull himself up until he was nearly standing on the horse's head.

The thundering of hooves ceased as the Black Knight brought his mount to a halt directly in front of them. The spritely creature riding in front lifted one stick-like arm in a wave, the gossamer tatters of his clothing following the movement.

"Well met, Fair Jennet," he said in a clear, high voice. He grinned at them from his vantage point, his brown eyes sparkling. "And to this brave yet untried champion. Greetings, Tamlin."

Tam blinked up at the creature. "It's, er, Newrin."

Wasn't it? Seemed like the character creation in this game was badly bugged. That's what he got for playing the beta version. Still, it was very weird that the little creature addressed him by name.

"Well met, Puck." Jennet made a small curtsey, but Tam could see her hands trembling. "What brings you so far from the pleasures of court?"

The sprite folded his arms. "The queen desires to know who has entered the realm. I come with a message - and a warning."

Behind Puck, the knight sat motionless, as though he were an inanimate object. It was eerie. Usually the devs built in some kind of movement to in-game characters. Maybe they had missed coding this one.

"What message does the queen have for us?" Jennet asked, her voice higher-pitched than usual.

Tam was glad to let her do the talking - she knew the

rules, after all. It was good to get a bit of the storyline, even though it seemed disjointed. Was this queen the final boss they would have to defeat to win the game?

"She bids you remember that the realm does not give up its secrets lightly." Puck leaped, making a sudden somersault from the horse's head, and caught the top of Jennet's staff. He clung there, hovering before them, and lowered his impish voice. "It is never simple to regain what was lost."

"I know." Jennet sounded way more unhappy than Tam would have expected from a bit of scripted dialogue. "Tell the queen I have come for what is mine."

She shook her staff, as if to dislodge the sprite, and Puck frowned at her. "Your champion still must prove himself, foolish Jennet."

"He will," she said, sending Tam an anxious look.

"Ha!" The sprite laughed, and the sound sent prickles down the back of Tam's neck. "Then he may do so this instant. Black Knight, I summon thee to battle!"

There was a blur of motion, and suddenly the Black Knight was standing before them, menace emanating from his faceless visor. His black sword hissed out of the sheath, and Tam leaped forward, making sure he was between Jennet and the knight. He drew his own weapon - barely in time. Dark metal clanged against silver, the shock jarring him to the teeth.

The knight feinted left, then thrust forward with a strength that sent Tam stumbling back. Whoa - for a first fight, this game was pretty serious. Behind him, Jennet let out a cry, but all Tam's attention was focused on his adversary. He had a feeling he couldn't afford to lose this fight, but how could he possibly win?

He stabbed at the knight, who blocked his sword with a bone-shaking counterstroke. Damn, the guy wasn't even using a shield. A series of hard blows rained down on Tam. Breath scraping his throat, he fell back under the power of that relentless assault. His shield arm began to ache from the jarring impact of the Black Knight's blade.

Slowly, the knight pressed forward. None of Tam's attacks seemed to touch him, though he was pretty sure he'd dented the guy's armor in a couple places. Tam couldn't let him get to Jennet. He risked a quick glance at her, to see that she was somehow frozen in a block of clear ice. Her staff was raised and her mouth was open, as if she'd been caught mid-yell.

Clang! Another blow to his shield forced Tam's attention back to the battle. Ok. This was just an in-game fight. An intense one, sure, but there was a pattern here. Every game had a certain level of predictability, if you paid enough attention.

One, two, three sweeping strikes, then the Black Knight lifted his sword for an overhand slice. It wasn't the first time the knight had made that series of moves. Tam scrambled out of the way, saving his strength. He wouldn't attack again until the moment was right - but he still had to keep those deadly sword strokes at bay. He hoped his shield wouldn't crack under the force of those massive blows.

The knight's sword slid across his shield, then continued slicing down. Ow! The blade nicked him in the vulnerable area just above his gauntlets. It didn't feel like a dangerous cut, but it stung. Tam sucked in his breath and kept fighting, kept watching. That combo of moves had to come soon.

Sure enough, after another punishing rain of strikes, the knight began that same series of swings Tam had seen before. This was it - his opening. He backed up and took a firm grip on his sword.

Now! The knight lifted his sword for the overhand attack, and Tam lunged forward with all his strength, the tip of his blade pointed straight toward the Black Knight's chest.

His sword connected with a hollow thunk, then stuck right in the center of the knight's armor. The Black Knight froze in place.

Silence descended, marred only by Tam's ragged breaths. Slowly, he pulled his blade free. It was unmarked by blood, but there was a hole in the knight's chest plate. Had he won?

"Tamlin," the Black Knight said, his voice low and grave. "First fight to you." He raised his sword in a half-salute. Then, just as suddenly as he had dismounted, he was once again astride his horse.

"Well well!" Puck cried, a merry note in his voice. "A fight fairly won." He gestured at Jennet. The ice block cracked open, and she took a quick, stumbling step forward.

She glared at the sprite. "Unfair! You didn't need to—"

"Of a surety, I did." Puck swung about at the end of her staff. "A noble impulse, to aid your champion, but forbidden nonetheless. But you, Tamlin..."

"Yes?" He sheathed his sword, but kept his hand resting lightly on the hilt.

"You are a truer champion than I would have guessed. Well fought, indeed. And now, in parting, I have a gift to bestow on you." He brought one cupped hand to his mouth and puffed.

Glittering dust blew across Tam's face.

"What the...?" He coughed and took a step backward.

Through blurred vision, he saw the little creature vault back onto the horse. In one smooth motion, the knight turned his steed and they galloped away, Puck's mischievous laughter trailing behind.

"What was that?" Tam rubbed his eyes. "Was he trying to blind me or something?" Things slowly started coming back into focus, and he let out a breath.

"Fairy dust," Jennet said. "It usually confers some kind of gift. I guess we'll have to wait and see what, exactly. That is *so* like Puck." She laid a hand on his arm. "Tam - you were prime, fighting the Black Knight like that. I would have helped, but," she made a face, "you saw what Puck did. You didn't need my help, though. You did great on your own."

He shrugged, though pride warmed him through. "If I won, that was a weird way to show it. Usually stuff dies at the end, you know?"

"Feyland is, well... it's unique."

"Yeah - I'm gathering that." He was also getting the feeling Jennet hadn't told him a few important things about how Feyland worked. There was a totally different mood to this game, and he couldn't quite figure it. Probably as they kept questing it would get clearer to him, but right now it was hard to sort. "Is Puck on our side?"

She tilted her head. "Puck is sort of a free agent, from what I've seen. Sometimes he helps with quests. Sometimes he doesn't."

"Speaking of quests - about this fetching water in a sieve..."

"What about it?"

"Where *is* my sieve? How does the inventory system work in here?"

"Oh - I should have explained earlier. Sorry. I was just so excited to get you in-game." She gave him a repentant look. "Basically, you think of the thing you need, say the name, and it appears."

"Anything? That's a pretty advanced database."

Jennet nodded. "There's a couple catches, though. You can't summon anything while you're in combat. And the main thing is, calling anything saps your energy for a little while afterward, makes you vulnerable. The more complicated the item, the longer the recovery." She glanced around. "Now is probably an okay time to try it, though."

"Ok. *Sieve.*" He blinked in surprise as the metal mesh bowl appeared in his hands. A second later, a wave of weariness washed over him, weighting his arms and legs. "Now how do I get rid of it?"

"That's easy —imagine your hands empty again and it will dematerialize."

Sure enough, the sieve disappeared as soon as he imagined it gone. Freaky.

"Can I try some other stuff?"

"Sure," she said. "Just don't tire yourself out too much."

"What about ... *Chocolate-chip cookies*. The big ones, with lots of chips." A stack appeared in Tam's upturned hand. "Hey - these look great."

He let himself collapse, cross-legged, on the ground, then lifted a cookie to his mouth. The interface was so good, he swore he could taste it. Except...

"These cookies taste like bananas," he said.

"Yeah." Jennet shook her head. "Apparently that's the synthesist's favorite flavor. They're working on it, but right now, everything in-game tastes the same."

He swallowed. "Good thing I tried it with cookies. I'd hate to take a big bite of banana-flavored pizza."

She laughed, and the sound felt like warm rain on his skin. Tam liked the way she looked when she smiled. Maybe this playing together was going to work out, after all. She hadn't been lying when she'd said the game was hard and she needed help. *His* help.

"That reminds me," she said, her expression growing sober. "Except for food you summon, don't eat or drink *anything* that someone here gives you."

"No candy from strangers. I get it."

"No, really." She knelt to face him, her blue eyes serious. "Promise me, out loud."

He vanished the cookies. Already he was feeling better - ready to get to their quest. "All right. I won't eat or drink stuff that people here give me."

"People or creatures. Promise it."

"Fine. I won't eat or drink anything that people or *creatures* give me. I promise." As he spoke the last word, the air vibrated, as though somewhere far off a bell had tolled.

Jennet nodded. "Good. It's a true pledge."

# CHAPTER 11

JENNET GLANCED AT TAM. SHE DIDN'T WANT TO EXPLAIN that he could get trapped in-world if he ate anything here. That would open up an entire barrel of worms that she wasn't ready to talk about now. If ever.

She exhaled, letting the last of the fear leave her lungs, and pulled in a deep breath of sweet air. This first level of Feyland was supposed to be safe. She'd brought him in without much explanation because they weren't supposed to get into any trouble at the beginning. Boy had she been wrong about that.

Nothing was going the way she'd planned. The elation of finally making it back in-game and picking up a quest that would lead to the next level had quickly curdled to fear when the Black Knight had shown up. She'd been sure he was going to pound Tam into the ground, then turn and fling her back outside the borders of Feyland.

But thanks to her champion, that hadn't happened.

Tam had bested the Black Knight. She had been so afraid. So proud. She wished she could have helped, instead of being bound into frustrating immobility by Puck, but it made crazy sense. It was Tam's test, after all.

"So, which way is the river?" Tam asked. He turned in a slow circle and the sunlight glinted off his armor.

She should call it now, and send him home. He'd done what he was supposed to - helped her reactivate the game quests. She could handle it from here. Besides, the Dark Queen was dangerous. It was Jennet's responsibility to make sure Tam didn't get too deep in-world.

"Well... we should probably log off."

"What?" He turned to her, surprise in his green eyes. "We can't just quit *now*. We have a quest to complete. Besides, I'm having fun."

"Fun. Right." She shook her head. Her idea of fun didn't include being pummeled by ferocious knights. But then, guys were different that way.

Would it hurt if he came with her a little further? If they completed the quest together? It would be quick and easy, and it was so nice to have someone along. Someone strong. Someone she could trust.

"Come on, Jennet," he said. "Let's keep going."

"All right," she said, and was rewarded by a flash of his smile. "I think the river is this direction. There should be a trail."

She took a firm grip on her staff and set off, away from Fynnod's quiet cottage. The grasses around them swayed in the wind, and the sky was once more clear and bright.

Tam strode beside her, glancing to either side. "This is really tight world-building. Though I'm glad everything doesn't *smell* like bananas too. Hey." He paused. "Do you hear that?"

She cocked her head, but heard only the breeze rustling in the tall grass, birds chirping. "I don't hear anything."

"Someone's calling for help." He set his hand to his sword and turned to their left. "This way. Come on."

"Tam, wait. Things here aren't always what they seem..." She was talking to his back.

Stifling a sigh, she hurried after him. He was a good hero, but couldn't he be a little more cautious? Then again, he didn't truly understand what they were dealing with. And whose fault was that?

Guilt twisted through her.

All right. As soon as they got out, she'd talk to him and explain how, exactly, Feyland was dangerous. Whether or not he'd believe her - well, that was a risk she had to take.

She caught up to Tam, who was turning a slow circle in the waist-high grass.

"I hear a voice," he said, a note of frustration in his tone, "but there's nobody here."

Jennet lifted her shoulders. "Feyland can be strange that way. Things don't always make sense. Come on, I see the trail. Don't you want to finish our quest?"

"Wait." He held up a hand, and then a startled look crossed his face. "Really? You are? Alright, let me see."

She had the feeling he wasn't talking to her - but she still didn't hear anything except some bird calling nearby.

Tam dropped to his knees and began parting the grasses around them. "Look, here he is."

"What? Who?" She peered over his shoulder.

He'd uncovered a hollow in the grasses, and there was something moving there. It was a small brown sparrow, flapping its wings desperately, but going nowhere. She bent forward, to see that one delicate foot was caught in a tiny snare. Poor thing.

"Shh," Tam said, holding out one hand toward the bird. "Don't be scared. We'll get you out of this, no problem."

"Is this who you heard calling for help? I mean, obviously he needs some assistance, but..."

"Yeah." Tam's nimble fingers worked on the twine that bound the bird, while a series of tweets and chirps issued from the little beak. "Can't you understand him?"

"Um, no. But obviously you can."

Tam nodded. "This is Skyward. Hold on, buddy, almost got it." He worked the snare free and carefully slid it off Skyward's tiny foot. The bird let out a few more chirps, and Tam dipped his head. "You're welcome."

With a startling flurry of wings, the sparrow shot up into the air. In moments he was just a brown speck against the blue. A cheerful trill drifted down to them, and then he was gone.

"Hm." Jennet stared up into the empty sky, thinking. "I bet that was Puck's gift - understanding the speech of animals."

"That could come in handy."

"Or be totally annoying, depending. What about

insects?" She glanced around, then pointed to a dragonfly skimming the grasses nearby. "Can you talk to it?"

Tam stepped over to it. "Hey, bug," he said in a loud voice. "'sup?"

The dragonfly hovered for a moment, then flew off, its wings making a shirring sound.

"Well?" Jennet asked.

He shook his head. "Nope. Guess I don't speak bug."

"That's probably best. I mean, you don't need every little speck trying to have a conversation with you. Hey, look. There's the river." She gestured down the hill to where water made a sparkling line of silver between the trees.

"And here's the trail. Come on." Tam led the way, his movements confident and relaxed.

Jennet watched him. Like her, his avatar was an improved version of his real-life self. Even though there was a character selection menu, it turned out that the game somehow picked up on how you *actually* looked, with a few modifications. Good thing there weren't any mirrors here, or she'd have even more explaining to do.

It didn't take them long to reach the woods lining the river. Dappled light filtered through the fresh green leaves, and up ahead the river chuckled to itself.

"I wonder if fish talk," Tam said. "And whether they have anything interesting to say."

"Are fish even animals?"

"Guess we'll find out. It's peaceful down here."

Jennet glanced at Tam. His eyes shone with interest as he looked around. It was nice, being able to see his face. He had good, strong cheekbones, and a sharp nose that wasn't too big. But his best feature was his green eyes, the color of the leaves overhead.

It was interesting, too, the way he opened up in-game. It felt like he'd said more to her in Feyland than he had the whole rest of the time she'd known him.

"Let's try this sieve thing," she said, pausing at the river's edge. An ancient willow grew there, its leaves trailing in the current. She materialized her sieve, and Tam did the same. He held it up to the light and turned it back and forth.

"Fetch water in this?" he asked. "If you hadn't noticed, there's a million holes in it."

"Well, that's the quest that Fynnod set us."

Tam stepped down to the river and bent, scooping up water. It immediately flowed back out, sparkling and dripping through the mesh of the sieve.

"Yeah," he said. "Of course it couldn't be that easy."

She set her staff down and knelt next to the willow, then dipped her own sieve in. A wavery reflection looked back at her. A reflection that suddenly grew long teeth and green hair.

"Jennet, there's something in there... look out!" Tam yelled.

Long arms erupted out of the water, grabbing hold of her. Fright thumping hard in her chest, she tried to scramble back, but sharp nails dug into her arms. She couldn't get free, and the creature was dragging her forward, into the water.

"Tam!" she cried.

The bank was slick. Nothing to hold on to but slender

reeds that slipped through her fingers as the creature yanked her down.

"Jennet!"

Tam lunged for her, but the creature gave a last, vicious tug and Jennet tumbled headlong into the river.

Chill water closed over her head, the cold shocking through her, and she kicked out wildly. The river was deep here, by the roots of the old willow. Deep, and treacherous, and the domain of a water hag. Fear shuddered through her.

Her staff lay uselessly on the bank above - she couldn't fire blue mage-bolts at the creature. Instead she jabbed her fingers into the tough green skin and tried to kick against the current. But no matter how she struggled, the water hag gripped her tighter and kept towing her down. Down. Dizzy panic tightened her throat.

"Hee hee," the creature burbled. "Wicked Peg found a morsel. A sweet tasteling." She smacked her lips as she pulled Jennet into the submerged shadows.

Jennet's limbs felt heavy. Her body was an echo of her own heartbeat, slowing, slowing. Bubbles escaped her mouth, little pearls lifting from between her lips to float up and away. The sky was wavery splinters of light above her.

Then silver exploded into the current beside them. Air and a flash like lightning - Tam diving in after her, his weapon shining. His sword darted, faster than she could have dreamed, stabbing the green-skinned Peg and making her howl. She lifted one hand from Jennet to claw at Tam's blade.

"Away, away. Prick me not, foul beast of the air!"

Tam kept slashing. Trickles of blood bloomed, clouding

the water like green algae. With a last screech, Wicked Peg released Jennet and wriggled away, disappearing into the murky depths beneath the willow.

The last bit of breath escaped Jennet. Her lungs were screaming for air, and Tam's arm was around her, urging her up. He kicked, strongly, and pulled her from the depths. They emerged together in a gasping spray of light.

"Come on." Tam half-carried her onto the bank. He kept his arm around her, even when they had gained solid ground.

Jennet knelt on the mud, coughing. Even though her mind was screaming at her to get away from the river, her legs wouldn't hold her up. She pulled in a rough lungful of air, then coughed again as it scraped her throat. Shivers chased through her.

That had been way too close. What was a high-level monster like that water hag doing here? Feyland was getting more dangerous than she had dreamed.

She crawled forward a few feet and grabbed her staff, then pulled herself to her knees. "Let's get out of here." Her voice was hoarse.

Tam nodded and took her hand, helping her to her feet. Her legs trembled and he gave her a concerned look. It warmed her up a little, inside.

"Yeah," he said. "Some distance is a good idea. You sure you're ok?"

"I'm fair." All she wanted was to get away from the river, and the green terror lurking in its depths.

"Let's head over there," he said, waving to a sunny

clearing just visible between the trees. "It seems far enough to be safe."

She nodded. He put his arm around her shoulders, helping her when she nearly stumbled. By the time they reached the clearing, her breathing had evened out and her steps were less shaky. Flowers dotted the grass - blue bells and spangles of daisies. It looked pretty and innocent, and she desperately hoped there wasn't some evil creature hiding in the trees, ready to pounce on them.

Tam surveyed the area, and seemed satisfied. "Here. Sit down a minute."

She sank down in the soft grass and looked up at him. Water plastered his hair to his head and dripped off his armor. He looked a mess, and she certainly wasn't any better off.

"I hope you don't start rusting," she said.

"Yeah. That could get awkward. But magical armor doesn't do stuff like that. Right?"

Jennet glanced down at her soaked gown. "If you don't rust and I don't mold, I think we'll be all right. Anyway, well... thanks." The word seemed inadequate.

Tam gave her a crooked grin. "Hey, I'm a Knight. It's what I do. In fact, give me your sieve and stay here. I'll figure this thing out."

"No." She climbed to her feet. "I'm coming with you. If Wicked Peg comes back, it might take both of us to defeat her again."

She was not going to let Tam out of her sight.

There was a stubborn set to his jaw, but finally he nodded. "Ok, but let's stay away from deep water."

"Yeah - you don't have to convince me of that."

They headed upstream, and she was relieved to see the bank flatten out and the river grow shallow. The water ran around large rocks, making a cheerful babble.

"It seems safe," she said.

"Maybe." Tam kept one hand on the hilt of his sword and gave the river a wary glance. "At least the bottom's easy to see - it can't be more than a few inches deep."

"You stand guard and I'll get my sieve." With a thought, she summoned it, and then braced herself against the surge of weariness that followed. "Maybe if we put mud over the holes, the water will stay in."

"Anything's worth a try at this point." He spoke to her, but stayed facing the river, his eyes scanning the shallows.

She scooped up a handful of dark, gooey mud from the edge of the bank and plopped it in the mesh. So far so good. She smeared it around until it coated the inside of the sieve then, fingers crossed, carefully scooped up some water.

For a second, it held. Then her triumph turned to disappointment as the mud dissolved. Brown water ran out the bottom, and the sieve emptied.

"Great," she said. "Now what?"

A trill of birdsong filled the air, and Tam jerked his head up. He nodded, then turned to her, a smile in his eyes. "Skyward's back. He says it's safe here. And he says to use ashes in the sieve."

"Ashes? Like, from a fire?"

"That's right."

Another flurry of chirping, and this time Jennet saw Skyward, perched on a nearby branch. Ashes, hm? She thought a moment, letting her mind come up with the picture. Ashes - thick gray flakes that would lie over the mesh, with the weight of the water holding them in place.

"It could work." Holding her sieve out, she imagined ashes settling into it, covering the holes. In an instant, the thought became reality. She swayed. "There. The tricky part will be scooping the water in without dislodging them."

"We can do it." Tam sounded completely confident. He summoned ashes into his sieve, then marched to the edge of the water and tilted it into a quiet eddy of current. His lips curved into a full smile as he held up his sieve, brimming with water. "Quest complete."

The hardest part was trudging back to Fynnod's without spilling the water. Skyward kept pace with them, twittering what Jennet imagined was encouragement. When they reached the thatched cottage, Fynnod was sitting in his usual place on the front steps. He watched them approach, his close-set eyes gleaming. She let out a silent breath of relief. Their earlier misadventure with the milk hadn't ruined the quest, after all.

"Greetings, Fynnod." Jennet gave him the proper words.

"Fair Jennet. Knight Tamlin. Have you completed the quest I set you?"

"We have," Tam said, stepping forward. The sky reflected off the water brimming in his sieve, a circle of blue bounded by metal.

The Brownie nodded, his ears flapping at the movement. "Then you have won access to the second circle. Prepare yourselves."

"Hold on," she whispered to Tam. "He's going to transport us there."

A golden glow surrounded them, and she caught a glimpse of Tam's surprised face. Then the world spun, a sudden vortex of glittering light. She reached, blindly, and caught Tam's hand in her own. It wasn't dangerous, traveling the rings, but it could be disorienting your first time.

The whirling stopped, the light dissipating to show a deep forest. As usual, they stood in the center of a ring of mushrooms.

"Where are we?" Tam let go of her hand and slowly surveyed the dark pines surrounding them.

"We're at the next fairy ring - the second level of Feyland." They had done it!

When Tam had defeated the Black Knight, she'd been pretty sure, but this was more proof. She was back in-game - though there was no way they could make it to the Dark Court in just one play session. Even if Dad didn't get home from work until his usual late hour, it was time to get Tam out of Feyland.

"Now what?" He sounded ready to quest all night.

"Now..." She visualized the interface, mentally pressing the exit button. "Now, we log off."

"But—" Tam's protest was lost as the game-world dissolved around them.

# CHAPTER 12

TAM LIFTED THE SIM HELMET AND BLINKED. HE FELT like he was waking up from some crazy dream - the kind that left your mind and body sluggish and overly warm. In the chair beside him, Jennet peeled off her e-gloves and ran her fingers through her hair. She looked....

Huh. She actually looked better. Less worn-looking. Her eyes were sparkling, and bright blue. Why had he ever thought they were pale?

She smiled at him, the glow and relief in it making him dizzy. "So - what do you think of Feyland?"

"Really amazing. Those fights..." he shook his head. "I could *feel* so much in there. Thanks for showing me the Full-D. Let's do it again - soon."

Her smile dimmed. "Tam... I really need to tell you—"

"Oh no!" He glanced at the clock blinking on the wall, and then read it again to be sure. "No - it's not really six-thirty, is it? I promised Marny I'd be home by six. She has to leave by then. Jennet, I have to go. Now."

He slid out of the chair, apprehension tightening his lungs. What a crappy thing to do to Marny. Hopefully she'd be able to stay a little longer. He didn't like the thought of the Bug on his own, even for a short time. There was no end of trouble that kid could get into.

"I'll call the car." She hit the blue switch beside the sim systems, turning off the jamming field. "HANA?"

*"Yes, Miss Jennet?"*

"Have George bring the car around front. Mr. Linn needs a ride home, as soon as possible."

*"Right away, miss."*

"I'm sorry," Jennet said, leading him down the hall. "Time is weird in-game. I knew you had to go, but..."

"It happens." He had lost plenty of hours in the past, had emerged from simming to find that the whole day had spun away. The consequences this time couldn't be that bad. He hoped.

Outside it was dark, the air quickly cooling into night. Jennet waited by the grav-car as he climbed in.

"So, see you at school tomorrow?"

"Yeah."

"Thanks for playing, Tam." Her voice was soft, almost wistful.

"See you." He let the door slide closed and told George where to head. The man didn't raise an eyebrow, which, considering their destination, was impressive. He must have some weaponry in the car - maybe even attached to it - if the thought of driving into the Exe didn't worry him.

It was full dark when the grav-car slid to a stop in front of Tam's building. He mumbled his thanks and got out as fast as he could. People were watching from the shadows and boarded-up windows - he could feel their stares. He hurried up the rickety stairs, not bothering to look back as the car slipped away.

It was quiet upstairs. Too quiet. A quick glance around the living room confirmed that his little brother wasn't there.

"Hey," he called. "I'm home. Come out now."

There was no response - and the Bug wasn't any good at hiding. He always laughed and gave himself away.

Tam peeked into the tiny room where his mom's bed was, did a quick check of the cramped bathroom - nothing. He pushed back the panic creeping up his throat.

There was a note on the dingy table. Tam picked it up, trying to keep his fingers steady. It was in Marny's round handwriting.

*Hey Tam, it's 6:20 and I really need to head out. I gave your evil kid brother the rest of the Sugar Crunchies and made him promise to chill until you got home. Hope you get here soon. And that you had fun.*

*--M*

Tam checked the faded green readout on the kitchen clock. Half-an-hour since Marny left. That was plenty of time for the Bug to get into trouble. Or for someone else to show up, and get him into even worse.

He sniffed - no telltale smell of matches or smoke. Not

like the last time he'd left his brother unsupervised. He'd come upstairs after simming a little too long, to find a pile of paper smoldering in the middle of the kitchen.

"Bug?" he called, "Peter?" Maybe his brother would answer to his given name. Nothing, and the fear really began to set in.

Should he call the cops? No - they'd only blow him off. The first few times Mom had gone missing, he'd tried to get them to come help, with no luck. Why would this be any different? He lived in the Exe.

His stomach twisted and he tried not to picture all the hurt his little brother could be in. The Bug was pretty random. The medicine he had to take for his blood disease made him act on impulse - not that an eight-year-old had a lot of sense to begin with. In the last year he'd started with the whole pyromaniac thing. He said the flames made him feel good. Tam was sure he'd hid all the matches where Peter couldn't find them, but still....

Maybe the people hiding out in the old shop down the street had seen something. They scared the piss out of him, with their crazy yellow eyes and the sickly-sweet smell of whatever they were smoking filling the air, but he had to start somewhere.

Tam was partway down the stairs when he heard it. A muffled clang, then a scrape of metal, coming from close by. He flung himself down the rest of the stairs and pelted to the back. Sure enough, the big door was unlocked. And inside -

"Peter!" He scooped his brother up in an awkward hug. "I was so worried about you."

"Yeesh." The Bug squirmed in his arms. "Let go, Tam. And don't step on anything."

Tam let his brother slip free, and finally saw what the kid had been doing. Disbelief hit him hard, right in the gut.

"Oh, god."

He turned in slow circles, trying to take in the destruction. Disconnected cables were half-unwound in coppery spirals over the floor. The visor of his helmet was propped against the open side of his CPU - which looked like it had been visited by a bomb. His gloves were turned inside-out, the sensors dangling like broken spider-webs.

Anger rushed through him, and a horrible sense of loss. "My system! What do you think you're doing?"

The Bug scuffed his shoe against the cement floor. "Marny said it was all messed up."

"Well, now it's *really* messed up. Damn it!"

He wanted to take his brother by the shoulders and shake him. Hard. So hard he'd fly into as many bits as the computer scattered across the floor. Instead, Tam took a deep breath. The Bug was too fragile for that - and besides, Tam was the one who held the family together.

"I'll put it back." His brother sounded on the verge of tears. "I didn't think it would be so hard to fix, Tam. I thought maybe, you know..." He curled his shoulders forward.

"Aw, man. Don't cry." There were enough other things in their life to cry about. "The system was about to die completely, anyway."

He tried to make himself believe it. And maybe the Bug

could actually get the thing up and running again. Stranger things had happened.

"Ok." His little brother sniffed, his voice still strained.

"Here." Tam pulled him into a rough hug. "Let's get you upstairs and ready for bed. You can work on putting it back together tomorrow after school."

Just before waving off the lights and locking the door, Tam couldn't help glancing once more at the ruins of his system. So much for his gaming.

Everything around here was falling apart. The stairs were getting more treacherous by the day, the neighborhood was disintegrating, and his brother had a disease nobody could fix. His mom was barely functioning. And now his sim-system was officially dead.

Tam shoved his anger deep down.

"How'd you cut yourself?" the Bug asked, one hand on Tam's arm.

"What?" He glanced down, to see his brother was right. There was a red gash on his forearm. It wasn't bleeding, but it was long and deep. "Oh, that. Don't worry about it. Jammy time, Bug."

While his little brother was getting into bed, Tam went into the bathroom and examined the cut. It throbbed, now that he knew about it. He didn't remember cutting himself.

For a second, the image of the Black Knight flashed before his eyes. That faceless black visor stayed there, floating in his vision, as if it were looking at him. With uncanny clarity Tam recalled their battle - the moment the knight's sword had slid into the gap between his armor....

A sick, shaky feeling moved through him. No way. You didn't get injuries that carried over from computer games into real life, no matter how intense the virtual reality was. It just didn't happen.

He had cut himself getting out of the grav-car, or downstairs, and just hadn't noticed. Yeah, that was it.

He gulped back a glass of water, and then splashed more on his face.

"Tam?" The Bug's voice was lonely.

"Coming." He slapped some all-purpose ointment on the cut, then went out to tell his brother goodnight. It was time they both got some rest.

"'Night to you, too," his brother murmured sleepily.

Tam curled into his old sleeping bag, and weariness hit him heavy in the chest. A crazy mosaic of his day flitted through his head. Jennet, smiling at him. The hairy brown man. A ring of pale mushrooms. Marny, stuffing his cash in her pocket. His system, the guts of his life, spilled everywhere.

Just before he slipped into sleep, he thought he heard the Black Knight's laughter echo in his mind, low and menacing.

# CHAPTER 13

JENNET SMILED AT HER REFLECTION AS SHE GOT READY for school the next morning. Hair a brighter shade of gold, eyes that sparkled - yes! She felt better than she had in weeks. Somehow, being back in Feyland had restored some of her energy.

Conviction rushed through her. She was going to win, going to make it all the way to the Court and get back the piece of herself she had lost.

Then her mood dimmed, the glint fading from her reflection's eye. That was, assuming she could enter the game by herself. She'd been so certain she was in - but then she'd tried to go in-game again, after Tam had left.

Once again she'd been stuck, trapped at the first level with no quest-giver and no way forward. Which meant that she still needed Tam.

And she had to tell him the truth about Feyland - that it was an actual place, somehow connected to the real world.

She couldn't ask him to go any further in-game without knowing what he was getting into. Though there was no guarantee he'd believe her, and the thought of telling him made her feel sick. She squeezed her eyes tight and concentrated on keeping her breakfast down.

"*It is time to depart for school, Miss Jennet.*" HANA's even tones rang through the bedroom intercom.

"Ok, I'm coming." Jennet hurried out of the bathroom and grabbed her satchel, then paused in front of her bookshelf. Her dad thought she was crazy for still wanting the paper books that lined the shelves.

"It makes no sense," he had said, watching the hired movers carry the last of the heavy boxes of books away from their old house. He'd slipped his tablet out of his pocket and waved it at her. "*This* is where all those books could be - plus thousands more. Instead you're going to give the workers a hernia."

"I like old tech, Dad." Especially since some of those books were too old, too rare. They didn't exist in e-form. Neither she nor Dad would mention Thomas, or the fact that some of those books had belonged to him. Since he'd died, they never, ever talked about him.

She ran her fingertips along the bumpy spines until she found *Tales of Folk and Faerie*, a collection that was nearly three-hundred years old. It had belonged to Thomas. She'd salvaged the aging binding and done what she could to reinforce the delicate paper. With a whispered apology, she slid the book out and tucked it into her satchel. Tam needed to see this, needed to look at the stories and illustrations and have it all start to make sense. The way it finally had for her.

"*Miss Jennet? Is there a reason to delay?*"

"I'm on my way." Sometimes she wished HANA would lose that machine patience and sound irritated. Just once. So that Jennet could pretend there was a real person there, who actually cared if she was late to class.

SHE MADE it to school on time. The only problem was, Tam wasn't there. She was sure at lunch, when she saw Marny sitting in the cafeteria. Alone.

Jennet took a deep breath and swallowed back the bitter tang of worry. There could be a hundred reasons Tam hadn't made it today.

Too bad all the things she could think of went from bad to horrible. Something had happened, she just knew it - somehow the game had harmed him already. Feyland had been completely unpredictable last night. It wasn't such a stretch to think the game had done something to Tam.

And it was her fault.

Maybe Marny knew something. Jennet grabbed her tray and walked over to where Marny sat. Without waiting for an invitation, she set her lunch down and took a seat. A shocked little buzz of attention followed her, making the back of Jennet's neck prickle - but there was no way she was waiting until the end of school.

"Hi," Jennet said.

Marny had set her fork down as soon as Jennet approached, and gave her a level gaze across the table. "You sure you want to be over here?"

"Yes. Unless you want me to leave."

Marny lifted one shoulder. "As long as the gossip won't bother you. I don't care. Sit where you want."

Jennet looked across the cafeteria, saw the faces quickly turned away, the giggles hidden behind lifted hands. "It's not like I'm exactly popular. Being a Viewer and all. Listen, do you know—"

"Where's Tam today?" Marny's question collided with hers.

"What?" Her worry spiked. "I thought you'd know."

"I had to leave before he made it home last night. If he made it at all. What did you do with him?" There was a challenge in her voice.

"Nothing! Okay, he was a little late, but my dad's driver dropped him off at his house no problem. Really, you don't know where he is?"

"I'm not his keeper. Like I said, I had to leave. I hope everything's all right."

Jennet pushed her tray aside. "I have to go find out."

"He never answers his messages - reception in the Exe is way spotty. There's no way to get in touch with him."

"I'm going to his house." Jennet stood. Having a plan helped clear some of the anxiety, made her feel a little more in control.

"What - now?" Marny glanced side-to-side. "You don't seem like the type to ditch your classes."

"This is more important." She had to make sure Tam was all right.

"Maybe he just got sick," Marny said, though she didn't sound very certain. "Or his brother did - their mom isn't around a lot, so stuff falls on Tam. It could be no big deal."

"Could be."

"Look. You can't just head into the Exe and hope to find Tam."

"Come with me, then." That would make things a lot easier.

"I wish I could, but..." Marny made a face, like she'd bitten something sour. "I can't miss the test in World Markets today, or they'll flunk me out. I'll take you over there after school though."

The anxiety sizzling through Jennet wouldn't wait. "No. It has to be now."

"You're not big on sense, are you Fancy-girl?" Marny blew out a breath, then pulled a piece of paper out of her bag and scribbled something down. "Look, here's a map. That's my number at the bottom. Message me if you get totally lost. And when you find out what's up with Tam."

Jennet folded the paper and tucked it in her pocket. "I'll let you know." She grabbed her tray and stood up.

"One more thing," Marny said.

"What?"

"Try not to get killed out there." The big girl gave her a wry smile.

"Um. Okay, I'll do my best."

Jennet scraped her lunch into the bin, then set her tray on

the stack with a clatter that seemed to echo around the room. People were still looking at her - but she had bigger things to worry about. There was only one person who mattered right now, and the sooner she slipped away, the sooner she'd know if he was all right.

BOARDED-UP buildings loomed on either side of Jennet. She swallowed back the metal taste of fear and glanced at the directions Marny had scribbled out. Did that line there mean she was supposed to go left, or right? According to the sort-of map, she was getting close to Tam's. So far things had been quiet in the Exe.

Before leaving the school grounds she'd taken off her jewelry and folded the cuffs of her sweater down over her wrists, trying to hide her chip. True, she still stood out, with her too-clean designer clothes, but so far she'd been left alone. If her luck held, in a couple minutes she'd be knocking on Tam's door. Provided she could find it.

George knew how to get there, but she couldn't call him and say, "Hey, I'm ditching my classes, could you give me a ride?" Dad would send her straight back to Middland.

A clank of metal-on-metal drifted from down the street to the right. Okay then, she'd go left. The pavement had chunks missing. The smell of something rotten lodged in the back of her throat, but this felt like the right place. The empty, brownish building on the corner seemed familiar. Wasn't Tam's just down -

"Hey, girly." A man stepped out into the street in front of her, his voice hoarse and low.

Jennet took a step back, her whole body going tight with fear. Run! She whirled, only to find another man flanking her. Oh god. Oh god. This was severe. Stomach clenching, she sidled toward the middle of the street.

The first man spread his arms wide. He and the other guy both had weird, yellowish eyes, where a crazy wildness lurked. They smelled, too - a thick, cloying stench that made her head spin.

"You look like you got loot," the first man said.

"No." She fought to make her voice firm, the way you'd talk to a menacing dog. "Go away."

"Nuh-uh. Not until you hand over that fancy purse," said the one behind her. "Hey man, check out her wrist. I think we just hit the jackpot." He laughed, a rusty caw.

The first man's eyes gleamed and his hand went to his belt. He had some kind of weapon there. Gun, knife - either way she was in deep trouble.

Jennet's body was a drum, filled with the heavy thump of fear. She should've waited for Marny. If only she had a weapon, just a stone or a stick, something to fight with. Or her staff. She could almost feel it in her hands - the heavy, comforting weight, ready to zap whatever creatures menaced her.

Wait. She *could* feel it. She glanced down to see the smooth, dark wood, the crystal glowing blue-white at the tip. Her mage staff from Feyland.

No way. Fear was making her imagine things. But the

man in front of her was staring at her hands, too. Staring at what she now held.

"What the..." He took a step back and drew a knife. "Where'd that come fr—"

Jennet hit him with a sizzling bolt of light, square in the chest, sending him flying backward ten feet. He lay moaning on the broken pavement.

Never hesitate when confronting your enemies - she'd learned that in-game. Pivoting, she leveled her staff at the second man, but he was already running away, down the street. She nearly went after him, but caught herself. She had to find Tam. And this wasn't Feyland.

It was the real world - so what was her staff doing, appearing in her hands and shooting magical bolts? Things like that just didn't happen. They couldn't.

As if sensing her disbelief, her staff disappeared. There one second, gone the next, leaving her fingers curved around empty air.

Jennet blinked and lowered her hands. Had she been dreaming? The guy lying on the street was pretty convincing evidence that it had happened. But her staff had vanished. No explanation.

The man moaned and Jennet ran, sprinting past him down the street. She didn't look back. She skidded around the corner, and her breath whooshed out in relief as she saw the old mechanic's shop with the rickety outside stairs. Tam's place.

She checked the big metal door in back first, but it was locked. All right - upstairs it was. No matter how treacherous the stairs looked, they would be easy compared to the guys she'd left behind.

The railing swayed when she touched it, and the treads creaked wearily under her feet, but Jennet kept going. Maybe Tam wasn't home, but she couldn't stop now. The thought of going back through the neighborhood alone... no way. A shiver shook through her. At least it was the middle of the day. She couldn't imagine how creepy the Exe would be at night. Maybe even worse than the Dark Forest in Feyland. She didn't intend to find out.

No wonder Tam was so brave, if this was what he lived with every day.

A small landing at the top of the stairs led to a warped front door. There was a window in the wall beside it, but it was made of thick glass imbedded with wire, impossible to see through. Well. No use just standing here. She lifted her hand and knocked.

# CHAPTER 14

A SHADOW CROSSED IN FRONT OF THE WINDOW, AND then a metal cover in the door slid open a bare inch. An eye regarded her.

"Hi," Jennet said. "Um - Tam, is that you?" Somehow she didn't think so. Unease tightened the back of her neck and prickled down her spine.

The eye looked at her a moment more, then the peephole cover closed abruptly. Jennet waited, but there was nothing else - no greeting or dismissal, no opening door. She bit her lip. Should she knock again? Maybe it had been the little brother, and he didn't know what to do. Although, whoever had been looking at her, it hadn't felt like a kid.

"Hello?" she called. "Is Tam home?"

The silence continued on the other side of the door.

She waited for what felt like forever. Finally, Jennet turned away. Disappointment was sour in her mouth. She took one step down the rickety stairs. Then another.

Behind her came the quiet jangle of a chain, the clunk of a deadbolt being drawn back. Whoever had been standing there was opening the door. Half-afraid to look, she made herself turn around.

The door swung back to reveal a woman on the threshold. She clung to the knob, as if it were the only thing keeping her upright. She was tiny, and not just because she was emaciated, though that didn't help. Her green eyes were ringed with weary circles. Brown hair, cut raggedly short, framed her too-thin face.

"Who?" she whispered, the question a bare thread of sound.

"I'm a friend of Tam's," Jennet said, making her voice soothing. This woman looked like she could be knocked over by a loud voice, an abrupt move. "Is he home?" Please, let him be here.

"Mom?" It was Tam's voice, calling from inside.

Thank god - he was all right. Relief poured through her, making her knees weak. Tam was here. Not collapsed on the floor because the game had ripped out a piece of his soul. Not bleeding away from some game injury that crossed the boundary into real life.

"Hey mom, where are you?" he called again, sounding worried.

The woman glanced over her shoulder, and then looked back at Jennet. She nodded, once, and then Tam was standing beside her.

"What are you doing?" he asked, all his attention fixed on

the wraith of a woman still clinging to the doorknob. "Come back inside now, Mom. You shouldn't be up."

Then his gaze moved past the woman. He looked unhappy to see Jennet standing there.

"Hi," she said. "I wanted to see if you were okay."

"I'm fine." He put a protective arm around his mom and steered her back into the house.

Jennet took a hasty step forward, before he could close and lock the door in her face. "Can't I come in? There are some crazies out there, you know."

"Whatever." He didn't sound at all pleased about it. "I'll be right back. Close the door, and make sure it's locked." Without looking back, he guided his mom inside.

"Nice," Jennet said under her breath.

She hadn't thought Tam would throw a party when she showed up, but she hadn't expected this borderline hostility. Especially after running together in Feyland so successfully the day before. She'd thought they were allies, at the very least.

After closing - and bolting - the door, she stepped into the middle of the room. Tam's place was slightly better than a shed, but to call it a house would be a stretch. It smelled musty, with an underlay of old grease and rust. The main room had a thin couch along one wall, with bedding pushed down at the bottom. In the corner was a sleeping-bag and worn pillow. Pretty obvious that Tam and his brother slept here. A bathroom was wedged in beside the kitchen, but it was too small to even qualify as a room.

Next to the sleeping area was an overflowing bookshelf,

made from rough boards nailed together. Comics and computer repair schematics spilled out of the shelves in messy stacks, sandwiched in between old game manuals, kid stories and some novels. It reminded her of the other reason she was here - to give Tam the book in her satchel. And - her breath caught - to tell him about Feyland.

In front of the couch, taking up part of the floor, was spread a thin webwork of wires. Jennet took a careful step closer. They seemed to be attached to Tam's gaming gloves. Was he doing some modifications? There was nothing he could do to make his gloves respond like the VirtuMax ones. He shouldn't even try.

Tam came back into the room, closing his mom's door quietly behind him. He folded his arms.

"So," he said, "what do you want?"

Jennet tried not to look like his attitude was bothering her, but the unfriendliness in his voice and expression hurt. He'd gone back to being the wary stranger with hair in front of his eyes.

"Nice to see you, too," she said. "I'm glad you didn't get jumped by the crazies last night, or break your neck on the stairs, or something like that."

"My mom came home," he said, like that should explain everything.

Which in some ways it did. Obviously his mom was a wreck, and Tam was taking care of her. Jennet couldn't blame him for missing school - it didn't seem like he had much of a choice. Even though it had put her in a severe panic.

"We need to talk," she said.

He gave a sharp nod. "You first."

She swallowed. "Could we sit down?"

"Ok. Watch the wires." He stepped over the eviscerated gaming gloves and pushed the bedding off the end of the couch, then perched there.

Jennet sat at the other end and leaned her satchel against her legs. She nodded at the floor. "Are you re-configuring your gloves?"

His expression tightened even more. "You could say that. The whole system is down for maintenance right now."

"Oh. So - you can't play at home?"

"Look." He pushed the hair out of his eyes and gave her an angry glare. "Why did you come here?"

"I have something to show you." She pulled the old book out of her bag and handed it to him.

He stared at the cover a long moment, and then opened the book, turning the pages with a care that eased some of her tension. Familiar faces flashed past. Fynodderee. Puck. At the illustration of Peg Powler, the water hag, he stopped.

"This is the inspiration for Feyland," he said. "Where'd this book come from? Is it yours?"

"It belonged to the lead developer who worked with my dad on the game. His name was Thomas Rimer."

Tam slowly closed the book. "What happened to him?"

His expression was serious. Would he still trust her, still believe her, when she told him the truth?

"He..." Jennet twisted her fingers together. "My dad would tell you he died of a stroke, but... I think somehow the game killed him."

"Wait a minute," Tam said, rubbing at his forearm. "How can a game kill someone? That can't happen, not literally."

Jennet took a deep breath. "Feyland isn't just a game, Tam. I know it sounds crazy, but I think it's somehow connected to the Realm of Faerie."

"Get real." He pushed the book onto the couch and stood. "There's no such thing."

"If it's not real then what is that book all about?" She pointed to *Tales of Folk and Faerie*, sprawled on the faded blanket.

"Fairy tales!" Tam jammed his hands in his pockets. "It's just a book. Stories to frighten kids, made-up stuff - they're not real."

She used to think the same thing. "That book is hundreds of years old, Tam! Those stories aren't made-up - they're collected from real people who had real experiences with something beyond our world. Did you know that in Europe, stone circles used to be recognized as portals into Faerie? Burial mounds, sacred wells - all of those were doorways to somewhere else."

"So?"

"So - those places are gone now."

"And what?" He gave a disbelieving laugh. "Now the faeries are trying to get to us through *games*? You're insane, Jennet."

His disbelief stabbed through her. She'd thought - she'd hoped - that Tam would believe her. He was the only one who might.

A muffled cry from the bedroom made them both turn.

"Damn - she's waking up." He turned on her, a fierce look in his eyes. "You need to go. Now."

"Fine. I'm leaving you the book."

Another cry, louder this time, followed by a thump. Tam took her arm and marched her to the door. "I don't have time for your wacko theories about Feyland, Jennet. Just, stay out of my life from now on. I have more important things to deal with."

She blinked hard against the sting of tears. He wasn't worth it.

Except that, he was.

"Tam—"

"Bye." He closed the door in her face. The bolt chunked back into place. From inside came the sound of something breaking.

Jennet sank down on the top step. It took a minute for her to blink away her tears. School was almost out. She'd wait a little longer, then call George to pick her up. She didn't think Tam would let her back inside. She wasn't welcome, that was beyond clear, but she wasn't about to walk back alone through the Exe.

She stared at the grey sky and took a shaky breath. All right. So much for her gamer hero. It was better this way - for both of them. Feyland was too dangerous, especially for someone who didn't take it seriously.

She was on her own. Again.

# CHAPTER 15

It took longer than usual for Tam to soothe his mom back into sleep. Maybe it had been his argument with Jennet, or just having someone else in their house, but she was restless and manic. He'd coaxed her back onto her meds, but it always took a while for them to kick in and stabilize her crazy mood swings.

He swept up the shards of the plate she'd broken. Next time he'd remember to bring her food on plastic dishes. It would be another two, three days before she'd be back to functioning. Then he and the Bug would have a mom for a while.

His brother was still young enough to treasure those times, but Tam had learned to hate them. A week or two, maybe a month, and she'd stop taking the drugs that made her sane. Then she'd steal whatever money was left and leave - only to stumble home a few days or weeks later. And then the cycle repeated.

He still couldn't forgive her for taking the travel money he'd worked so hard to earn. The money that would have gotten him to the national gaming tournament. It had been his ticket out - prize money, sponsorships, a little fame. All gone. He still felt sick when he thought about it.

At least this time she had brought some cash. Tam didn't ask where or how she got it, he just hid most of it. They needed food, and cheap fuel for the generator, and anything else they couldn't put off. This time around, it would be a trip to the clinic for the Bug, to get his quarterly shot.

Would there be enough for a new system? Yeah, right. No way was that going to happen. Tam laughed bitterly at himself for even having the thought.

Not only did he have no system, he'd just ended his friendship with the girl who had the best set-up he'd ever played. He was an idiot.

Forget about her sparked system, and her blue eyes. He'd go back to Zeg's - when he got some time and some extra coins.

Not soon, that was for sure.

He didn't have anything else to do, other than stare at the mess of his gaming gloves, so Tam picked up the book Jennet had brought. What a nutcase.

*What about that cut on your arm?* a voice inside him whispered. He ignored it. There was no overlap from virtual reality to real life. None. To think there might be - that was craziness waiting to happen. It was surprising the authorities hadn't taken Jennet in for psych testing.

Or maybe they had. What did he know about her, after

all? She was new in town. She could be hiding all kinds of things.

Well, he'd never know. They were done. Though at some point he supposed he'd have to return her stupid book. Might as well take a look, now that he had it.

It was old - she hadn't been lying about that. The few color illustrations had a dreamy, saturated feeling, similar to Feyland. Jennet said the lead programmer had owned this book. Obviously he'd used it for some serious inspiration.

There were black-and-white drawings, too. Gnarled figures perched in tree-branches, lovely women who called men to their deaths in deep water, winged sprites darting through a clearing. And the Black Knight. Tam's gut clenched as he stared at the picture of the knight. The cut on his arm started hurting. Hastily, he turned the page.

*The Faerie Queen.*

For a second, Tam couldn't breathe. So, this was the queen. Her face was delicate, her eyes haunted and compelling. She wore clothing that looked insubstantial as mist, the flowing gown revealing the curve of her hip and baring one shoulder. Pointed ears were just visible through her midnight-dark hair, gems tangled like stars in its silky blackness.

She was beautiful. He couldn't imagine *wanting* to fight her, even as the final boss in a game.

"Tam?" It was the Bug, home from school. Tam hadn't heard him coming up the stairs.

"Hey there. Want a snack?" He shoved the book under his sleeping bag and went to distract his brother.

THAT NIGHT the Dark Queen moved through his dreams. She whispered to him of his bravery and offered him a goblet of deep red liquid. His lips touched the edge - and he woke, tangled and sweaty in his sleeping bag. First light was sifting through the windows. He got himself a drink of water, and then went to check on Mom.

She was sleeping - a restless, unhappy sleep from the looks of it. He could sympathize. Even though he was tired, he wasn't going back to bed. The alarm to get the Bug off to school would ring in an hour, and it wasn't worth it to lie there trying to rest for most of that time, only to get yanked back out of sleep again.

He missed gaming. It had only been two days since simming at Jennet's, and there was a big aching hole in his chest.

He'd told Jennet to stay out of his life. Remembering the look on her face made him wince. Maybe he'd been a little harsh. But it had been too much - her just coming over, showing up while he was trying to deal with Mom, looking around his house like it was no better than a cardboard box some street bum slept in.

And then that freaky talk about Feyland and some guy named Thomas. Obviously his death had hit her hard, but that was no excuse to go off the deep end about what was real, and what wasn't.

Still, maybe he shouldn't have told her off. Even if that game had made her crazy, she was a nice person. Too good for him, really, with her fancy life and all. Not to mention that amazing system.

He let out a deep breath, then went into the kitchen to heat water for instant coffee. It was going to be another long, tough day.

## CHAPTER 16

JENNET WALKED INTO THE MEDIA ROOM AND STOPPED, her heart sinking. The room held a cluster of netscreens, an old console, and a dismantled moto-sense setup. She'd assumed the Gaming Club would have basic sim equip. But no. Not in Crestview.

A clump of boys and a purple-haired girl were sitting around screens showing a battle RPG. They hadn't noticed Jennet yet.

She took a careful step backward, trying to breathe softly. This had been a mistake. Maybe she could still get away unseen.

"Hey. Rich girl," a voice called. "You in the right place?"

Jennet halted and looked across the room, meeting the gaze of a large girl with fierce eyes. She looked familiar, and her name rolled into Jennet's mind - Marny. They shared a few classes. The rest of the gamers lifted their heads, fingers on their pause buttons, and the air in the room went heavy and cold.

Great. An invisible exit was out of the question now.

"So, you're too good to answer?" Marny asked. "What are you doing here, anyway? Looking for a cheap boyfriend?"

The other kids laughed, though the big girl's words hadn't been entirely kind to them, either.

Jennet took a deep breath. This was her last chance. If there wasn't a 'leet player here, she didn't know where she'd find one.

"You guys aren't the only ones who game, you know," she said. "I'm a simmer."

The tension in the room gained an interested edge. One of the boys pushed his yellow hoodie away from his big-nosed face.

"You? A simmer?" He looked her up and down. "Right."

The skinny boy next to him let out a high-pitched giggle. "Yeah, like I'm sure she's really prime at Unicorn Fantastic. Or RainbowGems."

The other kids laughed, ready to dismiss her.

Jennet gestured to the netscreens. "Do you guys play Rumble?"

Yellow-hoodie's eyebrows went up. "What, you're gonna challenge one of us to a duel? If you hadn't noticed, princess, these are screens, not sims."

"Ease up, Fernald," Marny said, leaving her solo screen and walking over to the other gamers. "If she wants to duel, let her. Maybe she could show you a thing or two."

"Right. You really want to duel?" The boy named Fernald folded his arms, then glanced at the skinny kid next to him. "Clarc would be a good pick - he's fairly dud."

The skinny boy flushed, but he didn't say anything. Clearly Fernald was alpha dog in the Gaming Club.

"Or you could face off with Shella." Fernald nodded to the purple-haired girl. "You know, stay at the female level. Girl on girl."

This guy was an idiot. Jennet stepped forward. "Who's the best player here? That's the one I'm dueling."

Fernald gave her a mean smile. "You're looking at him."

"Then we're on."

She was glad, actually. Fernald was too full of himself by far. And he was in for a serious battle, whether he knew it or not.

There was a general scramble as the gamers shifted, and an empty chair opened up for her. Jennet sat, put on the headset, and gave the 3D-mouse a couple test swipes.

It had been months since she'd played Rumble, but it was a pretty simple PVP combat game. The worst that could happen was that Fernald would end up beating her. She pressed her lips together. If he proved to be the best gamer in school, she wasn't sure she wanted to ask his arrogant face for help - let alone spend time in Feyland with him.

"We'll go Basic Mode, just for you," Fernald said. "How's that sound?"

Jennet shook her head. She wanted to push him, and herself, to the limit. "Hard Mode. Best two out of three."

"You really want to eat cement twice in a row?" Fernald gave her a look of mock sympathy. "I'm not gonna cut you any breaks."

"Whatever." She selected the Rumble icon and pressed the play button.

The pre-set characters popped up, a dozen of them on the selection screen. She didn't hesitate in making her choice - Nika, the ninja assassin. All that time spent dueling her friends last spring was about to pay off. If she wasn't too rusty. She had one chance to remember how to play - one loss she could absorb. After that, she'd better be on.

"Ready," she said, meeting Fernald's stare.

"Ok, princess. Show me what you got."

The arena appeared, a big walled circle enclosing the characters. Inside were the usual obstacles and traps: randomly scattered mines, a pit, some pillars, and a couple floating platforms. Jennet clicked through the function bars, reminding herself of Nika's combat skills. Slice, Leap, Throwing Star, Dash.

Then Fernald's character materialized - a massive tank-bot called Reaper. Good. That thing carried a lot of armor and some serious weaponry, but it was clumsy. She had the advantage of speed and maneuverability.

The tank-bot moved forward, bladed hands snicking together, but Jennet was faster. She leaped Nika onto one of the platforms and got a couple throwing-stars off. One of them stuck into the metal side of Reaper's head, like a jagged earring, but it didn't cause much damage. For that, she'd need to hit the vital spots - eyes, neck, under the ribs.

Reaper lurched forward, one arm now transformed into a laser-cannon. Red beams sliced the air, and she somersaulted Nika out of the way. Adrenaline zinged through her, and she felt her focus tighten up. Every shift of her fingers sent her character dancing away from the tank-bot.

Fernald let out a vicious laugh. "Fancy moves aren't going to win this for you. Listen. You can still surrender."

"I don't think so." Jennet dodged away, keeping far enough that Reaper couldn't hack at her, but not so far that he could use his cannon again.

Just in time, she realized Fernald was backing her into the pit. Certain death from razor-sharp stakes waited at the bottom. For a moment Nika teetered on the edge, and she heard the other gamers suck in their breaths. She twisted the mouse violently and managed to fling her character to the side. Too slow. She'd evaded the pit, but the tank-bot was on her, clashing and slicing. There was no escape. Her screen flashed red, and Nika went down in a splash of blood and flutter of black cloth, defeated.

Jennet let out a silent breath. Okay. One round gone. She had to do better than that. She *would* do better than that.

"Yeah!" Fernald leaned back and cracked his knuckles. "You like that? Want some more?"

She was getting the rhythm of the game back into her body. This next fight she'd go on the offensive, take the tank-bot down with a quick assault. She didn't think Fernald would expect that.

"Best two, remember?" She batted her eyelashes at him. "If you can beat me again, that is."

"Heh. In your dreams."

This time, when the arena opened, she didn't hesitate. In two fast moves, she blocked Reaper's clashing hands and slid a blade into his right eye. With a clank and groan, the tank-bot tilted and fell backwards. The ground shook when he landed, and a puff of dust rose in the air.

The gamers were silent. Most of them were staring at Fernald's screen, but Marny was looking straight at her. A smile lifted the corner of the big girl's mouth.

Fernald's expression was as black and stormy as a tornado. "Lucky break. It happens. Even the worst noobs sometimes win - by a fluke."

"But, dude," the skinny boy began.

"Shut it, Clarc," Fernald gave him an elbow to the side. "And get out of my way. It's time to take the princess down." He shot Jennet a narrow-eyed look. "Here comes your loss."

He'd be on guard now, but Jennet knew she could take him. She grinned at him over the screen.

"In *your* dreams," she said. She heard Marny smother a laugh.

Fernald scowled at her. Good. She had no doubt he'd rush her character and try what she'd just done. A quick and bloody death.

Sure enough, the tank-bot charged forward, this time carrying a huge axe. The weapon whistled down - but Nika was already gone, sliding around the side of Reaper, her blade seeking the weak spot under his ribs.

Fernald pivoted his character and tried to pound her

again. At least he wasn't a hopelessly bad gamer. Just an annoying one. She swallowed, and danced Nika back a few paces.

*Click.* Barely heard - the sound of a mine, primed and ready. Adrenaline surging, she hammered the *dash* command and ran Nika across the arena in a blur of black. There was a sudden, fiery explosion right where she had been standing.

"Dammit!" Fernald wasn't as quick. The blast rocked Reaper, but didn't take him down.

Now she was in trouble. Nika was out in laser-cannon range again, and she wouldn't be able to *dash* for another ten seconds. Plenty of time for Fernald to hit her with a couple deadly shots. She had to keep him off-balance - and her character out of his sights. She dodged Nika behind one of the stubby pillars scattered through the arena.

"Hiding?" There was a sneer in Fernald's voice.

"Yeah, and you're it. Come and get me." She checked the cooldown on her *dash*. Eight seconds.

Reaper clanked to the side, trying to maneuver for a clear shot. She circled Nika around the pillar, letting a flutter of black cloth show. Red beams shot past, taking out a part of the pillar. Time to find a new hiding spot - the whole pillar was probably next. She imagined Fernald thinking the same thing. Focusing the cannon on the pillar. Pulling the trigger - now!

She rolled to the side, and kept rolling as the pillar exploded. Five seconds to go. And nowhere else to hide.

Nika scrambled to her feet and started zigzagging across

the arena. The earth around her was scored with holes as Reaper kept firing, tracking her path. He got an indirect hit, and Jennet winced as her screen flashed yellow. That was the warning that her health meter was plummeting. Three seconds. Time for a new plan.

"Shiiineh!" Nika's battle-cry rang through the arena.

She changed her trajectory and ran straight at Reaper, flinging throwing-stars like glittering confetti in front of her. When she ran out of stars, she started on knives.

"What the - ?" Fernald watched her crazy moves for the last crucial seconds. Then, with a chuckle, he raised his laser-gun. "Wow, you really are a noob."

Deadly red beams shot out … into empty air. Nika's *dash* had carried her past Reaper. She whirled, knives flashing, and sunk a lethal blow right between his ribs.

This time, Reaper crumpled into a heap of metal. Satisfaction swept through her like a warm tide.

"No way!" Fernald shoved his chair back and stood. "You used some kind of cheat. I should've known someone like you would use exploits. That was so—"

"Shut up, Fernald." Marny's voice was even. "She didn't cheat. You lost. Deal."

"I should've known. You freak girls stick together."

With a last glare, the defeated gamer turned his back on them. He punched Clarc in the arm, then stomped out the door.

"Uh. That was really prime," the skinny boy said, rubbing his arm. The admiration in his eyes was uncomfortably close to a full-on crush.

Jennet stood. "Well, thanks for letting me play. I sort of crashed your meeting."

The purple-haired girl gave her a tentative smile. "It was about time someone took Fernald down. Come back again, k?"

"Sure. Do you think you'll ever get some sim equip in here? That's what I do, really."

The girl shook her head. "Not in the next ten years, I don't think. Unless VirtuMax wants to donate some." She got a thoughtful look. "Hey. Maybe I should do a project on that."

Clarc nodded eagerly, giving the purple-haired girl the same look he'd turned on Jennet. "Good idea, Shella. You're so smart."

"Well, thanks again," Jennet said. "It's been... interesting."

She turned, to find Marny standing there.

"More than interesting," the other girl said. "Best afternoon I've had in a while. My name is—"

"Marny. I know."

There was a flash of surprise in Marny's eyes, quickly masked. Then her mouth quirked up. "Yeah. And you're Jennet."

"Glad we got that sorted out." Jennet smiled - one of the first real smiles she'd felt since coming to Crestview. "So... is Fernald really the best player here? Or was he just boasting?"

She had wanted to defeat him - to wipe that arrogant smirk off his face. But at the same time, she'd hoped, she'd *needed*, to find a prime gamer here.

Marny shrugged. "Fernald's as good as any of them are."

Jennet gave her a close look. She hadn't seen Marny play, but obviously the girl knew something about gaming.

"What about you? Do you sim?"

"Me? Nah." Marny shook her head, her bobbed black hair swinging around her face.

Too bad. Of everyone she had met so far, she liked Marny. They might have made a good team - if only the girl were a simmer. Jennet would much rather have Marny's solid presence beside her in Feyland than that jerk Fernald.

"Is there someplace else people go to play?" Jennet glanced around the Media Room. "I mean, someplace with sim-systems?"

"My uncle has a sim-café. Though you don't seem the type to go there, frankly. Don't you have a system at home?"

"Yes. I was just wondering," Jennet said. "Anyway. Good meeting you."

She felt her brief happiness fade, like an ember dying out. So much for the Gaming Club. Now what? The sim-café? That kind of place was for people who couldn't afford systems or pay the monthly access fees on the top games. She could try looking there - but she already knew it would be a dead end. Despair boxed her in, dark heavy walls with no windows, no doors.

"Hold on." Marny's brown eyes held a spark. "You know, if you're looking for a simmer you should talk to my friend Tam."

"Tam? Tam Linn?"

The sullen boy in her history class who never brushed the hair out of his eyes? The ragged kid from the Exe? No way.

"Yep. He won his system in a sim tournament. You should see him play. He's flawless."

# CHAPTER 17

THE REST OF THE WEEK, JENNET KEPT HOPING TO SEE Tam at school. If only she could talk to him again and say she was sorry for coming over. She shouldn't have gotten up in his space like that, but she had needed to make sure he was all right. Needed to try and make him understand.

Each day crawled by, the hours oozing past like old ketchup, and there was no sign of Tam. Marny couldn't tell her much, either. She just said that it was his life, his business, and that he'd be back. Eventually.

Every afternoon Jennet went home, turned on the jammer, and snuck onto the Full-D, trying to get back into Feyland. Every afternoon, she was stuck again at the starting lands, unable to find a faerie ring to take her deeper in. It was no use - she was locked out. Without a companion, the game wouldn't let her through. She could feel the extra energy she'd gotten back trickling out again, like a slow leak from a faucet. Pretty soon she'd start getting dizzy again - and how long would she last after that?

It was better for Tam if he were done with her, done with Feyland. She knew that, but panic still crawled up her throat at night, choking her, and her dreams were full of the Dark Queen's mocking laughter.

Then at dinner on Friday, Dad decided to get all parental.

"I hear you had a guest over," he said, setting down his fork. "A young man."

He seemed pretty calm. Maybe he was just glad that she'd made a friend. "His name's Tam. He's in some of my classes."

"Oh?" Her dad lifted his eyebrows. His voice was carefully neutral, in that way parents had of trying to get you to confide.

She let out a sigh. No doubt George and Marie had already given him their biased opinion. "He's nice. And he's a gamer. A good one. I thought he might like to take a look at the prototype system."

"Young lady." Dad's voice was suddenly hard. "I've told you Feyland is off-limits. That's not going to change."

"I know that, Dad." She pasted a smile on her face, trying to look like she had a major crush. "But the Full-D systems are cool to see, and I just wanted to show Tam..."

"Impress him, you mean?"

She didn't have to fake the blush heating her cheeks. "I guess. He's kind of sweet." And messed-up. And still a hero in every way that counted.

"I expect you to behave yourself." He picked his fork back up and took another bite of meat. A good sign that the interrogation was about over. "Does this Tam have a last name?"

"It's Linn. And don't worry. I mean, I like him, but we're just friends." Or had been.

"If you continue seeing him, I'd like to meet Mr. Linn. And Marie is insisting on a clearance check." His tone said there was no arguing around this one.

Luckily, it wouldn't be a problem. She wasn't seeing Tam at all - not even in the most basic sense of the word.

"All right." It was way past time to change the subject. "How's work going?"

He finished chewing. "We need to find a new lead programmer."

For Thomas. His death had been strange; even VirtuMax acknowledged that. They thought it had been some kind of corporate espionage, though. Suddenly the push was on to get the whole project relocated here, to Crestview, where the security was tight as clenched teeth. And where the buried cables of the 'net ran right through - ready and waiting for when the company was ready to market their new release.

"Maybe you should start something new," she said. She tried to keep it casual, though she wanted to grab Dad by the shoulders and start yelling that they must never, *ever*, release that game. "There has to be another way to showcase the system without finishing Feyland. What about a different kind of game?"

Her dad shook his head. "I don't know why you keep

saying that, Jennet. The company has already put millions into this project. And I thought you liked the idea behind Feyland."

"Not so much, any more."

Not since she'd been sucked through it into a place that was perilous, real, and full of dark magic. What would happen if her dad's team managed to finish the project? Once Feyland was released with the new sim-system, there would be millions of players. Would all of them fight the same battle with the Dark Queen that she had - and lose? Then what? Could the Dark Court somehow find a way to enter their world? The thought made her mouth go dry.

"I'm sorry." Dad's tone told her he was apologizing for everything: Thomas's death, their sudden move, even being such a workaholic that her mom had left for good five years ago.

Jennet took a drink of water. The liquid in the glass shivered under her unsteady hand. Some things you couldn't change. And some things you had to try, no matter how impossible.

"You should start playing Feyland." She couldn't keep the urgency from her voice. "You know, see what it's like *inside* this project you've been managing. It would help you get a feel for it. I could go with you, help you with the quests, show you around."

Maybe then he'd be able to see the danger, maybe then he'd listen to her. Although Tam had played, and he hadn't believed her. Her dad would be no different.

"I played the earliest version," he said. "You know that. It was enough to give me a solid idea of the concept. Gaming's not my strong point. Besides, I prefer to stay out of the artist's vision at this point."

"There is no artist! You can never replace Thomas. You shouldn't even try." Tears clogged her throat, and she stared at her plate, appetite gone.

After an uncomfortable minute, her dad let out a low breath. "How about we go see a movie tomorrow? There must be something good at the 3-Max."

"All right," she finally said, swallowing back her hope-lessness.

Not that going to see a movie would change anything. Dad would never come around, and banging her head against that brick wall wasn't going to solve her problems.

Monday was better, especially when she caught sight of Tam at his locker. Relief blew through her like a welcome wind. Should she go up and say hi? Did he have her book? What if he just ignored her? Or worse, snapped at her and told her never to speak to him again?

While she was still debating with herself, the first bell blared through the hall and it was too late. He didn't look at her once during Early World History. Good thing she hadn't said hello. She tried to ignore him in return, but despair settled over her like a thick cloak. When class ended, she moved blindly out into the hall.

"Hey." A touch on her arm.

She turned, to find Tam beside her. His eyes, half-hidden by his hair, looked wary. But not mad, not the way they had when he'd told her to get out of his life.

"What do you want?" She kept her voice even. No gladness. No anger. Students thronged past them, some talking noisily, others with heads bent to their tablets, barely watching where they were going.

"Can I meet you after school?" he asked.

She shrugged, like it didn't matter, but a flame of hope wavered to life. "I guess. I'll see you out front."

"Ok." He hesitated like he wanted to say more, then gave her a brief flicker of a smile. "See you."

He walked away, and her body was suddenly lighter, like she'd finally remembered how to breathe.

It still took years for the end of the school day to come. A few times, Jennet was certain the clocks had broken, their readouts stuck on the same numbers. But at last her final class ended.

She made herself walk slowly down the stairs and out the big double-doors. There was no guarantee Tam would be there. He could have changed his mind. Even if he was waiting for her, things might still be bad between them.

He was there, leaning against the brick wall with his hands shoved in his pockets, his mangy backpack at his feet.

"Hi," she said, stopping in front of him. It didn't seem enough, but everything else she could think of to say was too dumb - or too personal. Clearly his mom was a dangerous topic, as was Feyland. Her apology stuck in her throat, but she scraped it out anyway.

"I... I'm sorry I barged into your life like that."

"Yeah." He looked down at his scuffed pack. "I'm sorry, too."

Ouch. "I'll stay out of your life from now on, don't worry." Tears pricked the back of her eyes.

"Wait." He held out one hand. "I didn't mean it like that - I meant for telling you to leave like that. I, um, brought back your book."

"Did you read it?"

"Yes." His green eyes caught hers. "It was interesting. Look, Jennet. I'm sorry I said those things to you."

"Which things?" She needed it to be perfectly clear. Needed to know exactly which parts he was sorry for.

A shadow crossed his face. "That you should get out of my life. That you were crazy. Wait—" He held up a hand as she drew breath. "I'm not saying that you're right, either. But I do know that something strange is going on."

"Do you?" It was a start. She pressed her lips together, trying to keep from hoping.

He rolled up his sleeve and held out his arm. There was a red line marring his skin.

"I got this cut after the fight with the Black Knight. Yeah, I could have cut myself on something else, but..."

"But what? You think maybe the game can affect the real world?" Oh, god. He might actually believe her. The painful knots in her chest began to loosen. She'd been carrying this alone for so long.

"I'm also having weird dreams." He cleared his throat. "And the game, Feyland - there's something kind of off about it. So - I don't believe you. But I don't *not* believe you, either."

Jennet went limp with relief. She sagged against the wall, her whole body trembling. "Thanks."

The word wasn't big enough to convey the enormous wave of gratitude rushing through her.

He bent and pulled *Tales of Folk and Faerie* out of his pack, then handed it to her. "So, when do we go back in-game? I could come over almost any day this week. My mom," he looked away a moment, then back, "she's doing better. For now."

"That's good. But I don't think we should play again."

There was a flash of hurt in his eyes and he straightened. "What do you mean? I thought you needed my help. Or did you find somebody else?"

"No - nobody else. But Tam," she gestured to his arm, "you've already gotten hurt, and that was in the starting lands, where nothing like that is supposed to happen. It gets worse. A lot worse."

He pushed his hair away from his eyes and gave her a long look. She could almost see the thoughts turning in his head.

"Did something happen to you in-game, Jennet?" His voice held a rough note of concern. "Are you okay?"

She wouldn't cry - not here, in front of the school. In front of Tam. Blinking hard, she summoned up the words. "I lost... I lost the game to the Dark Queen. And no, I'm not okay."

A tear slipped down her cheek. Then another. All the

fear she'd kept inside was pushing out, making her skin hot, making her weep despite herself.

"Jennet." He reached out and touched her shoulder. "Don't cry. You aren't supposed to beat the boss the first time you try. It'll be all right, I promise."

She drew in a shaky breath. "It's not like that, Tam. You have no idea. The first level of the game—"

"Hey." He gave her a fleeting, crooked smile. "Give me another chance. I'm the best simmer around, remember? And this time, I know what we're getting into."

"You don't." She pushed away from the wall and stared into his eyes. "Feyland is dangerous!"

"Then show me." He held her gaze.

Stubborn idiot. He wasn't backing down. She wanted to hit him and hug him at the same time.

"Tam—"

"Let me choose whether I should keep playing or not. I get it, something's weird with the game. I'll be careful. Besides, don't you still need my help?"

She dropped her gaze and stared at the ground for a long moment. That was the worst of it. It was hard to argue that he shouldn't enter Feyland when she needed him so desperately.

"Yes," she finally said. "I do need your help."

"Then we're still playing," he said. "Together."

# CHAPTER 18

Jennet settled in the sim-chair and glanced over at Tam. Helmet and gloves on, he was leaning forward like a free-faller about to jump.

"Ready?" she asked.

Please, let nothing go wrong. She had the twisting feeling that Feyland was a trap, waiting to spring. They shouldn't be doing this - but she didn't have any other options.

"Ready," he said. His voice was full of anticipation that she couldn't share.

"All right. See you in there." She pulled down the visor of her helm and entered the game.

WELCOME TO FEYLAND.

The words scrolled across her vision, flared, then burned down to nothing. She braced herself for the transition, that queasy, whirling golden light that marked full entry into the game.

When the light stopped spinning, she was standing in a

ring of pale mushrooms. Tam was beside her, wearing his armor, his sword at his side. The sky was filled with the grey of early twilight, and the dark forest stretched away on all sides. Directly in front of them a thin trail cut through the pines.

He glanced around. "Where are we?"

"The second circle. We unlocked it last time." Proof, as if she needed it, that she couldn't go deeper in-game without Tam. "The path should lead to our next quest giver. And don't forget, each level is more dangerous than the last."

"Ok. Let's go." His silver armor gleamed as he strode out of the ring. She noticed he was careful not to disturb any of the mushrooms.

Taking a firmer grip on her staff, she followed. The silence was thick in the forest, the sound of their footsteps muffled by the layer of pine needles carpeting the path. Grey mist filtered between the trees, making everything dim and hazy.

"Will the sun come out?" Tam asked. "It was a lot lighter the first time we played."

"Every circle takes us farther into Feyland. In the center, at the court, it's night all the time." The memory of her moonlit battle shivered down her spine.

"I thought faeries were ok with daylight. They're not vampires, are they?"

"It's the Dark Court." Even saying the words made her feel cold. There was a sudden ache in her chest, as though the part of herself that belonged to the queen had woken and was tugging at her.

Tam was silent a moment. When he spoke, she could practically hear the thoughts tumbling into place in his head.

"In that old book you lent me, there were two main courts. They weren't called Dark and Light though."

"Unseelie and Seelie. We're in the land of Unseelie. Unfortunately."

"So why aren't the Light - er, Seelie - faeries around?" he asked. "Don't all these guys live in the same world?"

"From what I've read, it's kind of complicated." She stepped around a bramble bush that tried to snag her skirts. "It's not that any of them are good or bad, the way we think of it. This isn't Tinkerbell running around sprinkling pixie dust, you know."

"Actually, I've read that old story. Peter Pan. You know, she wasn't a very nice little faerie. She tried her best to kill the heroine."

"Exactly," Jennet said. "They don't have the same sort of morals as humans. The dark, the light, it's all fluid. So the Seelie Court may be involved, or may be content to let the Dark Court go about its business."

Something rustled in the underbrush, and Tam whirled, hand on his sword hilt. "Who's there?"

There was no reply.

Then motion erupted around them. Thick black roots whipped out of the earth and snaked around Jennet's ankles. Brambles grasped her skirts with spiky fingers, and the pines reached down, needles tangling into her hair and holding fast. Her mage staff was whipped from her hands and landed in a prickle bush, out of reach.

"Tam!" she cried, her heartbeat racing. She brought her hands to her head, trying to wrench her hair free. The trees held her fast, and her scalp burned from the pain.

"I'm trying!" Tam was slicing at the foliage holding her, but the bushes and vines were impervious. It was like his sword had been turned to useless plastic.

"Why aren't they grabbing you?" She tried to kick free of the roots, but they were iron manacles around her ankles.

"No idea. Maybe my armor protects me. Are they hurting you?" He kept slashing, but it was no use. The underbrush wasn't giving way at all.

"My head hurts, but I don't think they're trying to kill me." After the initial attack, the trees seemed content to just keep her imprisoned.

"We have to get you free." He slid his sword back in the sheath and grabbed her mage staff from where it had tumbled into the bushes. "Try this."

She took her staff from Tam and pointed the end at one of the thickest roots, at a safe distance from her feet. White flame sizzled, and for an instant it felt like her bonds weakened - but then they cinched even more tightly about her ankles.

"Ow," she said. "That didn't work."

"Look." Tam pointed through the misty trees. "There are lights over there - and can you hear that music?"

She listened. "No. I don't see anything."

"What if it's the Seelie faeries, Jennet? I bet they could help us. Anything that plays music like that has to be good."

A dreamy look moved across his face. He turned and took a step into the underbrush.

"Wait! Hold on - something's wrong."

She heard the music now. It whispered her name, sweet and low, promising help, promising that if she followed, everything she wanted would be hers. Jennet shook her head, sharply.

"Don't listen, Tam." It was hard to ignore the pull of the music - but she was hardly going anywhere, with the trees imprisoning her.

"They're just over there," Tam said, gesturing. "I'll be right back, with help."

"Tam, no... don't go!" She tried to take a step after him, and fell to her knees as the roots held her feet immobile. The pines wrenched at her hair and she blinked back tears of pain. "Tam!"

He didn't turn around, and now she could see the lights. Blue faerie-fire, glimmering and beckoning. The music was louder now, almost impossible to ignore. Obviously Tam had fallen under its spell. She called his name again, but he kept going without a backward glance.

She had to get free by herself - and fast.

Brute force wasn't doing it. She looked at the roots, then hefted her staff again. She needed a different spell. What would work against plants? She closed her eyes, trying to ignore the hammering of her pulse.

Heat. A soothing warmth that would coax the plants to wilt and droop like leaves on a hot summer day. Could she summon a gentler form of her lightning? Opening her eyes, she coaxed the spell to life, making waves of heat shimmer from the crystal set at the end of her staff.

For a long minute, nothing happened. Then the roots binding her ankles eased and the painful tangling in her hair lessened. Barely breathing, she kept sending warmth at the roots, the bushes snagged in her skirts, the pine branches overhead. At last, with a creaking sigh, the plants let go.

Yes! Jennet leapt to her feet and took a few hasty steps away. The roots lay quiet on the path, the pines no longer loomed over her.

But where was Tam?

The forest was utterly still. Heart pounding, Jennet picked up her skirts and ran in the direction he'd disappeared. Surely she'd catch sight of him just ahead.

But there was no Tam. Her fear swelled into the edges of panic. Deep in the forest something glinted. A flash of light, reflected off silver armor.

Lungs burning, she forced herself to go faster. The underbrush pressed against her, thorny brambles and thick-leaved skunk-cabbage, but she was getting closer to the lights. They resolved into glowing balls bobbing through the thinning trees. The ground softened, and in moments she was slogging through the shallow water of a bog.

A bog! Oh no. Wisps. Those were the pale balls of light, not help from the Seelie faeries. Tam was following marsh wisps, and they were luring him to his doom.

She caught sight of him up ahead, striding through knee-deep water.

"Tam!" she called, her voice high with fear. "Come back!"

He didn't give any indication at all that he'd heard her. Instead he marched on, his face turned toward the pale orbs that floated ahead. Panic gave her a spurt of energy. She splashed forward through the murky water and caught his arm.

"Stop," she cried, almost losing her footing. "Tam, you're following will o' wisps."

He still didn't look at her, but this time he spoke. "Can you hear it? It's the most beautiful..."

Clearly Tam was entranced. She circled in front of him and placed herself squarely in his path. Her feet were beginning to sink into the soft mud, and the water was almost up to her hips.

"You have to listen to me," she said, putting one hand out. "Tam Linn, you have to—"

He tried to slosh around her, and then stopped, shaking his head. The soft music seemed to grow louder and the wisps bobbed around them in a semi-circle of cold light. With a jolt of panic, she saw that the water was crawling up Tam's armor. He was sinking.

"No!" She pointed her staff at the closest wisp and shot a bolt of white flame at it.

The wisp flared, then disappeared, leaving behind the smell of rotten vegetables. Jennet tried not to breathe in the stench as she shot the next wisp, then the next. From the corner of her eye, she saw Tam was up to his chest. He was going down fast.

Calling on all her energy, she sent a wave of fire rippling from her staff. The rest of the wisps ignited, their reflections blurring the water. Then they were gone, burned away to nothing.

"Jennet?" Tam blinked, as if his eyes had been focused someplace else. "What happened?"

"Wisps." She gripped her staff tight and let out a shaky breath. "They lure people into the bog, to drown."

Tam grimaced. "Sorry - I shouldn't have followed them. That was dumb."

"You were ensorcelled. But yeah, it was." She grabbed his hand. "Come on, we have to get out of here."

"Um, we have a problem." He didn't move. "I'm stuck."

"Ok, here." She handed him her staff. "Use this for leverage. I'm going to push you from behind. Ready?" She went around him and laid her hands on the cool metal of his back. Chilly water lapped at her wrists.

"Stupid armor," he said. "Ok, go."

Her feet slipping, Jennet leaned and shoved and heaved, and finally, with a sucking splash, Tam stumbled forward.

"Keep going," she said. "There's solid ground just a little further on."

They sloshed toward the trees, pushing past lily pads and thin reeds, until the water was below their knees. Jennet let out a long breath and shivered. They'd come too close to disaster. Another minute, and Tam would have been a victim of the bog. Would he have woken in real-life, gasping and choking? Would she have logged off to find him limp and lifeless in the sim-chair?

She shuddered, grateful to step out of the slimy water to the firmer ground of the forest. Tam was right beside her. His feet came free with a disappointed squelch, as if the bog wasn't pleased to let him go.

"Thanks for the rescue," he said, ducking his head.

"Yeah, well, we have to look out for each other here. You saved me last time. I figure it was my turn, right?" Her gown was clammy against her legs, and her shoes were filled with mud, but a crazy relief moved through her. "We make a good team."

"True enough." A smile flashed through his eyes, quickly gone. "Now what? Back into the forest?"

"I'm not sure I could find the path again. And I'm not a big fan of the trees attacking us, either." She glanced around. The misty light made it hard to see, but to their right she thought there was some kind of a structure. "Do you see something over that way?" She gestured. "A bridge, maybe?"

He squinted. "Yeah, I think so. Let's go check it out."

As they got closer, the shape resolved into a stone-arched bridge. Which meant a road. Which meant that they could find a quest-giver and start progressing to the next level of the game - before it caused them permanent harm.

The bridge was tall, the road running on an embankment high above the murky bog. Deep shadows filled the spaces between the arches, and Jennet eyed the darkness. Anything could be lurking in there.

"Hm," Tam said. "Did you ever hear that old story about the three goats trying to cross a bridge?"

"I was thinking the same thing. I bet there's a troll - or some kind of guardian - under there."

"Then we better give it something if we want safe passage across. What do you think - a goat?"

"I don't think I can summon a goat. Besides, that's just wrong." She thought a moment, and then summoned some bread, honeycomb, and berries. Her hands overflowed with the offerings.

"Here." Tam held out a basket. "Put them inside and rest a second. I'll take it up to the edge of the archway."

She placed everything in the basket, then wiped the stickiness off her hands with her damp skirt. The usual weariness from summoning twined around her, making her arms feel heavy.

"Do you think it's going to be enough?" she asked.

"If I were a hungry troll under a bridge, this would be a feast. Throw in a pizza or two, and an army could cross over - even if everything's banana flavored."

"Hopefully it's not too picky about taste." She held her breath and watched as Tam carried the basket up to the shadowy arch.

"Hey, troll," he said, setting their offering of food down. "We'd like safe passage over your bridge. Here's a little something for you to eat."

There was no response. Had they been wrong?

"Try again," Jennet said. "Maybe it's sleeping."

He raised his voice and repeated the words. This time, there was movement in the dark recesses. Tam slowly backed up until he was standing beside her. He pulled his sword from his sheath with a low hiss.

A large, pasty-looking hand reached out from the shadows. It seized the basket, thick yellow fingernails curving around the handle, and drew it under the bridge. Jennet caught a glimpse of a doughy face and a mouthful of long, pointed teeth.

There was a chewing noise, and then a low sigh, like wind over stone.

"You may pass," the creature under the bridge rasped.

"Quick," Tam murmured, taking her arm and pulling her up to the embankment. "We don't want it to change its mind."

They hurried across the bridge, following the stone blocks stretching over the bog. With every step, the back of Jennet's neck prickled. Halfway across, the bridge shivered. The troll was getting restless.

"Faster," she whispered to Tam. "I don't want to be dessert." It was too easy to imagine that yellow-nailed hand reaching up and grabbing her ankles.

She and Tam sprinted the last few feet to safety as the bridge gave a final shudder. Then she looked up, and blinked in surprise.

The landscape had shifted while they traveled across the bridge, the rough-hewn stones of their path giving way to a dirt road bounded by low rock walls. The bog lay shrouded in mist behind them, while ahead, fields stitched the countryside. The setting sun was caught in the clouds.

"Sunset," Tam said, nodding at the rays slanting red across the sky. "What does that mean?"

"It means we're not as deep in as we were." She let out a low, shaky breath.

"Is that a good thing?"

"It depends. If we complete another quest at this level, the next ring will lead us closer to the Court. But we have to find somebody to give us one, soon."

"Yeah." He rubbed his forearm. "So, where does this road go?"

"I'm not sure." She glanced at the winding lane ahead. "Nothing seems familiar."

"I guess we follow it and find out," Tam said. "Stay close."

"Hey! I'm not the one who wandered off into the forest."

"We still have to stick together." He lifted one eyebrow. "A team, remember?"

Despite the seriousness of their situation, Tam was always more relaxed in-game. It made her smile a little, inside.

It didn't take long before the road dipped into a valley. At the bottom was a standing stone, a huge sentinel at least thirty feet high, gilded red by the setting sun. The wind lilted around them, almost a melody.

And then it *was* a melody - a sweet plucking of strings, the humming of a baritone voice.

Tam stopped. "Do you hear that? Is it more wisps?"

"It's not wisps." Shading her eyes with one hand, she squinted down the lane. There was a figure seated at the base of the stone, playing the guitar. Her heart gave a lurch. "Oh god. I think it's..."

She leaned forward into a tilting run, her legs pushing hard against the earth while her pulse hammered through her. It couldn't be. And yet, in Feyland, who could say what was possible?

# CHAPTER 19

"Wait!" Tam called from behind her. "Who is it?"

As she hurtled down the road, the man set aside his guitar and rose. He opened his arms and she flew into them.

"Thomas!" Tears ran salty into her mouth. She clung to him, her father's old friend, so familiar despite the odd clothes he wore. "I can't believe it. You're all right."

"Well, now." He gave her a final squeeze, then set her back at arm's length. "You might want to tell your friend with the blade not to chop off my head."

Jennet whirled to see Tam running toward them, his sword gleaming at the ready. "Tam, wait! This is a friend." She couldn't stop crying.

"Really. You don't look too happy about it." He didn't sheathe his weapon.

She pulled her sleeve across her face, trying to dry her eyes. "Tam Linn." Her voice still wobbled. "Let me introduce you to Thomas. Thomas Rimer."

Tam's expression went wary. "Wait a minute. Isn't that the programmer - the guy you said died?"

"But he didn't!" She turned to Thomas. "You're here. We have to get you out of Feyland and back into the real world."

"Jennet, stop." Thomas's voice was full of sorrow. "There is no return for me."

"What? Of course there is." She grabbed his arm. It was solid, real.

Thomas shook his head. "I'm the Queen's Bard now. I made a bargain with her, and it cannot be broken. I belong to the Court."

"What do you mean?" But there was a chill in her stomach. She knew how it felt to lose a part of herself to the queen. Had Thomas given away everything?

"We could help you get free," Tam said, sliding his sword back into the scabbard.

"My thanks," Thomas said. "But even if you could break the bonds that hold me here, I have no form in your world to return to. My body is gone, is it not? I left it behind when I followed the queen's call."

"But..." Jennet swallowed hard against the grief shaking through her. How could she have found Thomas here, only to lose him again?

"So," Tam said, "You don't really exist?"

Thomas gave him a weary smile. "What is real? What is illusion? Am I just a memory conjured from Jennet's mind? Am I a wayward bit of programming, hidden deep inside a computer game? Am I one of the fey-folk now? It is for you to decide - and there may be no true answer."

"I'll never see you again?" Jennet tried not to wail the words.

"Of course you will." Thomas ruffled her hair in an old, familiar gesture. "I will help you in every way I can. But tell me. What month is it, what day, in your world?"

"October nineteenth," Tam said. "Why?"

Worry creased the bard's forehead. "The days grow short - but there is still time."

"Time for what?" Jennet asked. "What's going on?"

"Come sit with me," Thomas said. "I will tell you what I know."

He took up his guitar, and then leaned against the weathered standing stone. Bits of melody drifted around them as he strummed the strings, coaxed free by his nimble fingers.

Jennet sank down beside him, but Tam remained standing in the middle of the road, his arms crossed. Thomas continued to play, as if there was nothing urgent or remarkable about the situation - two kids in the middle of a computer game, talking to a man five weeks dead.

"Tam, come on." Jennet frowned at him. "Don't you want to hear this?"

"It is better if he does," Thomas said, still strumming his guitar. "I cannot speak loudly, in case someone, or some*thing*, is listening."

"Fine." Tam stalked over to them. His green eyes were wary as he glanced at Thomas.

The older man nodded. "It's good that you have such a champion, Jennet. You're going to need every bit of his courage in order to win free of the Dark Queen. And you must do so - before the end of the month."

"But why?"

"Samhain." Thomas played a minor chord, and Jennet shivered at the sound. "The faeries remember when they could pass freely in and out of the mortal realm, making mischief, taking lovers, sowing ill deeds and magic in their wake. The Dark Queen has promised them that time will come again."

"So, what happens at the end of October?" Tam asked. Then he shook his head. "You're kidding me. This is some cheap horror vid isn't it? Something creepy happens on Halloween?"

"It is much older and deeper than that," Thomas said. "All Hallow's Eve is a time when the walls between the worlds grow thin. The time when a gateway to the human world could be opened. Under the right circumstances."

"What circumstances?" Jennet asked, swallowing the fear climbing up her throat. She was afraid she already knew the answer.

"A tiend." Thomas's voice was sober.

"English, please," Tam said.

"A sacrifice," Jennet whispered. "And... I'm it." She turned to Thomas, suddenly cold to her bones. "Aren't I?"

He nodded, his eyes infinitely weary, infinitely sad. "The Realm of Faerie is dying. It's slow, almost invisible, but the rulers of the courts know it is happening. They cannot survive without an infusion of human energy."

"Energy?" she asked. "Is that what the Dark Queen took from me?"

"And is taking. You must feel it, Jennet, the slow drain on your soul. That is the faeries' need."

"Right." Tam folded his arms. "The computer game is stealing Jennet's *energy*. Faeries and dead guys and sacrifices. Come on, Jennet, this isn't Thomas. It's some broken NPC."

"Wait." She glared at him. "We need to hear this, to figure out what's going on." She focused back on Thomas. "So, the faeries are some kind of psychic vampires? I don't remember reading anything about that."

Thomas kept strumming his guitar, the chords a soft backdrop to his voice. "These are desperate times for them, Jennet. And human energy can mean many things. A dream. A prank. A maiden's kiss, a bowl of milk, a stolen child. Music. And sometimes, a life."

"I don't believe this." Tam pushed away from them and began pacing. "I mean - this is just a *game*. A computer program. Stuff like that doesn't happen in the real world."

Thomas followed him with a sad gaze. "But this isn't the real world, is it? The between-places have always been the province of the faeries. Dusk and dawn. The cross-quarters of the year. Why not the space we call virtual reality? It's as *between* a place as you will find. Real, but not real. You are here, but not quite here. And here does not quite exist."

His words fell like stones into a dark pool. Jennet could see them rippling inside Tam. He was smart - surely he would see that Thomas was right.

The red sun touched the horizon, and a sound echoed

across the fields - a low, mournful call that sent a shiver through Jennet.

Tam whirled. "What was that?"

"The summoning horn of the Wild Hunt," Thomas said. "They will ride at dusk, and the two of you must be gone from here." He stepped away from the tall stone and slung his guitar over his back.

"What about you?" Jennet grabbed his hand. She wasn't ready to let Thomas go again, so soon.

"Do not worry for me." He smiled down at her. "As the Queen's Bard, I will come to no harm. But you and your knight must make haste."

"I can't leave you," Jennet said.

"You must." Thomas squeezed her hand, then turned and pointed. "Follow the road east until you reach a stand of white trees. The passage to the next ring is there. And Tam Linn - follow your heart, and keep your lady safe. Now, go."

Before Jennet could say goodbye, Tam grabbed her arm and pulled her down the road. She twisted, waving to Thomas, but the sun was in her eyes. All she could see was a shadow beside the standing stone.

"Come on," Tam said. "Your crazy friend said we needed to hurry."

To underscore his words, the deep horn sounded again. The last bit of light was caught on the crests of the stone walls. Soon it would be twilight. And the Wild Hunt would be after them.

# CHAPTER 20

TAM KEPT HIS GRIP ON JENNET'S ARM, KEPT HER MOVING forward. That was some insane stuff going on back there. The 'dead' programmer... he wasn't sure he believed it, that someone could get sucked into a game like that. And the dark faeries creating some kind of gateway into the human world by sacrificing Jennet? Totally crazy.

Yet it all made a kind of creepy, convoluted sense. He needed time to think.

Right now, though, they needed to get out of Feyland.

"Jennet - what is the Wild Hunt?"

"It's a ghostly gathering of huntsmen and hounds. According to legend, if you see them you either go crazy or die." She glanced back over her shoulder. "I don't know what happens if they catch us."

"We're not sticking around to find out."

The last bit of light slipped out of the sky. In the distance behind them, he heard a series of excited yips, then the baying of hounds. The worst part was, he understood the cries. *Scent! Blood! Our prey!* The Hunt was on their trail.

"Now, we run," he said.

He let go of Jennet's arm and took her hand. He didn't think she'd turn around and try to go back to Thomas, but no way was he letting her fall behind. Thomas's last words repeated in his head, matching the pace of his running steps, the push of breath through his lungs. Keep your lady safe. Lady safe.

She wasn't *his* lady, of course - except in the sense that he was a knight, and her in-game champion. Or something. But no matter what, he would keep her safe.

Maybe the faeries *were* planning to use her life to open a gateway between the worlds. His blood chilled at the thought. No way did he want the creatures in-game showing up in the real world. Games weren't fun if you couldn't turn them off.

"Slow... down," Jennet panted.

"We can't." He scanned the edge of the road. "Do you see anything that looks like white trees?"

A sound like far-off thunder rolled through the air. Tam looked behind them. There was a growing darkness in the sky. Shapes, forming out of the clouds. But these weren't the kinds of things kids saw in clouds - no dinosaurs or cartoon faces. These were spectral hounds with huge, shining eyes, and half-human figures on galloping black horses. And at the front, the leader of the hunt, a huge dark figure with antlers spiking up above his head. The Huntsman turned and Tam felt his attention focus on them, like a spear of black ice.

The entire Wild Hunt was visible now, a dozen mounted figures riding hard toward them. He could see the flash of hooves, the glowing eyes of the hounds. Panic pushed him and Jennet forward. The breath rasped in and out of his throat. Trees - where were the damn trees? There! A scatter of white up ahead marked the grove.

He risked another look behind them, and then wished he hadn't. The hounds were too close, tongues hanging from their mouths, black paws eating up the distance. He and Jennet weren't going to make it.

He let go of her hand and turned to face the hunt. Fear and adrenaline pumped through him as he drew his sword. If he made a stand, slowed the hunt for even a minute, she could get away.

"Go!" he shouted. "I'll hold them off."

"No. Not without you." She stopped running and doubled back to stand with him.

"Jennet!"

"Together or nothing, Tam."

There was no more time for arguing - the Hunt was upon them. Tam pointed his sword at the nearest hound, waiting for it to get in striking range. The wind whipped Jennet's pale hair around her face and she raised her staff. She gestured, and a searing white light flashed out from where they stood, making Tam wince.

The hounds yelped and tumbled and the riders milled confusedly, but Tam could feel the Huntsman's attention still fastened on them.

"Come on! That will only hold them for a minute."

Jennet grabbed his shoulder and they sprinted into the shelter of the trees.

The white bark glowed softly, lighting their way. They dodged around the trunks, and finally, finally stumbled into the faerie-ring clearing. Nothing had ever looked as good as the circle of mushrooms before them.

Jennet leaped into the center, but before Tam could follow, something took hold of his leg and yanked. Pain slammed through his senses and he glanced down to see a coal-black hound, its teeth locked around his calf. He pulled his sword and slashed at the hound, who twisted its body out of the way.

"Tam!" Jennet cried.

She had her staff pointed at his attacker, but he didn't think she could get a clear shot - not with the way the creature was shaking and pulling at him. He cut downward again, connecting this time. The hound let out a muffled yelp, but didn't let go.

On the outskirts of the trees, dark figures were silhouetted. Then the leader strode forward, the shadow of his antlers reaching toward Tam. Fear seized him in its strong fist.

He took his sword in both hands and drove it down, point-first. There was a spray of something hot and sickening across his face, and the hound let go with a screeching whimper.

"Hurry!" Jennet's voice was high and panicky.

He scrambled to the ring, his left leg not quite working. Jennet reached for him with both hands and he managed to get inside without trampling any of the mushrooms.

An angry cry resonated through the clearing. Just before the swirl of golden light surrounded them, Tam saw the Huntsman. His cloak billowed out and his antlered helm was lit with an eerie light. The figure lifted one hand and pointed at them, but it was too late. The Wild Hunt's prey had escaped.

"Ow!" Tam tried to pull his leg away, but Jennet held him firmly. He slouched back on the gaming-room couch and tried not to look at the bloody bite in his leg.

"Hold still. We have to disinfect this." Jennet swiped again at the punctures, and he tried not to flinch.

Good thing she'd had an emergency kit in her bathroom. Of course, this was the kind of house that would be well-stocked for any eventuality. A bite from a nightmare hound? No problem. He sucked in his breath as she poked at his injury.

"Hey," he said, "you'd complain too, if your leg had just been used as a chew toy by some demon dog. How come, when things get rough in-game, we can't just hit the exit button?"

"There isn't one." She frowned. "It's one of the things the designers are working on. We could 'escape' out, but that re-sets the whole game. We'd be back at Fynnod's cottage again."

"It might be better than being run to ground by the Wild

Hunt. Although - that spell you used on them was pretty effective. What was it?"

"A light flash with a sonic blast. Too high for us to hear, but I thought it would get to the animals."

"Nice choice - I never would have thought of something like that."

She smiled a little, then rummaged in the emergency kit. "I don't think you'll need stitches. Just a little plas-skin to get you through."

She lifted the can and sprayed, the contents sealing and soothing the bite. Welcome numbness spread through his leg, and Tam let out a low sigh. Jennet laid a bandage over his wounds and tucked the can of plas-skin away. When she looked at him again, her expression was serious.

"So, are you convinced now?" she asked. "Feyland is dangerous."

"Yeah - it's dangerous. To you, to me, maybe even the whole world, if what Thomas said is true."

He glanced down at the bandaged bite. There was no fooling himself that he'd somehow gotten hurt on the way home - not like last time.

"I'm sorry, Tam. I never meant for you to get hurt. I was just so afraid, and I couldn't get back in alone..." She looked away from him.

"I don't blame you, Jennet. But this isn't just your fight any more. What if the creatures in Feyland got through? We can't let that happen."

For a moment he flashed on a horrible image of the Wild Hunt riding through the streets of the Exe. His little brother, his mom, chased down and savaged by hounds with glowing eyes.

"I... I never wanted to put you in danger, too," she said, her voice low.

She looked so miserable that he reached out and took her hand. It felt different than when he touched her in-game. The contact with her slim fingers jolted through him, but he didn't pull away.

"Hey," he said. "Sometimes we don't really have as much control over things as we think. We're in this together now. Ok?"

"All right." She squeezed his fingers and an odd, breathless silence fell between them.

Tam cleared his throat. "I think I can stand now."

Still holding his hand, she slowly drew him up. Their faces were close - so close he could feel her breath against his cheek. His heart raced, as if they were running from the Wild Hunt again. Her lips looked really soft.

*"Miss Jennet."* HANA's metallic voice sounded through the room.

Jennet jumped back and dropped Tam's hand. "Um, yes?"

*"Would you like to have the car summoned?"*

"Sure, go ahead and call George." Jennet gave him a weak smile and moved toward the hallway. "Guess it's time for you to go."

"Yeah, I should get home."

Home, where his mom was slowly pulling herself together. He didn't kid himself that she was better, but every day that she was around and functioning was worth remembering. He stuck his hands in his pockets and followed Jennet down the stairs. At least his leg felt good enough to walk on.

"See you tomorrow," she said when they got to the door. Her gaze met his and held, her blue eyes clear and full of honesty. "And Tam... thank you."

# CHAPTER 21

THAT NIGHT, THE DARK QUEEN HAUNTED TAM'S dreams. Her midnight hair brushed his face while she whispered promises in his ear. She smelled of stars and roses.

Tam woke in the darkness, the scent of her still caught in his mouth. He lay awake, the silence broken by his brother's soft snores, and tried to catch hold of the bits of dream floating in his mind. It was no use. He couldn't remember her clearly enough. The only thing left was her laugh, sparkling like moonlight on frost.

When he woke again, sunlight was trickling into the room. His alarm buzzed beside him like an angry bee.

"Get up," the Bug said from the couch, then yanked his own pillow over his head.

"You, too." Tam sat up and pushed out of his sleeping bag. He smelled coffee. Mom must be up already - and cheerful as only her medication could make her.

"Good morning to the best boys in the world," she said, coming in from the kitchen.

She handed Tam a mug of strong, milky coffee. Her hands shook, but Tam ignored the trembling and took a sip.

"Thanks - it's delicious." It didn't matter that both the coffee and the milk were made from powder. Coming from her, it was the best thing in the world.

"Mmf," his brother said.

"Hot chocolate for you." There was a teasing note in Mom's voice. She was so much better than he was at getting the Bug up and ready for school. When she was around.

When she wasn't, Tam always ended up yanking the covers off his little brother and resorting to threats. He didn't like it any better than the Bug, but nothing else seemed to work.

"Will you be home after school today, or are you seeing your friend again?" she asked.

"Uh." He shifted and took a minute to find a shirt that wasn't too dirty from the pile next to his bedroll. "Do you need me to come back right away?"

"Oh, honey." She gave him a smile that lit her eyes. "I don't mind either way. Peter and I keep good company. When he's awake that is." She cleared her throat, and his little brother suddenly sat up and started pulling on his clothes.

"Maybe I'll go over to Jennet's house again. If that's ok."

His mom spread jelly on a piece of bread for the Bug's breakfast. "Jennet. So that's her name. Do you still spend time with Marny, too?"

"Yeah. Though it's been a while." He hoped she wasn't too pissed about it.

"I'm glad you have friends, Tam. Have fun this afternoon."

Fun, yeah. Hopefully that wouldn't include more in-game mangling. "I'll be back in time for dinner."

"That would be nice. I'll make your favorite potatoes. And if your friend Jennet wants to come, she's welcome. I'd like to meet her."

Tam stared at the floor. Guess Mom didn't remember opening the door for Jennet, or the wrist-chip that was so out of place here in the Exe. Didn't remember the patina of wealth that lay over Jennet, making their place look dingy and derelict in comparison.

He sighed. "Ok Mom, thanks for the offer. I'd better get going."

"Bye, honey." She gave him a kiss on the cheek as he went out the door.

It was painful, her affection - it made the emptiness when she was gone even worse.

"So what's up with your system?" Marny asked Tam at lunch.

"Spread out all over the floor, that's what. The Bug's working on it though." The kid was even making some progress, though it was going to be a long time before his rig was playable. If ever. He took a bite of mushy noodles.

"You going to Zeg's to play, then?"

"No." He finished chewing. "I've been simming at Jennet's."

"Ah." There was a world of understanding in Marny's voice.

He didn't have to say that his mom was back, or defend his actions. No explanations necessary.

Marny glanced past him. "Speaking of Miss Fancy-pants..."

"You calling my name?" Jennet asked, setting her tray beside Tam's.

She sat down and flashed a quick smile across the table at Marny. Then she looked at Tam and her smile tilted a little, unsure.

Marny pointed her fork at them. "You guys simming this afternoon?"

"Yes," Tam said, at the same moment that Jennet said, "No."

The other girl raised an eyebrow. "That kind of mutual understanding is really inspiring, you know. Keep it up."

Tam sent Marny a warning glance, but she just looked at him, like she was trying not to grin.

Jennet touched his arm. "How's your leg feeling?"

Her eyes were troubled, and he knew she was trying to remind him of how dangerous Feyland was. But it wasn't her choice. Not only did she need his help, things would get severe for *everyone* if the Dark Realm opened a gateway between the worlds.

"My leg is great." He swiped his hair away from his eyes,

so that Jennet could see how serious he was. "What are you doing for Halloween? Got plans?"

She stilled and her blue eyes widened. Yep - direct hit. He didn't think he'd hear any more argument from her about how he shouldn't play.

Marny was looking back and forth between the two of them. "Planning a party or something?"

She clearly could tell they were talking in layers here, but there was no way for her to guess how very deep they were.

"Something," Tam said. "We'll let you know."

Too bad Marny wasn't a simmer. She was smart and level-headed - two things that would be assets if she ever set foot in Feyland. But that wasn't going to happen.

She gave a quick nod, her black hair swinging above her shoulders. "Okay." Her gaze moved to Jennet. "Whatever's going on, watch out for each other."

"We will." Jennet's voice was steady, though he knew she was worried.

He'd be worried, too, if he were marked as a human sacrifice.

# CHAPTER 22

JENNET TRIED NOT TO GLANCE AT TAM TOO OFTEN during the drive to her house after school. Something had changed between them. Or at least, she thought it had. Yesterday, after escaping the Hunt, after Tam finally and truly believed her, she had felt so close to him. She had even wanted to kiss him.

Heat crept into her cheeks and she made herself look out the window so he wouldn't notice. It was just a crush. And no wonder - he was her knight in shining armor. In a virtual sense, anyway. Plus, they were good together. Solid partners in-game. Getting to be friends, out.

She wasn't getting the same interested vibe from Tam now, though - not like she had yesterday. Which was good. Really it was. Boy-girl stuff would just make things too complicated.

Maybe later, after they had defeated the queen and figured out how to deal with Feyland, she could go thinking about kisses. But right now it was dumb of her to be so aware of Tam sitting quietly beside her in the back seat. Dumb to notice how his leg touched hers when the grav-car took a corner. Dumb to imagine brushing the hair out of his face and getting a good, long look into those guarded green eyes.

"So," Tam said. She felt him turn to look at her. "What now?"

She hoped her blush had faded. "We finish the game."

"No. We *win* the game."

"Ideally, yes." She glanced at the front seat, to where George was piloting the grav-car, then raised her eyebrows at Tam in warning. Better they not say too much where he could overhear.

Tam nodded. "So. How'd you do on that surprise quiz in history today?"

They talked about school for the rest of the ride. It wasn't until they were in the gaming room, with the jammer on, that Jennet felt secure.

"We have the rest of the month to get to Court and defeat the queen," she said. "It's going to take three, maybe four game sessions. Provided we succeed at each level, and don't get in serious trouble." Like running into the Wild Hunt again.

"Two weeks." Tam frowned and leaned against one of the gaming chairs. "That's cutting it close, if what Thomas said is true."

"And how 'true' was your gnawed-on leg, yesterday? Or have you forgotten that part?" Worry circled in her stomach.

"Ok." He pushed his hair out of his eyes, only to have it

fall back down again. "Obviously the game is interfacing with another world. One that can affect our reality, at least a little."

"More than a little," she said. "The day I came over to your place and met, um..." She didn't want to mention his mom, and by the shuttered look on Tam's face, neither did he. "Anyway, on the way there, two zombed-out guys tried to give me trouble."

"Hell." He fisted his hands. "Did you run?"

She tasted her remembered fear. "No, they had me boxed in. But - and this is the weird part - my mage staff appeared."

"Your staff? As in, a long piece of wood with a crystal on the top?"

"I know. I didn't believe it either."

"What did you do, whack them with it?"

"No. I blasted them."

Tam had a way of drawing his eyebrows slightly together when he was thinking hard. She could just see it behind the scrim of his hair. Abruptly, he straightened. Concentration clear in every line of his body, he held out one hand, fingers curved.

"Are you - ?"

"Shh," he said, his hand still extended. After another few, silent, moments, he shook his head. "No luck."

"You were trying to summon your sword?"

"Yeah. Maybe it only works if there's great need."

"However it happened, it saved me. I knocked one guy out, and the other one took off. Maybe, like Thomas said, the boundaries between the worlds get thinner around this time of year."

He let out a low breath. "I'm still trying to get how Thomas - or his spirit, whatever - could be inside the game."

"He's not *in* the game. He's in the Realm of Faerie, but can interact with us through the game. You read that book I lent you. Faeries are great at enticing humans into their world. And their realm is every bit as real as ours."

Tam got that thinking look again. "So, Feyland is just an anteroom between our world and the Dark Realm of Faerie?"

"You have to admit, it makes a weird kind of sense."

He nodded. "Then, after we save you, how do we make sure the door on our side stays locked?"

It was an excellent question.

"Maybe Thomas will have some ideas," she said. "Because I sure don't."

"We'll figure something out." He slid into the sim chair. "Come on. We have a game to win."

## CHAPTER 23

Tam felt himself relax as the game's golden light surrounded him. The moment of disorientation he felt when entering Feyland made sense now. It wasn't some trick of the visuals. It was an actual transition from the real world to - what had Thomas called it? A *between* place.

This time, they arrived in a ring full of twilight shadows, with not even a hint of sunlight. That was good, right? Jennet had said the darker the level, the closer they were to the court. The thought sent a shiver through him. A dream-fragment caught in his memory; the satiny texture of the Dark Queen's hair, her midnight voice whispering forgotten promises.

"Tam? Are you coming?"

He gave himself a mental shake and looked up. Jennet had already stepped out of the mushroom ring and was watching him, her head tilted. The crystal on the end of her staff shed a bluish glow, illuminating the pale forest around them.

"You brought a flashlight," he said. It was a weak joke, but she smiled anyway.

"No following wisps this time, okay?"

"I expect you to poke me with that if I do." He nodded to the staff. "Lead on."

The pale trees grew farther apart here, interspersed with clearings full of silvery grasses. They hadn't walked for long when Tam became aware of a sound - a humming buzz coming from up ahead. Jennet halted.

"Do you hear that?" Her voice was hushed.

"Trouble?"

"I... I don't know. I've never seen this place before. Everything in the game is changing."

He set one hand on the hilt of his sword. When she started walking again, he was at her shoulder. If something jumped out at them, he could get between her and it in a heartbeat.

Nothing sinister happened, though. Just the noise getting louder until they reached a larger clearing, illuminated by a lantern set on a post. On the far side was a tumble-down hut, and just outside the door sat a bent old woman. The sound they had heard was coming from her spinning wheel.

"Come closer!" the spinner called, not pausing in her work.

The wheel in front of her turned at a furious pace as her foot worked the pedal. She had a handful of something that looked like cloud, which she was feeding into the wheel. Luminous white thread came out the other side.

"Greetings, goodwife," Jennet said.

The old woman looked at them then, her eyes deep-set and piercing. She nodded her lace-capped head and let the wheel slow.

"Fair Jennet. And bold Tamlin."

"Greetings." Tam made a bow, and then glanced at Jennet, waiting to follow her lead. Was this a threat, or just a diversion? It was impossible to tell if this was originally part of the game, or if it was all Faerie, or a combination of both.

The old woman let out a cackle. "Which of you will help me spin, thus further in the world to win?"

"I will." He took a step forward. It seemed that the old woman was their next quest-giver.

"Tam, no." Jennet caught hold of his arm. "It's too dangerous."

"All the more reason for me to do it."

A half-remembered bit of story snagged at his brain. Something about pricking a finger and falling into a deep sleep. Well, if he did, Jennet would just have to blast the old spinner by herself.

"We'll do it together," she said. There was a stubborn set to her jaw that said she wasn't backing down.

"Heh!" the old woman said. "Four clever hands will lead you into faerie lands." She stood and gestured to the wheel.

Tam perched on the stool and set one foot on the pedal. His booted foot looked cumbersome and strange beside the delicate wood. Hopefully he wouldn't break the thing.

"Ok." Jennet took up the downy stuff the old lady had laid aside. "Ready?"

He nodded and pushed down with his toes. The wheel began to spin. Jennet eased bits of the fluff forward between her hands, a look of concentration on her face. The thread they made wasn't smooth, but lumpy and awkward-looking. As it wound onto the wheel, it was obvious where the old lady's spinning had stopped, and theirs began.

"Faster," the crone cried. "Spin and turn, spin and turn."

Tam swore he wasn't pressing any harder, but suddenly the wheel sped up. The humming noise began again, vibrating down to his bones.

"Tam!" There was a panicky note in Jennet's voice.

"Keep going," he said.

Somehow he knew that if they stopped, they failed. And they couldn't afford to lose.

The wheel was a blur of motion - everything around them was twirling. He heard the old woman's voice, as if from far away, call, "Round and round, then reach the ground."

The stool vanished from beneath him and his teeth clacked together as he sat down hard. It was completely dark. He felt around in front of him, but the spinning wheel was gone.

"Jennet?" Fear stabbed through him. If they were separated....

"Here." She sounded breathless.

A moment later, bluish light bloomed as the crystal from her staff illuminated their surroundings. Rough-hewn rock enclosed them on three sides. The fourth led into the shadowy dark of a tunnel. Jennet stood beside him, both hands wrapped around her staff. He was sitting on a dirt floor, next to a heap of bones.

"Nice. Any idea where we are?" He clambered to his feet and nudged the pile of bones with his boot. They didn't look human.

"Some kind of cave - and I don't think much of the décor." She made a face at the bone-pile. "Let's get out of here."

Side-by-side they stepped forward into the dark opening. The tunnel was big enough that Tam didn't need to duck his head, and wide enough that their shoulders just brushed as they walked. He kept one hand firmly on his sword.

The way twisted and turned, and they came to a place where the tunnel split. There wasn't a clear choice - both tunnels were equally wide and dusty.

"Which way?" He kept his voice low. Just because they hadn't run into any creatures yet, didn't mean they were alone in here.

"Hm. Maybe this will help." Jennet extinguished her staff's light.

The darkness pressed against Tam's senses. He blinked a few times, to make sure his eyes were open. Then, very faintly, he saw a glow coming from the left-hand side. It was reddish and didn't seem too friendly, but it was better than nothing. Even if it led to trouble, fighting monsters would be a change from wandering lost in some dark and dusty cave.

He felt Jennet's hand on his shoulder and he nodded, though it was too dark for her to see. From here, they'd go without a light. No sense in advertising their presence. He stepped forward, keeping his pace slow in case they ran into any obstacles. Her hand was steady where she touched him, and she seemed happy enough to let him lead the way. Ahead, the red glow was a sullen smudge against the shadows.

The light grew imperceptibly brighter with every step, but no more welcoming. The tunnel curved, and he heard sounds - a low thumping, the strange sibilance of a language he couldn't recognize. A foul reek filtered through his nostrils; rotten food and singed hair. Eerie shadows danced on the rock wall, and the back of his neck prickled. He inched forward and quietly drew his sword. The ruddy light reflected off it like blood. What lay ahead?

## CHAPTER 24

Jennet's hand tightened on his shoulder as they rounded the curve. Tam swallowed, throat suddenly dry, and peered around the corner. His heart was pounding, deep and low, like some big tribal drum. This was like going through the Exe, where at any second bad things could leap out at you. Except that the bad things here were straight out of a nightmare.

His hand squeezed the hilt of his sword and a shiver crawled down his back. He was staring into a huge cave full of grotesque, green-skinned creatures.

Some of them were dancing beside a bonfire filled with bones. Others scuffled and fought, their gnarled fingers clawing, their sharp teeth gnashing. They had long, pointed ears and wore a motley assortment of coverings. Tam saw the tatters of a velvet dress, a crudely-tanned hide with half the fur still stuck on, and the glint of haphazard bits of armor.

They all had one thing in common, though. Every one of

the creatures was wearing a skullcap or hood the color of old blood. Behind him, he heard Jennet's sharp gasp.

"Red-cap goblins," she breathed into his ear.

Tam nodded, keeping his gaze on the creatures fighting and cavorting. The air was full of their guttural, hissing language. They looked like they wouldn't hesitate to tear him and Jennet to bits.

The fire flickered, and the goblins sent up a sudden rough cheer. A second later, Tam saw the source of their glee. There was another tunnel on the far side of the cave, and emerging from it were five goblins, dragging the corpse of a deer behind them. The creatures closest to it leapt on the dead animal, knives and teeth flashing.

A loud command made them back away, and from the right-hand side of the cave a figure rose. He was a little taller than the other goblins - which still made him shorter than Jennet. On his hideous head he wore a crown studded with rubies.

"Goblin King?" he mouthed to Jennet.

She nodded, her eyes wide and scared.

He looked at the far side of the cave again, to the dark tunnel the hunters had come from. That had to be the way out. But how were they going to get there?

The king was making some sort of speech, punctuated by thumps of his wickedly-barbed pike on the stone floor. Jennet pulled on Tam's shoulder and he slowly backed up until the goblins were hidden from view. Without a word they kept retreating until the red light was no more than a smudge against the darkness.

Jennet's staff shed a faint glow, just enough to see their way.

"We need a plan," she finally said, her voice low. "Got any ideas?"

"We can't just fight our way through - there are dozens of them. Even if they're afraid of my sword, or your magefire, they'll overwhelm us with sheer numbers."

"And the Goblin King won't let us just traipse past, either. Unless..." She pressed her lips together.

"What?"

She shook her head. "I was thinking we could offer him a bribe - but he won't accept anything conjured, and that's all we have. Next time, remind me to wear lots of jewelry."

"Do you think it will come in-game with us?" he asked. "Never mind. Ok. Fighting is out, so is bribery. So somehow we're going to have to sneak undetected through a cavern full of hungry goblins."

Jennet took a strand of her pale hair and wound it around her finger. "Do you remember reading something in that book I lent you, Tam? Wasn't there a way to avoid the notice of evil faeries by wearing your clothing backwards?"

"I'm going to have to borrow that book again - and pay more attention." He hadn't known how essential the information in it would be. He squeezed his eyes shut and tried to recall the page that listed protections against the faeries. "Let's see. Cold iron: we know that my sword works, but probably not against a whole roomful of creatures. Holy water: like we have any of that lying around. Oh wait, yeah. Clothing worn... not backwards, but inside-out."

"Do you think it will work?" She sounded nervous.

"We have to try." He pulled off one armored gauntlet. "I can't imagine trying to put my armor on inside-out. Do you think if I vanish this stuff, it will come back when I need it?"

"I don't know why not. All right, turn your back." She leaned her staff against the wall and gave him a look, eyebrows raised.

"Hey. No worries." He vanished his gloves, then turned to face the rough-hewn rock.

There was a silky swishing sound. Despite himself, he wondered what Jennet would look like in her underwear. Did these characters even have underwear? He'd find out in a minute, when he switched his own clothing.

"Done," she said.

Tam turned, fingers busy with the buckle of his sword-belt. "Are you sure you changed it? Your robe looks the same."

"Of course I changed." She smoothed one hand over the front of the silvery garment. "All the seams are showing - can't you tell?"

Not really. He shrugged off his breastplate, relieved to find he was wearing some kind of homespun shirt beneath. Next were his boots and the armor covering his legs. Brown pants - good. He didn't want to be flashing Jennet. Without waiting for him to ask, she turned away.

Quickly, he stripped off the simple clothing. There was underwear after all. He flipped the pants and shirt inside-out and put them back on. Then the sword. He was careful to twist the belt around, too, re-buckling it from the inside.

"Ok," he said. "Let's go find out how legit that old book is."

Jennet turned back around and nodded at him, her eyes big and scared-looking.

Way too soon they were back at the end of the tunnel. The Goblin King was still standing, and the deer had been dragged in front of him. It looked like the creatures were getting ready to have a feast. Tam glanced at Jennet, who looked even paler. He hoped the goblins would cook the deer and not just dismember and devour it on the spot. If she threw up it would break their cover for sure.

He jerked his head to the left, where the cavern was quieter. Most of the goblins were looking at the other side, where the king was. If he and Jennet stayed close to the wall, they should be safe.

Provided this clothing thing actually worked.

Fingers wrapped firmly around the hilt of his sword, Tam stepped into the ruddy light. He took a slow step forward, then another, barely daring to breathe. Five feet in. Then ten. The nearby goblins didn't seem to know he was there. He looked back to where Jennet stood in the shadows of the tunnel, and beckoned to her.

He could see her fingers clench around her staff, and for a second he wasn't sure she'd be able to take that first step. Then her shoulders straightened and she came forward, as slowly as he had. Once he was sure he wasn't leaving her behind, Tam started moving again. Maybe the goblins couldn't see them, but he wasn't betting on the ugly creatures not hearing or smelling them.

His nerves sparked, urging him to hurry, to run, but he kept his pace deliberate, forced his breathing to stay low and quiet. This was going to be a slow, dangerous journey.

Halfway around the cavern, he paused to let Jennet catch up. So far it had been simple enough to stay along the rock walls, but just ahead two goblins crouched against the stone. They were throwing white twigs on the ground, then scooping them up again in some kind of complicated gambling game. Tam looked closer and a chill snuck up his neck. Not twigs, but bleached finger-bones, knobby on one end.

The festivities on the other side of the cave were growing louder. He tried not to see what they were doing with the deer carcass. As soon as Jennet got close, he began edging out into the cave, giving the bone-throwing goblins a wide berth. Jennet followed him. When she was directly in front of the goblins, one of them stuck his long pointed nose in the air, nostrils flaring.

The goblin leaped to his feet and said something in the garbled language to his companion. It sounded urgent, and both Tam and Jennet froze. Had the creature scented them? The first goblin was waving his arms around. Then he pointed directly to where Jennet stood. The other goblin shook its head, and the first goblin leaped forward. Its arm brushed across Jennet's skirt, and both she and the creature let out a cry - though the goblin's was far more vicious.

Tam grabbed her hand and yanked her forward. Just in time. The goblin's knife hissed through the air where she had been standing. Tam and Jennet dashed through the cave, the two goblins following. They were making noise now, but they still seemed to be invisible. Distraction. He had to create some kind of distraction.

There - a battered copper pot lay against the wall. Tam caught it up with his free hand and flung it into the center of the feasting goblins. A lucky throw - it flew right past the Goblin King's head and struck the creature behind him.

The reaction was like kicking a hornet's nest. Chaos erupted in the cave. Goblins drew their weapons, and warlike shrieks filled the room. The two goblins tracking them began leaping up and down, waving their arms and pointing.

Jennet picked up a wooden shield and hurled it behind them. Screaming goblins converged on it, gouging it to splinters with their knives and claws.

"No more time for that," Tam said under his breath. "Run for it!"

Dodging and leaping, the two of them pelted for the tunnel. Almost there. Just a few more steps -

Clawed fingers sank into his arm, jerking him to a stop. He spun, to find he was face-to-hideous-face with the Goblin King.

# CHAPTER 25

"Go!" Tam yelled at Jennet.

He tried to wrench himself away, but he couldn't break the king's grip. Left-handed, he scrabbled for his sword.

The Goblin King drew Tam closer, his yellow fangs terribly sharp, his eyes gleaming with malice. The hilt of the sword slipped out from under Tam's fingers and he felt the edge of panic. *Come on, sword!* Finally, when it seemed the goblin was about to take a bite out of him, he got a solid grip and pulled the blade free.

"Ark!" the king screeched. He threw both clawed hands up to shield his grotesque face, and Tam scrambled backward into the tunnel.

From her place just inside the tunnel, Jennet shot a bolt of magefire at the Goblin King. He cried out again and staggered toward them, barking out commands. One long, crooked finger pointed toward the tunnel, and goblins surged forward.

"Let's go!" Tam shouted.

Jennet gave him a panicked look, then picked her skirts up with one hand and dashed down the tunnel. He was right behind her. The noise of goblins scurrying after them grew louder. At any moment, he expected to feel sharp claws digging into his back.

The tunnel branched, and Jennet went left. She didn't slow down, but he heard her panting for breath. Another branching, and she went right this time. They continued headlong, their way barely lit by the faint blue glow of her staff. The sounds of pursuit faded, but the back of Tam's neck still prickled. Those goblins didn't seem like the kind to give up easily.

"I have to rest," Jennet gasped, slowing down.

"Ok. I think it's safe for now." He faced back the way they had come, sword at the ready. The only sound was Jennet's breathing. After a moment, she stopped panting so hard. Tam's own breathing evened out, but he didn't let down his guard.

The tunnel was full of thick shadows. Then, suddenly, eyes shone in the darkness. A blur of sharp claws and red-capped creatures erupted toward them. Jennet gasped and began to run again, but Tam stayed behind. He swiped at the goblins, and the front ranks leaped back, yelping when his steel touched their flesh.

It was rapidly getting too dark to see. He whipped his sword at the goblins one more time, then whirled and sprinted after the faint blue glow of Jennet's staff.

It didn't take him long to catch up, which meant that the goblins would be closing fast, too.

"Quickly, come this way," a high, familiar voice piped.

"Puck!" Jennet said. "Where are you?"

A little brown hand beckoned from the shadows. Squinting, Tam could just make out a jaunty figure standing in a small opening in the tunnel wall. If the sprite hadn't spoken, they would have run right past.

"Are you sure that's Puck?" He was tempted to poke his sword at it.

"Hush your mortal mouths, and come," Puck said. "Or stay, and the redcaps will gnaw your bones."

"Tough choice," Jennet said, and slipped through the opening.

Tam hesitated. He didn't trust the little creature - or the company he kept. But it was either Puck or the goblins.

"Tam?" Jennet whispered.

He couldn't abandon her. He let out a breath and squeezed himself through the gap. It was a tight fit. Good thing he wasn't wearing his armor.

"Conceal your light," Puck said. "Softly now, softly." He waved his hands at the opening they had just come through.

Tam blinked. In the moment before Jennet's staff had vanished, taking its light with it, he thought he saw the tunnel walls close. Truth or trick?

Whether it was an illusion or not, the sounds of the goblins passing by were all too clear. Their guttural voices and the scritch of claws on stone made Tam's blood surge. His fingers clenched hard over his sword hilt and he held his breath. Finally, the last sounds of marauding goblins faded away. He let the air slip out between his teeth.

"You may summon your light again," Puck said.

A warmer glow pushed back the darkness this time. Tam looked over at Jennet. She was holding a glass lantern lit by a round ball of light.

She nodded at him. "You could summon one, too."

"Makes it too hard to fight." Still, he held the image in his mind. A moment later, a second lantern dangled from his fingers.

Despite the wave of tiredness that washed over him, there was something comforting about their twin lights. This part of the goblin tunnels seemed less menacing. Or maybe it was just having Puck with them, humming a tune as he led them forward.

"Um, Puck," Tam said, "Where are we going?"

"Here and there."

Jennet lifted her lantern. "As long as it's away from the goblins, I don't really mind where you take us."

"Don't say that." Tam gave her a warning look. "Aren't we trying to get closer to the court? I don't want to end up in the middle of a marsh again."

According to that book she had lent him, you had to be careful what you said around the fey-folk. There had been a whole chapter about bargains gone awry and the faeries' tricky ways.

"The knight can take you closer in," Puck said, "but if you need to go out, follow the stairway."

"Hold up." Tam stopped walking. "The knight? As in,

the Black Knight? That's a no."

"But..." Jennet paused, looking from Tam to Puck.

The sprite laughed, the sound like high bells. "Do you fear to face him in single combat again, bold Tamlin?"

"I'd be a fool not to. And I don't need any more souvenir cuts to take home, thanks."

"He has already tested your mettle, bold champion. But you will need an escort if you desire to meet his Lady."

An odd exhilaration swept over Tam. "You mean the Dark Queen?"

"Puck, are you sure?" Now Jennet was the one who sounded uncertain. "I don't think we're ready. There are more layers to go through, aren't there? Like the Dark Forest and the Fey Fields—"

"The land is ever-changing," Puck said. "The roads you once traveled have shifted, and the places laid by Thomas the Bard are all but gone. The realm returns to its own."

Jennet looked worried. "So, you're taking us to the Black Knight, who will take us to the queen?"

"Jennet." Tam set his hand on her shoulder. "This is it, right? Boss fight? Isn't that the whole point of the game?"

"It can't be that simple."

"Why not?"

"Because that's not how the faeries operate. It's never straightforward." She curled her fingers into her palms. "We're not ready. There are things about that fight - things you need to know."

Puck was watching them, head cocked to one side. "Ah, Fair Jennet. How is it that you have not told your knight what exactly happened when the queen defeated you? Why have you not described the bounds of that battle, and its consequences?"

"I thought," she sounded suddenly very unsure. "I thought we'd have more time. I was going to explain everything, as soon as we got out today."

"What?" Tam stared at her, feeling like the ground had tilted under his feet. "Jennet - didn't you think that information might come in handy? Sooner, rather than later?"

"I..." She stood with her head bowed.

The lantern light glowed golden in her hair. For an instant, his dreams of the Dark Queen receded. He remembered the odd stillness he had first noticed about Jennet. Her paleness, that waxed and waned like the moon. There was an otherworldly quality about her - but he had gotten used to it. Had practically stopped seeing it. And then his mom was back and, well, he should have paid more attention.

"Jennet," he said. He couldn't help the edge in his tone.

"Yes?" Her voice was thin.

Damn, he hoped she wasn't going to start crying on him. Not that it would change the questions he needed to ask.

"Children," Puck said, "We have no time for this. The Knight is holding a doorway open. We must not wait, or it will be too late to leave the goblins' kingdom."

"All right." Jennet turned away from him and headed down the tunnel. Puck danced at her heels and sent him a mischievous look.

"But..." He was talking to empty air. Fine. He vanished the lantern and stalked after them.

# CHAPTER 26

JENNET HURRIED FORWARD, BARELY NOTICING THE ROCK walls on either side. Why hadn't she been more honest with Tam?

Ok, she knew why. Secrecy was a hard habit to break. And she hadn't wanted to frighten him off by revealing the price she'd paid. Besides, Thomas had told Tam that her energy was being taken by the queen. She hadn't explained any further, and right after that they had run for their lives from the Wild Hunt, so maybe that bit of info had gotten lost. Plus, the right opportunity had never seemed to present itself.

There was another reason, too. She hated admitting it, even to herself, but she had made a few stupid moves. If Tam knew how badly she had lost to the queen, he could lose all respect for her. His good opinion mattered. Had mattered for a while, more than she wanted to admit. She could imagine the contempt in his eyes when she told him - so she hadn't.

And now it could cost her everything.

"This way," Puck said, tugging on her inside-out robe to get her attention. "The Black Knight awaits us."

She looked up, realizing that she had marched right past another, smaller, tunnel with a purplish glow emanating from it. The thought of meeting the Dark Queen again made her whole body go cold. Her chest ached, and she recalled with sudden clarity the queen's delicate fingertips holding a crystal sphere. Those star-filled eyes had held hers, the queen had declared victory, and searing pain had ripped through her.

Jennet took a quick breath. "I really don't think the queen and I—"

"Come on." Tam had caught up. "Much as I wish we'd talked strategy, didn't Thomas say we needed to do this as quickly as possible?"

There wasn't anything she could say to that. She pressed her lips together as Tam brushed past, one hand on his sword hilt. Did he have to be so drastically courageous about everything?

Well, that was why she had chosen him. It was just - they weren't ready, either of them, to face the queen. It was too late now, though. Swallowing back her dread, Jennet vanished her cheery lantern and summoned her staff. The blue light pulsed oddly against the purple glow in the tunnel. Tam and Puck had gotten a few yards ahead, but she couldn't make her feet go any faster.

In fact, it seemed as if the glow was pressing against her. After several steps, she felt like she was moving through syrup. She couldn't hear anything, but ahead she saw that

Tam and Puck had stopped in front of a glowing purple portal. The magical doorway was held open by the menacing figure of the Black Knight. He stood straddling the portal, one black-armored foot planted on the tunnel floor, the other set on a starlit hill. And behind him....

The Dark Queen.

Jennet couldn't breathe - until she realized that she wasn't the focus of that beautifully dangerous gaze. Tam was.

The queen smiled. High up in the air, faint frosty music played, borne by an invisible breeze. Her midnight hair stirred about her face, and she slowly reached her hand out. As if in a daze, Tam lifted his own.

"No!" Jennet pushed her staff through the thick air and sent a bolt hurtling toward the doorway.

It hit the purple light and sent up a shower of sparks. Puck leaped into the air and gave her an accusing look, then bounded across the threshold and disappeared. The Black Knight slowly lifted his foot from the rock floor.

Tam turned, a frown creasing the corners of his mouth. "Jennet, what the—"

"Don't go with her."

"I wasn't—"

*Too late.* It was a brush of sorrowful melody, breathed through the half-open doorway. Underneath it, Jennet could hear ice. She shivered.

Tam turned, but the portal was closing quickly.

"Wait," he called. There was something painful and yearning in his voice that Jennet pretended not to hear.

They watched in silence as the doorway shrank to a thin,

purple line. Then it was gone. In the light of her staff, Tam's face looked pale and young. She didn't like it - didn't like him looking so lost and vulnerable. He was supposed to be the strong one, the heroic knight, not the one who needed saving.

"Why did you do that?" he asked. "We could have—"

"What? Met the queen on ground of her own choosing and lost right away? Or let her lead you over the hills while the Black Knight lopped my head off? Something about that setup wasn't right, Tam."

He shook his head, but not like he disagreed. More as though he was trying to clear his thoughts.

"Maybe." He wouldn't meet her eyes. "Now what? Puck took off. We get to wander around until the goblins find us again?"

"We can't stay here." She waved at the blank rock wall facing them. "Didn't Puck say something about finding the way out?"

"He said follow the stairway. I haven't seen any stairs though. Have you?"

"Not yet. But faeries can't lie. They can bend and twist the truth, or make you hear what you want to believe. But if Puck said there's a stairway, then there must be one."

"Good. I'm getting pretty tired of these caves." His hair had fallen back over his face.

Jennet started forward, not bothering to make some cheerful remark. Either they would get out, or the goblins would find and eat them.

At the place where their tunnel connected to the bigger

one, she paused. Had they come from the left, or the right? All she remembered was pushing through purple light.

Tam came up beside her. He had re-summoned his armor, and it was a relief to see him ready for battle.

"Which way?" she asked.

He glanced both directions, frowning. "Wait a sec. Do you hear something?"

She held her breath. A faint sound, like dripping water or music, came from their right. "Yes. Let's follow it."

They walked quietly. The plunk and splash of single notes, single drops of water, grew louder, until it wasn't a hopeful echo in her ears, but something real and solid. It was both water *and* music, and soon the notes became a melody - something she almost recognized.

Tam leaned closer, keeping his voice soft. "Is that an old ballad or something?"

"An old song, anyway."

The name of it teased her memory. With each step, the tune grew louder and more familiar. When she finally remembered, she almost laughed out loud.

"What's so funny?"

"It's a song called *Stairway to Heaven*. Thomas used to play it. In fact, that's probably him up ahead." For the first time since they ended up in the Goblin Kingdom, she felt like they were safe. Almost safe, anyway.

"Puck." Tam made a face. "Follow the stairway. Right."

Ahead, the tunnel grew lighter. In a few moments they stepped into another cavern. She sucked in her breath at the beauty of it. Delicate white stalactites draped from the roof.

To one side, a bright blue pool of water reflected a ball of glowing light drifting in the center of the room. Music swelled and surrounded them, guitar notes played by a figure sitting on a pale boulder.

"Thomas!" she said. "I was right."

The bard smiled at her and finished the last run of notes. "Well met, Jennet." His expression sobered when he looked at Tam. "Tamlin. Beware the enticement of the Dark Queen. She weaves a shroud of enchantment that's nigh impossible to break."

Tam shifted, but didn't reply.

Thomas sighed. "What day is it in your world?"

"Just the twentieth," Jennet said. "We were here yesterday. Plenty of time still."

"I hope it is so." The bard's deep gaze rested on her a long moment. "The next time you enter the world, you will be at the edge of the Dark Court. Do not tarry. You must defeat the queen and reclaim what is yours, before the gateway opens."

"Yes, you've told us that before." Tam folded his arms. "Got any ideas about *how* to defeat the queen? And what about making sure the door stays locked from our side?"

"Magic has a treacherous nature," Thomas said. "Coming from the mortal world as I do, I know little of it, nor the *how*."

"Some help you are."

"Hey." Jennet took a step forward. Why did Tam always get so irritated around Thomas? "He's helping us the best he can."

"The two of you must depart," Thomas said. "There is a faerie ring in the back of this cave that will take you home.

But you must promise me that you will speak together. There are things each of you knows that are of great import."

Tam gave her a narrow-eyed look. "Like the details of a certain defeat at the hands of the Dark Queen. Little stuff like that."

"All right." She swallowed the dry fear in her throat. No putting it off any longer.

"Fare well, brave adventurers," Thomas said. He set his fingers on his guitar again, played a flourishing chord, and disappeared.

"Thomas..." She was talking to an uninhabited boulder.

"Come on." Tam jerked his head toward the back of the cave. "I can't wait to hear your explanation."

## CHAPTER 27

JENNET LIFTED THE GAMING HELM. SHE FELT WOOZY from the passage back through the golden light.

"Well." Tam had unhooked from the system already. He stood beside her chair, arms folded. "I'm ready for that explanation."

"Give me a minute. Jeez." She sat up, then clambered out of the chair, on the opposite side from where he waited. "Want some tea? We could heat some water—"

"No. Talk."

There was no avoiding it. She let out a slow breath, then went across the room and perched on the couch in the sitting area. Tam slouched down in a chair across from her.

"All right," she began, but no more words would come out.

She bit her lower lip until it stung. Her stomach felt like she had swallowed a mouthful of that disorienting light. Tam just watched her from behind his hair, his green eyes wary.

God, she hated how this was going to feel. She grabbed a pillow and hugged it across her middle.

"Ok," she tried again. "You know the kids with chips, the rich ones..."

The silence stretched between them, until he spoke. "The ones like you?"

"Yes." She squirmed inside. Time to lay it all out. "The snobs, the bullies, the *privileged*. The ones who will kick you for being a loser, the ones who know everyone else is worthless. Those kids. Exactly like me."

He frowned, though it wasn't directed at her. "You're not—"

"I was, though. Before." She drew in a deep breath.

"Before what?"

"Before we moved here. Before I lost to the queen. I was arrogant, just like that. I thought that appearance mattered more than what was inside. I mean, I knew better, a part of me did, but when you're surrounded by it..." She squeezed the pillow tighter. "Well, thinking like that becomes as natural as breathing. There was a kid at our school - and you need to know that it was a much richer school than the one here - anyway, she was so obviously poor, such a misfit. We made fun of her, all the time, of her raggedy clothes and hair that stuck out all over the place. She was different, and that made us, the privileged, that much tighter. Does that make sense?"

He nodded. That thoughtful expression was back on his face. At least he didn't look like he hated her. Yet.

"What happened to her?" he asked.

"Nothing too dire, if that's what you're thinking. But we treated her badly, in lots of little ways. She was still there when I left. Maybe things are better now, since I told the teachers and admins about the bullying before I moved."

"So - what does this have to do with losing to the queen?"

Jennet swallowed. "Thomas warned me about being unkind, but it's a hard habit to break. Anyway, when I started playing Feyland, there was this little hob-type creature. Raggedy clothes and hair that stuck out all crazy-like. She kept showing up asking for my help, but she wasn't acting like a quest-giver or anything."

Tam sat up a little straighter. "So you refused?"

Regret burned through her. "I wish I could go back and change that. It was only little things she needed. Sweeping out a cottage. Hanging some clothes. Fetching water from a well. It would have been easy to do, but I blew her off."

"Three times?"

"Three. Yes, the magic number. Because she was odd and poor and even in-game seemed worthless."

"Like the girl in real life." He shook his head. "Like me."

"No! Not like you. Tam, I—"

"You found a poor boy who would be easy to use, huh? A loser." His expression hardened into dislike - for her? For himself?

"It's not like that!" She flung the pillow on the floor. Leaning forward, she grabbed his hands. He didn't pull away. "No. Not a loser. I found the best gamer in the school, who turned out to be a pretty decent guy."

He met her gaze, the hard look in his eyes easing. The

feel of his hands in hers tingled through her. After a long moment he cleared his throat and sat back, slipping free.

"So. Your fight with the queen."

She fished the pillow off the floor, but didn't hug it again. "It wasn't a normal kind of battle. Even then, I could tell things were getting odd in the game. Anyway, it started out with fighting. I was zapping the queen with my staff, and she was casting these dark spheres that floated around and protected her while doing damage to my character. But then things changed."

The memory was hard to catch hold of, a hazy wisp of half-dreaming. There had been stars and a gibbous moon, and a silver goblet full of dark, perfumed liquid that she had almost, almost sipped.

"Changed?" Tam prompted.

"We weren't battling any more. We were sitting together at a high table, and the queen asked me a riddle. I tried, but... I couldn't answer it."

"Do you remember what it was?"

She folded her hands into fists. The problem was, she had been trying for months to *forget* the whole thing. "She told me the answer at the end - it was Life."

"Ok." He gave her a cautious look. "What happened next?"

Jennet closed her eyes, pulling the memory up from deep shadows. "The queen smiled at me, a terrible, beautiful smile. She beckoned to a figure in the shadows, and there was the pathetic hob-creature. *Show your true form, my handmaiden,* the queen said, and the creature shuffled forward. She trans-

formed, right in front of me, into a beautiful faerie maid."
Jennet shivered. "She laughed at me. Laughed and said that
my own arrogance and blindness had cost me dearly. If I had
helped her, she would have helped me in turn to solve the
queen's riddle. But I had not. And so I lost."

Lost. Lost. The word echoed in her mind. She kept her
eyes closed, hoping Tam didn't hate her.

He was silent for a long time. When he finally spoke, his
voice was sober. "You lost. And not just the game."

"No." She made herself open her eyes, but kept her gaze
fixed on the plum-colored upholstery. "The queen said a part
of me was now forfeit to Feyland. She inscribed some
glowing runes in the air, and there was this ripping cold.
Next thing I knew, I was out of the game. I was really sick -
spent a week in the hospital. The doctors called it 'summer
pneumonia,' as if they had any clue. And..." Her voice trembled, but she had to say this next part. "I think Thomas must
have figured out what happened. I think he went in to get
that part of me back, and ended up trapped forever. Not only
did I lose, I... I was responsible for his death."

Grief hit her, hard and sudden, like a punch to the stomach. She curled up and gasped from it. Tears of regret, of
blame and loss, etched down her cheeks.

"Hey, shh. Hey there." Tam was suddenly beside her, his
arm around her shoulders, his hand stroking her hair.

He didn't tell her everything was all right - they both
knew that wasn't true. He didn't tell her not to blame herself,
or to stop crying. He just was there, accepting. Somehow that
made it easier to bear.

Finally she pulled herself together and breathed away the tears. She sat up and pulled her sleeve across her face, trying not to think about how she must look - her eyes red from weeping, her hair stuck to her cheek with tears. Tam didn't seem to notice, or it didn't bother him. Either way she was grateful.

"Better?" His voice was gentler than she'd ever heard it.

She let herself lean against him and took a deep breath. He was solid and safe, and for a minute, she let herself believe that things were going to be all right.

"Yes," she said. "Thanks."

"Give me a couple days to sort all this out," he said, dropping his arm and scooting a couple inches away. "Feyland is intense, and what you just told me, well - somehow it all fits together. But I'm not ready to go charging in quite yet."

"Me either." She wished he would hug her again. "Anyway, it's okay. We can take a day or two off. There's still time."

# CHAPTER 28

Tam slept late on Saturday. He was vaguely aware of voices - Mom and the Bug - before dreaming pulled him under again. When he finally woke, the house was quiet. Too quiet. No smell of coffee. No clacking of tools as the Bug messed with his hard-drive.

He kicked off his sleeping bag and scrambled to his feet. Mom had only been home a few days. Surely she hadn't run off already? Worry clenched through him, but he forced it back. Maybe she left a note.

He checked the table three times, but there was nothing. With fear crawling up his throat, he stepped into Mom's tiny bedroom. It was painted a soothing blue that did nothing to stop the worry hammering through him.

The inlaid box on the bookshelf, where Mom kept the money, was empty. God, she was gone again. But why did she take Peter? Or was his brother downstairs?

He pulled on his jeans and flew down the rickety staircase. The heavy metal door was locked. Finally the stubborn key turned and Tam heaved open the door. Empty, dark and quiet. No annoying little brother to be found.

Ok, breathe. Think. Mom loved Peter - she wouldn't do something dumb like sell him for medical parts or turn him over to a gang boss.

So where were they?

His pulse roared. No, wait. That was some kind of motorcycle, the sound bouncing around from the street. It stopped outside the building. Tam went outside and locked the door, then looked around the corner.

A cop, in body-armor and a faceless helm, sat astride a cycle. The motor throbbed in time with Tam's heartbeat. When the cop saw him, he cut the engine and glanced down at his hand-held.

"This 1329 Bittern Street?" he asked in a gravelly voice. He slanted a look up, at the shack they called home. The weak sunlight slid across his polished helm

"Yeah." Tam shoved his hands in his pockets. This had to do with Mom and the Bug, he just knew it.

"You Mister Tam Linn?"

"I am."

"Got ID?"

Tam lifted one shoulder. "Upstairs. What's going on? Uh, sir." It was like talking to the creatures in Feyland - best if you followed protocol.

"We got your family at the station. Your Ma's in lockup, and your kid brother wants to come home. Got any more kin here? Anybody else responsible for you?"

"No. What happened?" He barely remembered to add, "Sir."

"She tried a dump-and-run at the hospital. The orderlies caught her before she could get out. Most people do that with babies, though. Not bigger kids."

"My brother is... different." Oh Mom. What a stupid thing to try. He could figure out her reasons, though, and it made him feel queasy and heartsick.

"Well you gotta come up to the station and get the kid. Bring your ID."

"What about my mom?"

"We keep her a few days. Counseling, all that."

"But—"

"Station closes at three, and you don't want the kid there overnight. Trust me." Before Tam could say anything else, the cop fired up his cycle, patted his holster, and roared away.

Damn.

He trudged up the stairs. First thing to do was message Jennet and let her know their plans for playing over the weekend were dud. Then it would take a trip on three different buses to get to the station and retrieve the Bug. Would they let him see Mom? What would he even say to her?

Underneath the planning, part of his brain was kicking and screaming. How could she do this to him, to their family? How was he going to explain it to Peter? And how was he going to help Jennet defeat the queen when his own life was falling apart around him?

At DINNER, Jennet sat quietly across from her dad and pushed her green beans around on her plate. Worry had curdled her appetite, and she didn't know what to think of the terse message Tam had sent. :*Life stuff, can't come. See you at school*:

He knew how close they were to endgame, how important it was. Whatever had happened, it must be serious.

"You're quiet tonight," her dad said. "Anything you want to talk about?"

Yes. No. But how could she possibly explain?

"I miss Thomas." The words were out before she realized what she was going to say.

Dad's face shuttered. "Me too, Jen. Me too."

Well, that brought the conversation to a screeching halt. After a minute she pushed her plate away. "So, how's work going?"

"Slowly." He shook his head. "Without Thomas... well, we're behind schedule. And the CEO is pushing us hard. She wants a release in time for the holidays."

If only Jennet could get Dad in-game. She knew Thomas would convince him to drop the project altogether. But there was no chance.

Dad took another bite of meat, and then rested his hands on the table. "Isn't your friend Tam coming over this weekend? George says he seems pleasant enough."

Great. Her dad was grilling the chauffeur about Tam. She thought back - had they let anything about Feyland slip while in the car? Just because George was as quiet as rocks didn't mean he wasn't listening to everything they said.

"Um, Tam had something come up."

She wished she knew what it was, or if there was any way she could help him. He seemed too used to dealing with stuff by himself. Did he even know how to ask for help? Or that it would be okay if he did?

Marie came in to clear the plates, and Dad nodded his thanks at her. Then he turned his attention back to Jennet.

"I'm sorry to hear your friend won't be coming over," he said. "I'm looking forward to meeting him. Soon."

Marie let out a sniff, as if to say *he's nothing but trash*, but Jennet ignored her.

"He should be around sometime this week. Or maybe next weekend." He *had* to be - next Sunday was All Hallow's Eve.

Halloween. The knowledge sat like a cold lump in the middle of her stomach. One week. They had one week left to defeat the queen.

# CHAPTER 29

"Isn't Mom coming, too?" the Bug asked. He gripped Tam's hand as they walked down the wide grey steps of the police station.

"She has to stay a little while longer." Tam swallowed, dark worry sticking in his throat. "They need to talk to her and stuff."

It was bad news, the system noticing their family this way. They had made him talk to a family counselor before they had let him see Mom. Basically, if she didn't get herself together in the next couple days and promise to take her meds regularly, he and the Bug would be put in one of the state-run Homes. The counselor lady had made noises about eventually being placed with a nice family, if the system decided Mom was too unpredictable to take care of them. Yeah, right. Who wanted a sick little kid and his screwed-up big brother?

Not that it mattered, since there was no way he was

letting the state suck them in. Which meant he and the Bug would have go to ground for a few days, until things shook out with Mom. The only place they could do that was deeper in the Exe. At least the cops wouldn't bother looking too hard for them.

The only problem was, how would Mom find them? Assuming they let her out. Assuming she even wanted to find them. That thought cut his chest like he'd swallowed broken glass.

Figure the rest of the day, maybe tomorrow, to find them a place to hide out, get it stocked with everything they'd need, and then disappear. Leave a note for Mom, reminding her of their old signal system. Red flag in the window - danger. Yellow - things were ok. Then he and Peter would erase themselves from the system like missing pixels, blank spaces where two boys used to be.

*You can't live like that*, part of his mind insisted. *What about food? What about school? What about Jennet?*

One thing was clear. He sure as hell couldn't help defeat the Dark Queen if he were stuck in a Home. But they still had time. Hiding out with the Bug - that was only temporary. Until....

Well, until whatever. Right now, he couldn't see more than a day or two ahead. His chest ached when he thought about Mom, so he stopped.

He squeezed the Bug's hand. "How about an adventure?"

"What kind? I wanna go home." Peter was looking up at him with big, worried eyes. The kid was too smart for his own good.

"Yeah, home first. But then we're going to go exploring and, uh, build a fort."

"In the forest?" A tentative smile crossed his brother's face. "Like, in camping stories? Can we make a big fire?"

"No." There wasn't a forest around Crestview. The stand of woods in the park maybe, but it wasn't big enough for them to hide out in. Anyway, they had to stay close, in case Mom.... He shook his head. "We'll find a place in the Exe."

"But Mom said we should never go there by ourselves."

Tam stopped and bent down, so he was eye level with his brother. "Peter. We *live* in the Exe. Not in the middle of it, sure, but I go to school by myself every day after putting you on the bus. I go through the Exe all the time, and it's fine."

Liar. He went along the edges, like where their place was, and even there it wasn't safe. But staying safe wasn't an option any more. Only surviving. He'd heard stories about the Homes, and there was no way he was letting them get hold of the Bug. Or him, for that matter.

"It's just for a little while," he said. "We can pretend we're camping in the woods. I'll even get us some marsh-mallows."

Sugar bribery. Good thing he had hidden some of Mom's cash stash. He and the Bug would get through this. They had to.

It took the rest of the weekend to find them a bolt hole that wasn't dangerously deep into the Exe, but far enough that the system would give up looking. Their hiding place was a low-slung building open on two sides, but there was a corner that was dry and out of the wind. Yeah, it was sketchy, and Tam knew it, but he couldn't find anything better. There was some rank, weird smell coming from further down the block, and at some point rodents had taken over the building, but they were long gone now.

The hardest thing wasn't getting their stuff there, or rigging up a couple of low-tech alarms - wires and cans filled with rocks - it was getting the Bug to keep his voice down. He was excited about their adventure.

"I want to show Mom our fort when she comes home," Peter said from his makeshift bedroll, his voice rising. "Do you think she would let us build a fire? Hey, Tam—"

"Sh. It's time you were asleep."

"But we're on holiday, you said so. I don't have to sleep because I'm not going to school tomorrow. Can we go someplace fun? What about the park with the fountain, or the—"

"Peter, shush. We'll talk about that tomorrow." Another marshmallow would shut the Bug up, but it would only be a temporary fix. The sugar would keep him up even later. Tam let out his breath in a low sigh. "I'll take you someplace fun, but only if you stop talking."

"Ok."

His brother lay still for a half-second. He pulled in a breath, like he was about to say something, then stopped - remembering just in time that he was supposed to be quiet. Then he started wiggling again. His feet swished back and forth under his blankets, moving like wings.

Tam snapped off the thin beam of his flashlight. It was better if they were in complete darkness, anyway. Nothing to give them away. He scooted down in his sleeping-bag, then slipped his hand under his pillow. The cool plas-handle of their longest kitchen knife was comforting against his fingers. Not the best weapon, but at least they weren't totally unarmed.

Would his sword materialize if he needed it, the way Jennet claimed her staff had? He damn sure hoped so. Even more, he hoped it wouldn't come to that. They would spend a couple of nights here and the system would let Mom go. They liked keeping families together, didn't they? She would come back and leave the signal that it was safe, and they would go home.

Sure. Because everything always got better in their lives.

Tam squeezed his eyes shut. No way was he giving in to that hot prickle behind his eyelids. He made his breathing soft, and listened to the Bug's feet moving quietly back and forth under the covers. Finally the motion got slower and slower, and Peter's breath deepened into sleep.

The Exe was quiet. Well, quiet as it ever got. Random yelling from somewhere, too far away to worry about. The low rumble of motors and machines, and behind that, the hum of the bigger, better town of Crestview, bypassing the Exe. Going about its business.

Up on the rich people's hill, Jennet was probably going to bed, thinking she'd see him at school tomorrow. But she wouldn't. He and his brother had to be invisible for the next couple of days. Tam didn't even want to turn his tablet on -

everyone knew you could be tracked that way. Though at some point he'd have to message Jennet again, tell her not to worry. Too much. He could do that from the middle of the park, right before they left. Yeah, that would work.

He knew she'd worry. He could practically see the frown hovering on her face, pulling her brows together above her blue eyes. She'd tuck a strand of pale hair behind her ear and press her lips together. If he were there, he could touch the softness of her hair, coax her lips back into a smile.

For now she'd just have to wait, and he was sorry for it, but there was nothing else he could do.

A LOW, shivering noise woke him. Keeping his eyes shut, Tam slid his fingers around the hilt of the knife. He gripped it hard, his whole body taut with listening. Was somebody there? Had their hiding spot been discovered? Nothing had tripped the alarms.

The noise came again, and this time, Tam knew what it was. There was no mistaking that low, mournful call. It turned his bones cold and made his mouth dry up. The eldritch horn of the Wild Hunt. Hell. How could the Hunt be here, in the real world?

He lay absolutely still, trying not to breathe as the sound swept over the Exe - the high yipping of dogs, the pounding of hooves through the night sky, the wild skirl of bagpipes. The sound flowed through the air, filling it with shadows and things unseen. Images flowed, unbidden, into his brain.

A menacing, horned figure silhouetted against pale trees. The impudent grin of a sprite. A woman more beautiful than midnight stars, her eyes dark as sorrow.

Finally, the sounds faded. Tam exhaled, and it felt like the whole Exe breathed out with him. They were safe.

This time.

# CHAPTER 30

"Marny!" Jennet called as she caught sight of the big girl in the halls. "Do you know where—"

"No. I have no idea where Tam is this morning, if that's what you're asking."

Jennet's spirits sank. She had tried messaging him about a hundred times, but could never get through. "I just was hoping that you knew—"

"Look." Marny crossed her arms. "It's great that you and Tam are friends and everything. You probably know more about him by now than me, ok? So don't bug me. Anyway, probably half the Exe is sleeping late. It was a crazy night."

A chill crawled across Jennet's skin. "A crazy night? In what way?"

"In a freaky-noises-echoing-around-the-sky-like-a-night-mare way. I should be asleep right now, if I had any sense."

"Did it sound like... hounds baying and sort of screechy

music? A low, deep horn? Like that?" Jennet's throat was tight.

"Yeah, like that." Marny narrowed her eyes. "What do you know about it?"

"It's complicated."

There, Marny's warning not to pry, right back at her. No way was Jennet going to try to explain the Wild Hunt, here in the middle of Crestview High's halls. Even if Marny believed her - and Jennet had a feeling she might - it was safer for her not to know.

"Marny," Jennet said, "if you hear that again..."

She shivered, she couldn't help it. The Hunt was loose in their world. And she and Tam were their prey. Please, let him be safe.

"What?" Marny asked.

"Just, stay inside. And, um, make a line of salt under your windows and doors." She wasn't sure that piece of lore about protection from the faeries was true, but every bit helped.

"Salt. Uh huh." Marny gave her a searching look, and then shook her head. "I'll see you around," she said as she walked away.

Jennet took a deep breath as she watched the girl turn the corner. Tam was fine, he had to be. Maybe a little late to school, but she would see him soon.

Soon.

But soon never came. In Ms. Lewis' World History class, Jennet couldn't stop glancing at Tam's empty seat. She looked over there so often that stupid Rod Dermont thought she was flirting with him. He wiggled his eyebrows and pursed his lips into a kiss, so Jennet stopped looking behind her.

All right. She had to find Tam, which meant going back into the Exe. The Hunt didn't ride during the day, did they?

The last bell echoed behind her as she hesitated on the steps. George would be here soon to pick her up. Could she get him to take her to the Exe? Or should she call him and tell him to pick her up later? The rule was she had to be home by five. At least Dad trusted her enough to do what she wanted after school.

Well, if the Dark Queen opened the gate to their world, it would hardly matter. They had four days. Which meant she had to go find Tam.

She had her tablet out, ready to let George know to come by for her later, when the screen lit up. Message from Tam!

Her legs suddenly soft as dough, Jennet sank down on the steps to read. It was terse, like all his messages, but at least now she knew he was alive.

*:Jennet, don't worry. Need a day or two. Don't come find me. Sorry. Tam:*

Relief blurred into anger. Need a day or two? A day or two? They didn't *have* that kind of time. What did he think this was, anyway? Some delusional fantasy of hers? She jumped up and paced to the street. How could he take this so lightly? She could *die.* Thomas had said as much, and Tam didn't even care.

Ok, that was unfair. She tried to hold on to the anger, but it started tattering away. Behind its bright red curtain was a darker shape. Fear.

Whatever was keeping Tam, it had to be serious. Even more serious than defeating the Dark Queen. She had no idea what kind of trouble could be that bad. Didn't even want to imagine.

TAM POWERED off his messager and shoved it into his pocket. Good thing the regular part of Crestview had reliable signal. He'd kept his text short enough that it couldn't be tracked - he hoped. Even if it was safe to say more, he didn't know how he could explain to Jennet that his life had fallen apart.

He grabbed his brother's hand. Time to get moving.

"Hey, Bug. Let's go look at the fountain again."

It was on the far side of the park, right where they'd catch the bus back toward the Exe. No buses went into their neighborhood, of course, but they could get close, and both he and Peter were used to walking.

His brother smiled up at him, teeth ugly from the chocolate-coated ice cream he had just finished eating. "I like the fountain! Can I go in it?"

"No. That fence is there for a reason."

Not that six feet of wrought-iron would stop his little brother if he really wanted in. But they had to stay under the radar, which meant no climbing fences and playing in forbidden fountains.

They were watching the water shoot and spray when Tam heard the distant cry of sirens.

"Alright, time to go." He kept his voice even. Everything was fine. The cops could be going someplace else.

"But we just got here. Can't we stay a little longer? Please?" His brother looked up at him with pleading eyes. "Extra please?"

Tam tilted his head. The sirens were definitely coming closer. "Nope. We've been here all day, anyway. Come on. Race you to those trees."

Laughing, the Bug took off, with Tam close behind. He could feel the sirens wailing, prickling the back of his neck. When he reached the safety of the woods, he glanced over his shoulder.

The sirens abruptly cut out as two black and white grav cars pulled up to the fountain, lights strobing. Tam grabbed his brother's hand and ducked behind the closest tree. He was aware of every sensation; the rough bark at his back, the warm, sticky hand of his little brother clasped in his, the breath rasping in and out of his throat. The Bug stayed quiet for once, as if sensing trouble. Which he probably did. Growing up in the Exe, you had to have decent survival instincts.

Tam counted to a hundred, then back down. Nobody had come for them. Were the cops gone?

Slowly, he peered around the tree. Empty grass. The fountain, oddly cheerful under the late-afternoon sky. No cars. No cops. He blew out a breath.

The Bug tugged at his hand. "Is it safe?"

"I think so."

He surveyed the area again. The faint call of sirens

moving away shivered through the air. It sounded like they were going to the other side of the park. Probably the cops weren't after him anyway, but with the luck he'd been having, he wasn't going to take any chances.

"Ready to go home?" he asked his little brother.

The Bug nodded. His eyes were wide, but not with fear, or excitement. Knowledge, maybe, and the good sense to not ask any questions. Had he heard the Wild Hunt last night? Tam could have sworn his brother slept through it, but now he wondered.

They stayed backed-up to the bushes until the bus arrived, then got on, no problem. It was a quiet ride to the outskirts of the Exe. The few other people who shared their ride didn't pay any attention to the two of them, and the driver was supremely uninterested. The Bug didn't make a ruckus of any kind, but as soon as the bus turned the corner out of sight, he started hopping on one foot.

"Ow, ow!"

"What?" Tam's patience was melting like ice-cream.

"I stubbed my toe getting off the bus."

"Can you walk? Because I'm not going to carry you."

His brother hopped around a little more, then slowly put his foot down on the cracked sidewalk.

"It feels better. Can we go home? Not to our fort, but really home?" His voice tipped up, and Tam felt the yearning in it. It mirrored his own.

"Not yet. But tell you what. We can walk past it - as long as we stay out of sight." It was too early to check for the sign that Mom was home and it was safe. But maybe....

"Do we have to go to jail with Mom for the rest of our lives?"

"Mom isn't going to be in jail much longer. She'll be coming home soon." He hoped with everything in him that it wasn't a lie. He put his hand on his brother's shoulder. "Things are going to work out, Peter. Just a couple more days."

He couldn't promise that they were going to be fine. There was never any guarantee of that. Things were going to change though, one way or another, and he and his family were going to wash up on some shore. Whether it was a midnight faerie realm or the hard edges of the Exe remained to be seen.

They cut through the ragged alleys until Tam could see the ramshackle place they called home. See the empty window too. No point in getting closer.

"Tam? How will we know when Mom is home?"

"She'll hang a yellow shirt up in the window. If she hangs a red one, we'll know she's there but it's not safe." If she could understand the hints he'd left in his note. If she made it home at all.

# CHAPTER 31

THAT NIGHT TAM'S SLEEP WAS BROKEN AGAIN BY THE low call of the Wild Hunt's horn, the baying of demon hounds. They seemed closer this time, and he hunkered down in his sleeping bag and tried to think invisible thoughts. Not here. Nobody here.

Cold light was leaking into the sky when he finally fell asleep.

The Bug woke him up early, asking where they were going to go that day. For a moment, Tam thought about dropping him off at school and spending the day sleeping. But no - they had to keep together and out of sight for another day or two. The Bug was way too conspicuous, and the system could easily get to him at school. All it would take was one call from a teacher and, poof - little brother whisked off.

He was *not* going to let that happen.

So he pried his eyelids open and dug up a couple protein bars for breakfast, then took the Bug to the mall. Peter amused himself by looking in the windows of all the stores, and talking about everything he saw. Even though the money was running low, Tam bought them both ice-cream bars.

If - he swallowed hard - if Mom didn't get free of the system, he'd need to get a job. Not the errands he ran here and there, but something more serious. A steady job, that also gave him time to look after the Bug.

Sure. And money would just drip down on him from the trees, too.

At least there weren't any cops around at the mall. He didn't message Jennet, though he wished he could. Wished he could dive into Feyland with her and fight free of everything, the two of them emerging strong and victorious. Wished he could tell her how crappy his life was, how tired he was of being the glue in his family. Wished he could take her hand and touch the softness of her hair. He needed to feel something soft, in a life that was so full of hardness.

But the messenger stayed at the bottom of his bag, silent and dark.

HIS SLEEP that night was filled with restless dreams. The Dark Queen, so beautiful she made his breath freeze, stood before him.

*Tamlin*, she whispered, in a voice like smoke and snowflakes. She reached out, and her hand was cool on his cheek, her fingertips tingling along his skin. *I am waiting for you.*

His body yearned forward, but his feet were rooted fast. Frustration climbed up his throat. Why couldn't he go? He was ready, more than ready to obey her summons.

Laughter chimed about him, a shimmering silver light that coalesced into three faerie maidens, dancing. They pulled scarves made of cobwebs and moonlight behind them. Whenever one brushed against him he felt it, bright and aching. The touch made him shiver with fear, with longing.

The queen stood farther from him now, watching from the shadows, her eyes luminous with mystery. *I am waiting.*

Tam wrenched forward, but the faeries were gone. Instead, the Black Knight was coming at him, his sword raised. With a shout, Tam lifted his hand, unsurprised to find his own sword there. The two blades met with a furious clang - and he was suddenly awake, heart racing, in the darkness of their makeshift shelter.

A different kind of noise jolted through him - a clatter of metal. The alarm he had cobbled together, a precarious balance of metal scraps across the door, had fallen. Beside him he felt the Bug stir, and he knew his brother was awake, too, and listening.

He groped under his pillow for the knife. Slowly, silently, he drew it out and shifted his grip on the handle. Breath barely stirring in his lungs, he listened. No footsteps. No light. No sound.

Wait. A skittering across the cracked cement floor. A faint rustle. And then laughter, impish and otherworldly. There was something familiar about that chiming sound.

Tam sat up. "Who's there?"

A pale spark lit in the center of the room, then grew into a ball of light, cupped in Puck's hand. The sprite sat cross-legged in mid-air, his clothes like tattered oak leaves. Tam heard the Bug draw in a quick breath full of wonder.

"Greetings, mortal boys," Puck said. He grinned, sharp and feral. "What fancies invade your sleep?"

"I think you know." Tam didn't loosen his grip on the knife. "How did you get here? I thought faeries couldn't cross over to our world."

"Three days before All Hallow's, the boundaries grow thin. You have been touched with elfin magic, Tam Linn, and so I come to you. I bring a warning, and an answer."

A warning. Like he needed the sprite to tell him they were in trouble. On the other hand, Puck *had* helped them in the goblin caves.

"What is it?"

Puck stood and floated forward, coming to hover a foot in front of Tam's face. It was hard to tell for sure, but there was a blurring behind the sprite, as if he had wings moving ten times faster than a hummingbird's.

"The queen has marked Fair Jennet for her sacrifice," he said. "Yet in the darkest moment trust your heart, Tam Linn, and make the hero's choice."

Whatever that meant. The sprite was as oblique as ever. Tam blew his breath out in an exasperated gust. "Great. Thanks."

Quick as a blink, Puck zipped close to Tam's face and gave his nose a painful tweak.

"Ow! Hey." Tam brought his hand over his face. "That wasn't funny."

The sprite's chiming laughter was joined by the Bug, and Tam divided his glare between the two of them. He should have known his little brother would enjoy the faerie's tricks.

Puck floated slowly back, the ball of blue light glowing in his palm. "Farewell, mortal boys. Rest well, for the Hunt seeks elsewhere this night."

Were they after Jennet? Tam rose to his knees. He had to

—

"Tam?" The Bug's voice held a plaintive note.

Right. His brother. He sat back down. Even if he could convince Puck to stay around, he didn't think the sprite would be a very good choice of babysitter.

"I'm here," he said. "Not going anywhere."

The sprite looked at him, with luminous, knowing eyes. "Heed the old ballads, Tam Linn. Your lady awaits."

"Wait. Which lady..." Tam began, but Puck was gone. Between one breath and the next, he had vanished. Only the afterglow of his light remained, printing blue sparks on the back of Tam's eyelids.

"What was that?" the Bug whispered. "Was it magic?"

"Yeah. It was magic. You're dreaming, in fact. Now go back to sleep."

"But if I'm dreaming, how can I go *back* to sleep? I'm awake, Tam. Really I am."

Tam let out a low, quiet breath. "We'll talk about it in the morning, ok?" And maybe, if he were lucky, his little brother would believe that it had all been a dream.

Tam woke early. The morning air was cold, and he hunched down in his sleeping bag, hoping he could fall back asleep. His thoughts were whirling too much for that to happen, though.

Worry for Jennet circled, trading places with fear for Mom, and the looming shadow of the uncertain future. A future on the streets, looking after the Bug - a future where every night the Wild Hunt rampaged through the mortal world.

At least he could do something about that second worry. And he'd figure out a way to do it today. After school got out, he'd take the Bug over to Marny's. She owed him a couple favors - enough that he could get the rest of the afternoon free. He and Jennet had to get back into Feyland.

*I am waiting.* It was a cobweb whisper through his mind.

Did the queen have the power to send the Black Knight after him? Was that what his dream had been about? He shook his head. It didn't matter. Win or lose, he and Jennet would face the queen. Today.

They had better win. The consequences of losing were too dire. Chill air snagged in Tam's lungs. He would do whatever it took to keep Jennet from harm - even though the Dark Queen whispered in his dreams.

"Tam? Are you awake?" The Bug's voice was slow and sleepy.

"It's still too early, Peter. Close your eyes."

"Don't want to." His little brother pushed out of his nest of blankets and sat up.

His brown hair spiked out in funny tufts from his head, and

Tam tried not to smile. Although - his amusement dimmed - they didn't have any running water to clean up with, and Tam had forgotten the hairbrush at their house. Pretty soon the two of them would look, and smell, like the dregs of the Exe. He was already starting to feel that way. Grime and hunger and tiredness had a way of gnawing at you, like a feral dog with a bone.

"Ok then." Tam rummaged around in the pack by his bed. He pulled out two more protein bars and handed one to his brother. "Breakfast."

"Ew! I'm tired of protein bars. Can't we have eggs instead?"

"Look around you. Do you see a stove? A fridge? Don't be an idiot." Impatience made him snap the words out.

The Bug was quiet. Then a sniffle escaped him. Ah, damn. Tam scooted over to his brother and pulled him into a rough hug.

"Hey, I'm sorry," he said. "I wish we could have eggs, too."

"I want to go home. How come we can't just go home?"

Tam sighed and forced himself to speak gently. Inside, his own eight-year-old self was kicking his heels and demanding the same thing.

"I told you yesterday," Tam said. "If we go home and they decide Mom's not well enough to get out of jail, then they take us and send us to a State Home. And that would be even worse than this."

"Wouldn't we get eggs there?"

"If we did, they would be grey and slimy. Trust me, Peter.

Hang in there. We just have to play fort here a little bit longer." Please, let it be the truth.

The Bug's shoulder's drooped. Then he shot Tam a curious look. "Hey. What was that little guy, last night?"

Damn. He was hoping his brother had forgotten about Puck's visit. "What little guy? You must have been dreaming."

"I wasn't! Tam—"

"Tell you what." Tam gave the Bug's shoulders a final squeeze, then folded the empty protein bar wrappers and stuck them in his pocket. No reason to leave trash around that showed they'd been sleeping there. "Let's go by our house and see if Mom has left the signal yet."

He was sure she hadn't, but he'd rather deal with his brother's disappointment than his questions.

"Ok," the Bug said, scrambling out of his blankets.

They went quietly through the broken streets of the Exe. Fog hung in tatters, with no promise of burning off. A shambling figure blocked one alley, forcing them to make a quick detour, but nothing more dangerous appeared. Even the yellow-eyes down the street were silent.

Tam squished down the stupid hope that tried to spring up in his heart. Mom wouldn't be home. And even if she was, there was no guarantee it would be safe. No use wishing for a yellow shirt hung in the window.

"Tam!" The Bug tried to whisper, but his excitement was obvious. His hand tightened in Tam's, squeezing hard.

Tam blinked up at their window. Blinked again. His

heart squeezed too, like the Bug's grip had traveled into his chest. There, in the window. A yellow shirt.

"Come on!" The Bug started pulling him across the street.

"Wait. What if it's not really Mom? What if someone else figured out my notes? What if—"

"Sheesh." The Bug dropped his hand and pelted up the stairs, with all the confidence of a kid whose world has been restored. He flung the door open and disappeared inside.

Tam followed. He stepped carefully over the rotten tread near the bottom of the stairs. Hope wrestled with fear, like two epic monsters equally matched, teeth and claws ripping into him. He hesitated at the threshold.

"Tam. Honey." His Mom's voice was warm and soft and smiling.

She knelt on the floor, her arms around the Bug, and she looked good. Unafraid and peaceful, the way she hadn't for a long time.

Tam gave the rest of the room a quick glance. No authorities lurking in the corners, no hard-faced counselors ready to take him and his brother away. Just the three of them. Their family. Tears, hot and heavy, reared up at the back of his nose. He sniffed to keep them from spilling over.

Maybe things were going to be okay.

## CHAPTER 32

TWO DAYS. TWO DAYS. JENNET COULDN'T GET THE WORDS out of her head. Halloween was the day after tomorrow. Where was Tam? Was he all right? She hadn't heard from him in too long.

"Miss Carter. Pay attention please."

She jerked her gaze to the front of the classroom. Mr. Davis, the ever-grumpy math teacher, was pointing at a problem on the screen, clearly expecting her to solve it.

"I'm sorry, sir," she said. "I wasn't paying attention."

Admitting her mistakes made her squirm, but it was better than trying to fudge her way out of them. Feyland had taught her that much.

"I expect more than that, young lady." Mr. Davis scowled at her. Then he leaned forward, as though he were seeing her for the first time. "Go talk to the nurse at lunch. You're not looking well."

No kidding. Every morning for the last week, a paler and

thinner Jennet had looked back at her from the mirror. Getting up was hard - she felt as though she hadn't slept at all, tiredness weighted her bones so heavily. And last night....

She shivered. Last night she had heard The Hunt, close and insistent. The cry of hounds and horns had woken her, and she had spent the rest of the night curled under her blankets, clutching her old teddy-bear.

The teacher was obviously waiting for a reply, so Jennet nodded. "Yes, Mr. Davis, I'll do that."

Not that the school nurse could do anything.

She needed Tam. Needed to get back in-game. Needed to face the Dark Queen and defeat her, once and for all. If only she didn't feel so weary.

Getting from one class to the next left her out of breath. By the end of the school day, she felt bruised and exhausted. At least she was so slow the hallways had cleared by the time she made her way to the doors.

It was grey outside, and cold. She pulled her coat closer and took small sips of the air. If she breathed too deeply, she'd get a coughing fit.

The grav-car was waiting beside the curb. As soon as George saw her, he jumped out of the car and opened the side door for her. Wow. She must look even worse than she'd thought.

"Miss Carter?" His words burbled, as though he were speaking underwater.

The sidewalk stretched and wavered in front of her, and she suddenly had no balance. Was she flying? Was she floating?

Then strong hands caught her, clasping her upper arms and keeping her from falling. She stumbled forward, and landed against Tam's chest. Tam. Thank the universe.

She closed her eyes, and felt his arms slip around her. Warm. Safe. He smelled of fresh soap and, faintly, the dust of the Exe.

"Tam," she mumbled. "I was so worried. What were you—"

"Sh. I'll tell you later. Come on, let's get you in the car." His voice held a tender note she'd never heard before.

She pried her eyelids open, and saw Tam exchange a look with George - a look of concern and mutual understanding, as though she were highly breakable. She would have objected, but it was too hard to think of the right words.

Tam lifted her onto the seat, and she saw George nod at him.

"Tam's coming with us." It came out a whisper, but she needed to be sure they understood.

"Of course, Miss," George said.

"I'm right here." Tam took her hand. "No worries."

FEAR HAMMERED through Tam's chest as he studied Jennet. Dark shadows smudged under her closed eyes, her skin was translucent, and she weighed barely more than air. No wonder the barriers between the worlds were growing thin. The Dark Queen was obviously sucking out Jennet's energy, and fast.

They had to defeat the queen. Today.

They should have done it earlier, that much was clear. It was his fault that Jennet was in such rough shape - but there was no time for regrets now. Only action. And he had done what he had to, made the only choices he could.

The grav-car slid to a stop in front of Jennet's house, and the driver turned back to look at Tam.

"Perhaps we should summon an ambulance." George's voice was concerned. "Just in case."

Tam swallowed hard. They had to get in-game as fast as possible - but George didn't know what the hell was going on, or how that would help. All he saw was Jennet, looking like she was thinking of dying.

"Ok," he said. "But it's not an emergency." Yet.

"Then I will call a non-emergency team in." There was a touch of wry humor in the driver's voice, as if joking about it would keep the fear at bay.

"You do that. I'll take her upstairs." Tam brushed the back of his hand over Jennet's cheek. She felt as soft as the sky. "Hey," he whispered, "Wake up."

Her eyes fluttered open, pale blue, and she took a deep breath. "Are we there?"

"Almost." He knew what she was asking. Not if they were at her house, but if they were in Feyland. "You up to walking?"

Behind her eyes, he saw determination. Saw her summon her strength. "Yes. Just..."

He helped her, one hand under her elbow, one at her back. Balanced her as she got out of the car, supported her while she stood on the walk. He tried not to act like he was half-carrying her. It must have worked, because George gave them both a relieved look.

"I'm still making that call," he said.

"Good." Because there was always a chance that he and Jennet would lose. Not that Tam would give that thought any room in his brain.

Gently, he turned her toward the house. As soon as the door closed behind them, she teetered. He swept her up in his arms. Good thing she didn't weigh much.

"Hey," she whispered.

"Hold still," he said quietly. "It's just the quickest way to get you to the game room."

He settled her into the sim chair, locked the door, hit the jammer button, and then plugged in himself. Game. On.

# CHAPTER 33

THEY STOOD IN A PALE GROVE, THE USUAL RING OF mushrooms surrounding them. Tam peered at Jennet, but in the dim light it was impossible to tell if her character looked any different.

"How do you feel?" he asked.

She took a hesitant step, then leaped over the ring. Whirling, she grinned at him. "Good! Fabulous, in fact."

"Glad to hear it. Do you think we're close to the Dark Court?"

He stepped over the luminous mushrooms and glanced about. The sky above them was dusted with stars and the trees gave off a faint glow.

"Yes, we are," she said. "Do you hear that?"

He tilted his head. Music twisted through the air, pulling at his senses. Pipes and fiddle and the steady beat of a drum. "Yeah."

"Come on." Staff in one hand she stepped forward, down the shadowy path.

Tam hurried after her and took her arm, halting her. "Me first."

"Really, Tam, I'm—"

"This is my job. Besides, you know in a fight that the tank goes first and the spell-caster stays back. We have to do this right, Jennet."

"Ok. But don't go too slowly."

"I won't - but I'm not rushing into danger either, alright?" Without waiting for a response, he strode past her.

The shadows under the trees shivered as they passed, but nothing leaped out at them. The music was stronger now, the trees taller and more widely spaced. A silvery light gilded the branches, and Tam glanced up to see a crescent moon floating in the blackness.

There were lights visible before them now, too, floating glimmers that looked like fireflies. The path widened, and Tam curled his fingers around his sword hilt. This was it. The Dark Court of the faeries.

He and Jennet stepped forward, into a clearing. An odd purplish bonfire burned in the center, and figures moved around it, their silhouettes inhumanly graceful or oddly grotesque.

Just past the fire, directly across from where they stood, was a throne made of vines and shadows. On it sat the Dark Queen. She smiled at him.

His breath left his lungs, and forgot to return. Who needed breath when *she* was there? Half-whispered secrets, the taste of moonlight, a brush of midnight across his senses. Bright stars sparkled behind his eyes.

"Tam!" Jennet hissed.

Abruptly, his lungs decided to work again. He sucked in a breath and forced himself to look away. His gaze landed on the Black Knight, standing utterly still in the darkness behind the queen. Now *that* was an enemy he could fight.

Beside the knight were feasting tables covered with delicacies, and a group of musicians playing sweet music. Fabulously beautiful women with gossamer wings danced, small twiggy creatures swooped past, and laughter chimed like bells in the soft, dark air.

Then, sudden as a slammed door, everything stopped. The music cut off, the dancers halted, the laughter ceased. Tam felt every creature in the clearing turning to look at them, and fear skittered across the back of his neck.

"Fair Jennet. And Bold Tamlin," the queen said, her voice full of smoke and promises. "Have you come to issue a challenge?"

"We have." He took a step forward. "We are here to regain what was lost."

"Is it so?" The queen's voice took on an edge. "What I have, I won fairly. Now you would take it from me?"

"Not take," Jennet said, "Win. I need it back."

"Ah," the queen said. "Need."

The way she spoke that single word made Tam's whole body tighten. Need. It echoed through him.

"Yes." Jennet sounded scared, but defiant. It was her life they were talking about, after all. "I demand another chance."

"So much trouble," the queen said, "for something so simple. Are you quite certain, Fair Jennet? Are you willing to place your champion in such danger?"

"It's not—"

"Her champion chooses this freely," Tam said. He would not make this Jennet's fault, no matter what the queen said.

"Ah. So bold." The queen breathed the words. "Very well."

She extended one hand, palm up, and a glowing sphere appeared there, cupped in her hand. Jennet gasped, and the queen laughed her chiming laugh.

"I see you recognize yourself, Fair Jennet." The queen turned the globe back and forth between her slender fingers. Bright orange and pink flames were trapped inside the sphere, dancing desperately, seeking freedom. "But if you may have a champion, then so may I."

There was a flash of silver, like a lightning bolt had struck the clearing, followed by bone-shaking thunder. The purple bonfire snuffed out. Tam turned, sword drawn, to find that he and Jennet now stood on a raised, circular platform. The fey-folk gathered around the edges, their expressions avid.

The queen and the Black Knight faced them. Tam's blood surged, hot and scared. With a sharp smile, the queen lifted her hand.

"Begin!" she cried.

## CHAPTER 34

SOMETHING WAS WRONG. JENNET FELT IT IN THE STARES of the watching creatures, in the way her soul flickered within its imprisoning sphere. But most of all, she felt it when she looked at Tam.

He watched the queen with a determined expression, but underneath that was a yearning that scared her. They couldn't win if Jennet's champion was only halfway on her side. Okay, yes, the Dark Queen was gorgeous and magical, but she was the enemy!

Even as fear washed through her, the Dark Queen was casting a spell, the Black Knight drawing his sword. It was too late to do anything but fight. She only hoped, to the depths of her trapped soul, that Tam wouldn't fail her.

A wave of shadows pushed forward from where the queen stood. Jennet raised her staff and sent a bolt of light into it, and another, another. The shadows danced back, temporarily at bay.

From the corner of her eye, she saw Tam and the Black Knight raise their swords and clash together. Tam twisted and jabbed, his armor contrasting brightly with the flat black of his opponent.

"Ow!" A sharp sting lanced her ankle, followed by numbing cold.

Her moment's inattention had brought the shadows creeping back, to twine, frigid, about her feet. The Dark Queen laughed, the sound like velvet with pins sticking out of it.

Pointing her staff downward, Jennet let out another blast of energy. With a hiss, the shadows receded again. Enough of this. She leveled her staff at the queen and summoned all her fear and anger. Whoosh! A sheet of blue fire sped toward the queen. The queen's pale face glowed and her hair shimmered with sparks. She threw up her hands and shouted a command.

Jennet's attack slammed to a halt. Then the backlash hit, knocking her to her knees. Blue fire streamed past, dissipating into the night. The watching fey-folk cheered their queen, in syllables strange and strident.

Slowly, Jennet got to her feet. Her legs trembled beneath her and it was hard to catch her breath. That hadn't gone well. She sent a glance at Tam, still trading blows with the Black Knight. His shield arm sagged and he wasn't moving as fluidly as before. As she watched, the knight landed a blow to Tam's shoulder that made her wince and sent him stumbling back.

The queen raised her hands again, and Jennet jerked her attention back to her own fight.

This time, skeins of darkness flew from the queen's fingers, as though she were throwing black threads into the air. Jennet tried to knock them away, but they wrapped around her staff, then flowed to her hand and began twining up her arm. Sweet music and poignant regret filled her mind. She was weary. Better to lay down her staff and rest.

"You are too weak, mortals," the queen said, her voice lilting with pleasure.

"Jennet!" Suddenly Tam was there. His bright blade sliced through the strands clinging to her staff.

She blinked as the Dark Queen's magic slid away. Then, over Tam's shoulder, she saw the Black Knight rushing forward, sword raised for a killing blow.

"Look out!" Jennet lifted her staff and sent a crackling bolt of blue-white fire at the knight.

It stopped him long enough for Tam to duck away and pull her with him. Together, they scrambled partway around the circle. When they had a little distance from their foes, they halted.

"Are you ok?" Tam asked. He sounded out of breath.

"Yes. You?" Could he hear the uncertainty in her voice?

He shrugged, keeping his face turned toward their enemy. "We're not losing."

"We're not winning either. Tam - I think we should switch opponents."

He looked at her then, a flash of stubbornness in his green eyes. "No way."

"Yes way. As long as the queen holds my soul, I'm weaker than she is, don't you see? You need to be the one to face her."

"I don't—"

"We have to try." She put all her hope, all her trust, into the next word. "Please."

He frowned at her, but she could see him hesitate. From the corner of her eye, she caught movement.

"Ha!" Whirling, she shot another bolt at the approaching knight, pushing him back a few paces. "Look Tam, I can handle him. Now go. Go."

Tam shook his head. Then, giving her a look she couldn't decipher, he turned and sprinted past the knight, his sword leveled at the Dark Queen.

# CHAPTER 35

JENNET DIDN'T KNOW WHAT SHE WAS ASKING - BUT SHE was right about one thing. They sure weren't winning. Without giving himself time to think, Tam charged toward the Dark Queen.

Maybe if he were fast enough he wouldn't get caught by her ethereal beauty, or fall into the starry pools of her eyes. He had to stay strong, be a champion. He was here to save Jennet.

Holding that thought like a weapon, he kept his sword pointed straight at the queen and kept going. Her lovely face stilled, her eyes widened, and Tam felt his heart rip. It was too late to turn aside. He waited in horror for his blade to pierce her beauty, for a shocked cry of pain to pass those perfect lips.

It didn't happen.

One moment, the queen was before him, the next, his sword tip was jammed between the vines that made up her throne. He yanked at it, finally wresting it free. Smoky laughter sounded behind him. A touch, light as a whisper, on the back of his neck. He whirled, to find the queen standing there, unharmed.

"A bold champion," she said. "I would give much to claim loyalty such as yours."

Her words sparked pleasure through him. But he couldn't give in. Squinting his eyes mostly closed, he swung at the queen again. This time, his blade passed through her as if she were made of fog. Her laugh chimed through the air.

"It is not so simple is it, brave knight? But look, see how your lady fares." She gestured to the other side of the circle.

Jennet was illuminated by blue fire. She had etched a line of it in the ground between her and the Black Knight. He paced before it, unable to cross, while she sent flickering lightning bolts that burned and sizzled against his armor.

"You see?" the queen said, her voice a twilight caress. "They are well-matched. Just as you and I are, Tamlin."

"No," he managed to say, but somehow he was looking into the queen's eyes.

They were fathomless, full of secrets he hadn't even known existed. The scent of smoke and roses twisted around him, and his heart tightened. Dreams and longing pressed against his skin, against his soul.

The Dark Queen leaned forward. Her lips parted with promise, and for one fatal second he lowered his sword.

"Good," she whispered, sending her breath into his mouth.

Then Jennet screamed.

Tam wrenched himself away from the queen. "Jennet!"

She was on her knees, the blue fire gone, her staff on the ground beside her, broken. Despair shone in her eyes. The Black Knight stood over her. Slowly, he lifted his sword.

"You have lost," the queen said. She held up her right hand, showing Tam the sphere that held Jennet's trapped soul. "Now I take what is rightfully mine."

No! Defeat was bitter in his mouth, churned in his stomach. His fault. He had let the queen distract him, and she had done something to turn the battle – had used Jennet's energy against her. But it wasn't over yet.

"Wait," he said. "I'll offer you a bargain."

"Yes?" The queen tilted her head and watched him, her expression knowing.

He felt as though his mind were moving at the speed of light. There had to be a solution here, a way to save Jennet. He couldn't let her die.

"You've taken Jennet's energy," he said. "Practically drained her. There can't be much left."

The queen held the flickering sphere up and studied it a moment. The flames glinted in her eyes. "There is enough for my purposes."

"But you could have more. You could have mine."

"Tam, no!" Across the circle from him, Jennet gave him a wide-eyed look. "I'm the one who lost. You can't do this." Her voice hitched on a sob.

The queen smiled, as piercing as a shard of crystal. "You offer yourself instead? Bold, Tamlin."

"Yes. Take me, and let Jennet go." His mouth was dry.

Still looking at Jennet, he scraped the words out. "Jen. Take care of my mom and brother. Tell them I love them. And I'm sorry."

Tears glistened on Jennet's face. "No. No. Tam, you can't—"

"I accept your bargain." The queen opened her hand, and the flames of Jennet's soul flew free, streaming back to her. "Now, brave knight, you are mine."

Tams' senses whirled as the Dark Queen leaned forward. She placed her hands on his cheeks, her touch like cool starlight. He could see nothing but her terrible, lovely face. Hear nothing but the high skirling of pipes. Taste nothing but ashes.

# CHAPTER 36

"No!" Jennet ripped the sim helmet off and lunged over to the other chair.

Tam lay there, still and pale. She put a hand to his cheek. His skin felt clammy, and he was barely breathing. Panic roared through her like fire, red flames nearly choking her, blinding her.

"Help!" she cried, running to the door and throwing it open. "HANA - Call an ambulance. Quick!"

"*A medical team has just arrived.*" The cool mechanical tones sounded through the room. "*They will be with you immediately.*"

Already? Jennet blinked. Before she could sort it out, two women in white medical gear rushed into the room.

"Miss Carter?" The taller one took her arm. "Let's get you on a stretcher and down to the ambulance. We can—"

"What?" Jennet yanked her arm free. "It's not me, it's

Tam. Over here. Help him!" She hurried to the sim chair where Tam was sprawled, unmoving.

The med techs exchanged a confused look, and then the first one joined Jennet. She took one look at Tam and sucked in her breath.

"Willis," she said, "we need the full team up here. Stat!"

The second woman pulled out her cell, but HANA spoke first. *"I have already alerted the crew."*

"Good." The tech gave Jennet a sharp look. "Move away, please. We need to get him on the floor and start CPR. Willis!"

Jennet edged back as the other med tech hurried up. A minute later there was a flurry of white-uniformed activity in the room. She couldn't even see Tam any more, just hear some equipment beeping and the techs throwing around terms she didn't understand. At least Tam was still breathing. He had to be.

"Miss? Are you all right?" George set a hand on her shoulder. She hadn't seen him arrive, but she was glad he was there.

The rough sympathy in his voice was too much. Tears burst out of her, and she wrapped her arms around her stomach, trying to keep from falling completely apart.

She had failed. Failed and failed and now Tam.... Oh god, what was going to happen? What was she going to do?

George patted her back. "I've called your father. He's on his way, and so is a heli from the hospital. We'll get Mr. Linn the best possible care." He gave her a curious look. "But you're feeling well, yourself?"

Jennet took a deep, ragged breath. "Yes. I'm okay."

She was surprised to find it was true. Tam had succeeded in that. Her soul was restored, while he....

The tears threatened to swamp her again. She had to hold it together and tell Dad what was going on. He would know what to do - he'd helped build the game, after all.

She wanted to go over and hold Tam's hand, brush the hair out of his eyes, but the techs were busy putting him on a stretcher. They carried him out the door. Jennet followed, feeling useless.

The daylight outside came as a shock. The way she felt, she expected it to be night. Expected the whole world to be dark. It wasn't right that the sun was shining while Tam could be.... She couldn't even think the word.

Biting her lip, hard, she slipped forward until she could see him lying on the stretcher. There was an oxygen mask over his face, tubes hooked into his arms. His body was there. But his soul, his *self*, was not.

Was he sitting beside the Dark Queen in her court? Was Thomas offering advice and solace? Had Tam already forgotten about his life in the mortal world?

A sob choked her. Oh, Tam. It was all her fault.

A whooshing sound made her look up, to see that the med evac was starting to descend. Luckily the streets of the View were wide. Jennet edged over to the tall woman, who seemed to be in charge.

"Excuse me," she said.

"Yes?" The tech looked at her with impatient sympathy.

"Can I go with him? In the evac?"

"Are you an immediate family member?"

"Um." For a wild moment she wanted to claim she was. But they'd find out it was a lie soon enough. "No. I'm not."

The tech shook her head. "Sorry." She glanced around. "*Are* there any family members here?"

"No."

"You're a friend?" When Jennet nodded, the tech thrust a tablet at her. "Someone has to fill this out. If you don't know all the answers, do the best you can."

Of course - they needed to know who they were taking away. Pressing her lips together hard, Jennet filled out what she knew about Tam. There were a lot of blank spaces when she was finished. She didn't even know how to contact his mom, or what her first name was, or their address. But she knew how to get there.

Would George take her into the Exe? She wished Dad were home. There were too many things falling on her, all at once. She could barely stand up under the weight.

"Here." She handed the tablet back to the tech.

The woman hardly looked at it. "We're taking him to Central Hospital."

"Central? But that's not nearby."

"He needs more than the local facilities can provide." She lifted her head and called out, "Willis? We ready to go?"

The other tech waved an affirmative.

"But..." Jennet couldn't help the shaking in her voice, couldn't help the fear that grabbed her by the back of the neck and wouldn't let go.

"He'll be okay. We've got him on life support now." The

tech gave her a brusque pat on the arm, and then clambered into the evac.

Moments later the machine shot straight up. Jennet squinted until she couldn't see it against the clouds any longer. Still she kept her face tilted to the sky, to keep the tears from spilling down her cheeks.

"Miss Jennet, please come into the house." It was George, his voice soft as he took her arm. "Your father should be here soon. We can wait for him inside."

She moved numbly as he guided her back into the house and settled her in the downstairs living room. Marie was waiting, with a blanket and cup of hot tea. Not that anything could make Jennet feel warm. Still, she took a sip. It gave her something to do with her hands, her body, while her mind bashed against what had just happened like some kind of frantic animal inside a cage.

"George," she finally said. "We need to let Tam's family know what's happened. Would you take me—"

"No, miss."

"But, you don't know where—"

"You need to remain here until your father arrives." George got to his feet. "And of course I know where to go. I have driven Mr. Linn home, if you recall."

"Oh. Right." She had forgotten.

"I'll bring his family to Central Hospital. To be clear, Miss Carter, do you know how many people I will be fetching?"

"Just his mom and little brother. I'm pretty sure." That little apartment over the garage couldn't hold more than the three of them, could it? Tam had never mentioned anyone else.

"Very good." The driver paused for a moment and set his hand on her shoulder. "Tell your father everything that has happened. Everything."

She glanced up, startled. How much did George know? "I will."

"Good. Lars can drive you and your father to the hospital when you are ready. I will put myself at the Linn family's disposal. I am certain your father would instruct me to do so."

"Yes."

George was right about that. Something terrible had happened to Tam here, at their house. Dad would take full responsibility. That was one thing she could always trust about her dad. He was as dependable as granite.

No matter how mad he got when he found out what had happened, he would take care of Tam's family. The fear holding her neck picked her up and gave her a little shake, then set her back down.

George gave Marie a long look. "Take care of her."

"Of course." The housekeeper sniffed, as if she didn't need the chauffeur telling her how to do her job.

It was quiet after George left, a heavy silence that muffled everything. Jennet felt as if she was lost in the middle of a blizzard. Everything was white and cold, and she had no sense of direction.

Then the front door slammed open and Dad rushed inside. He didn't bother taking off his coat, but went right to Jennet and took her hands. His eyes were worried.

"I got an emergency notification from HANA," he said, "and a confusing call from George. Something about your friend, Tam, and an ambulance. But you're all right?"

She nodded, and his expression eased.

"Good. Jennet - what happened?"

## CHAPTER 37

THE QUESTION HUNG IN THE COLD AIR. JENNET BLINKED, trying to find the words.

"Jen?" Her dad squeezed her hands.

"I...Tam..." She swallowed the lump in her throat, then tried again. "We were simming in Feyland and...Oh Dad, I'm so sorry."

"In Feyland? You know that's off limits!" He took a breath, visibly trying to calm himself. "All right, you were gaming, and then?"

"Tam made a bargain with the Dark Queen - she's the last boss. And after the fight, he was just lying there unconscious in the sim chair. Dad, stuff that happens in-game affects real life. It sounds crazy, but it's true. We have to go back in, together, and save Tam!"

"No."

"But Dad, he could be dying!"

"Jennet, listen to me. Playing a computer game is not

going to save your friend. And nobody is going to be using the Full-D system right now. It's too dangerous." He rubbed the bridge of his nose, looking suddenly weary. "I never told you exactly how Thomas died."

A shiver ran through her. "You said he had a stroke - a blood clot to his brain."

"That's what the doctors thought. But I don't mean the exact diagnosis. When they found his body, he was hooked in to the Full-D system. He died while he was simming. And now your friend Tam... there's something terribly wrong with the hardware. The neural interface of the helmet, something."

"It's not the hardware, Dad. It's the *game*. Feyland is connected to another world, and I have to—"

"Jennet." He put his arm around her shoulders. "I know you're upset. But there's nothing we can do except trust the doctors to take care of Tam."

"But I've simmed a lot on the Full-D, and I haven't—"

"You were playing right before you got sick this summer, weren't you?" He gave her a penetrating look.

"I... well, yes, but—"

"And it landed you in the hospital for a week. So, no. No more playing. Those systems need to be examined, dismantled, and rebuilt from the bottom up."

Oh no. A sick shakiness trembled through her. How could she go back in-game and fight to free Tam if the systems were down?

"There's one more thing." Dad cleared his throat. "About

Thomas. He had recently found out he had invasive cancer. He was dying."

Shock pierced the cold surrounding her. "But - what about treatment? Chemo and radiation and all that?"

"By the time they discovered the cancer, it was too late. He chose to not even try. In a sense it was merciful, the way he died. It was fast, and likely painless."

Thomas had cancer? Terminal cancer? Had he made a deliberate choice to leave his body behind, and enter the Realm of Faerie? He hadn't been able to save her, but it seemed he had some influence over the Dark Queen. Maybe without him there, Jennet wouldn't have ever come home from the hospital that summer.

But Tam's choice was different. He had a family, a life, a body to come back to. She couldn't let him give all that up - couldn't live with the guilt of knowing it had been because of her.

"It's all right, Jen." Dad squeezed her shoulders. "I need to get to the hospital, meet Tam's family, and see what the prognosis is. Whatever happens, I bear the responsibility."

"It's not your fault," she said, her voice nearly breaking. It was hers. Hers. "Can I come, too?"

"Are you sure you're up to it?"

"Yes. I have to know."

Every beat of her heart was fear and guilt and worry, carrying his name. Tam. Tam. Tam.

Tam held a heavy silver goblet to his lips. The scent of wine and spices tingled in his nose, but he didn't drink. For some reason, he wasn't supposed to. A memory flashed deep in his mind, like a silver-sided fish. He chased after it, but it was gone, submerged again in shadows.

Around him, the clearing was filled with glowing lights and high, chiming voices. The faeries came and went, swirling about their queen. Music floated through the air. He set the goblet down on the leafy table beside him and looked for the musicians.

There, at the edge of the clearing. A tall, twiggy figure playing the flute. Next to it, a squat, dark troll beating a hand-drum with gnarled fingers, and in the center, a man with a guitar. Tam squinted. There was something familiar about the bard.

As if sensing his regard, the man's fingers stilled. He nodded to his companions, and then strode over to Tam.

"Well met, brave knight," the musician said. "And how do you find our fair land?" There was something sad in the question, a weight that Tam didn't understand.

"How should I find it?" He had a feeling he hadn't been here that long, but he couldn't remember where he had come from.

The bard turned wise, weary eyes on him. "You should remember that beauty and treachery exist in equal measure here. It is wise of you to take no food, nor drink." He nodded to Tam's untouched goblet.

Tam's brain felt strange and sludgy. He opened his mouth to reply, but was interrupted by the glittery edged laughter of the Dark Queen. One moment the air beside him was empty, the next she was there, luminous as the moon in a midnight sky.

"How now, Bard Thomas," she said. "What strange tales do you tell our guest?"

The musician gave a short bow. "My lady, I do but discourse on the wonders of the realm."

The queen smiled at him, but there was a sharpness to it. Tam shifted uncomfortably. He wouldn't want to be on the receiving end of that look.

"Enough talk," the queen said. "Play on, bard. We have a taste for your music this eve."

"As my lady commands." Bard Thomas inclined his head. "Fare well, young knight. I shall play you a ballad ere our time here is done." There was warning in his look, and a message that Tam couldn't decipher.

The queen waved her delicate hand in dismissal, then turned to Tam. "Are you well, bold Tamlin?"

"Yes." He couldn't imagine saying anything but *yes* to the queen.

"Good." She brought one hand to his face and set her fingers lightly against his cheek. A rush of heat and starlight went right through Tam. He barely heard her next words. "Tomorrow you perform a great feat for us, brave knight. Tomorrow we open the Gate."

Her eyes were full of magic and mystery. Tam fell into her gaze, and didn't bother looking back.

## CHAPTER 38

THE HOSPITAL ROOM WAS DIM AND SMELLED OF
disinfectant, but Jennet barely noticed. She rushed to the side
of the bed where Tam lay, and took one of his limp hands in
hers.

Her dad stayed by the door, talking to the nurse who had
shown them to Tam's room. Without taking her eyes from the
still figure on the bed, Jennet listened.

"What's the prognosis?" her dad asked.

"We can't say at this point," the nurse answered. "He's in
a coma now, and seems stable. If there's no change in the
night, we'll run some tests tomorrow."

"The doctor mentioned possible brain trauma?" Her
dad's voice was strained.

"Sir, we really don't know anything yet. Our specialists
will be in first thing to take a look at him."

Jennet squeezed Tam's fingers. It was horrible, the way
they were talking about him. Like he wasn't even a person

any more. Oh Tam. For the hundredth time, hot tears rose in her eyes. It didn't seem like she was ever going to run out of them. Her body could shrivel up and desiccate, and she'd still be crying for Tam.

"Did his family arrive?" her dad asked.

"Yes, Mrs. Linn and her younger son are here. They went to the food court, I believe, but should be back soon. If you'll excuse me, I need to get back to the station."

"Of course. Go ahead. We'll just..." Dad cleared his throat. "We'll wait here."

Jennet listened to the nurse's shoes squeak down the hall. Then there was only the quiet beeping of the machines Tam was hooked up to, the hum of technology. Despair sloshed through her. The hospital could run a million tests, and never find out what was wrong with Tam. Did they have a machine that could tell when somebody's soul had been sucked into the Realm of Faerie? She didn't think so.

She had to go back, confront the Dark Queen and get Tam free - before Dad had the system taken apart. Now that she had her mortal essence back, she felt so much stronger. But would she be strong enough?

Voices sounded from outside the door. Jennet looked up as two people walked into the room - a solemn-looking boy and the frail woman who had opened the door the time she had gone to Tam's. They halted when they saw Jennet and her dad.

"Mrs. Linn?" Her dad had his hand out. "I'm Steve Carter, and this is my daughter Jennet. Your son was at our house today when the, er, accident occurred."

Tam's mom ignored the outstretched hand. "What did you do to my boy?" Her voice was low and full of pain. She turned and fixed Jennet with a hollow expression. "What did you do to him?"

"Nothing." It came out a whisper.

How could she possibly explain to this fragile woman with dark-circled eyes that her son had sacrificed himself inside a computer game?

"Now, Mrs. Linn," her dad said. "I've arranged for you to stay in a hotel nearby, and all your meals until... That is, the hospital will do everything they can to determine—"

"I just want him back," Tam's mom said.

*Me, too.*

The little boy came to stand beside Jennet. He peered at the bed, then turned to look at her. Green eyes regarded her, so much like Tam's that her heart squeezed tight with pain.

"I'm Peter," he said. "But you can call me Bug if you want."

"Hi. I'm Jennet."

"I know." He looked at the still figure in front of them. "I think he's still in there."

"So do I."

Peter leaned forward. "Hey Tam," he said loudly into one ear. "Wake up. Mom will make you some eggs if you do. And your computer is almost fixed." He turned back to Jennet. "I broke his sim-system," he said. "Not on purpose. I was fixing it. But it didn't fix right. Tam says you have a really sparked system."

"Yes."

She didn't want to talk about this. Behind her, Jennet could hear Dad speaking to Tam's mom. His voice was low and reassuring, and she wished she could take some comfort in it. Knowing more than your parents was a terrible thing.

After a fidgeting moment, Tam's little brother spoke again. "So, do you know Puck?"

"What?" Shock ripped through her like lightning. She glanced over her shoulder, but the adults weren't paying attention. "What do you know about Puck? And keep your voice down."

Peter's eyes widened, but his reply was soft. "One of those scary nights, when we were in the fort, I woke up and it was still dark out, and Tam was talking to this little guy." He screwed his face up. "Puck. He was just floating there in the air. He looked like a Pokemon who got old."

"What did Puck say? Do you remember?" Jennet leaned forward. Her body felt like it wanted to take off, explode into action and run, run.

"Mhm." Peter nodded. He didn't say anything more.

Impatience flared, making her chest tingle with urgency. "Can you *tell* me what he said?"

"Yeah. He said..." Peter cocked his head to one side, clearly fishing for the memory. "He said *heed the old ballands 'cause your lady waits*."

"Anything else?" There had to be something more. Puck was obscure, but he'd give more than this slim hint. He had to.

"Nope. What's a balland?" Peter's green eyes were wide,

full of questions. If Puck had said anything else, the kid wasn't remembering.

Jennet wanted to kick something and yell. Instead she squeezed her eyes shut, folded her hands into quiet fists, and concentrated on what Peter had told her. *Heed the old ballands.* Ballads? That made more sense. One of Thomas's old books was filled with ballads about the faerie-folk. She hadn't thought to look through those. They were just songs.

"Are you ok?" Tam's little brother took her hand. His grasp was sticky and warm.

Jennet opened her eyes. "Maybe. A ballad is an old song that tells a story."

"What's a *heed*?"

"It means to pay attention to something."

Maybe, just maybe, there was a ballad that could help. She glanced at Tam. His expression was still, his hair, for once, pushed back from his face and staying that way. The machines surrounding the bed gave off steady blips and beeps.

Ok. Halloween wasn't until tomorrow. There was still time. Crazy hope sputtered to life in her heart. She had to get Dad to take them home, so she could start looking through her books right away.

"Who's waiting?" Peter asked.

"Who what?" She pulled her attention back to the kid holding her hand.

"Puck said *your lady waits.*" He gave her a tentative smile. "Are you the lady? I hope you are. Your hair is pretty."

*I hope I am, too.*

## CHAPTER 39

In the grav-car on the way home, Dad talked. Jennet let the words wash over her. He'd explained things to Tam's mom. Tam's family would be taken care of, and VirtuMax would pick up the bills.

"Obviously it's the Full-D hardware." Dad was thinking aloud. "The wiring, the interface - we have to figure out what's gone wrong. The company can't ignore this. We can't go into production."

At least the game wasn't going to be released. But what would happen when the company didn't find anything wrong with their system? Would Dad believe her then?

Back at their house, they had a quiet dinner. As soon as she had pushed her food around enough to look like she had eaten, Jennet pleaded a headache and retreated to her room. She went straight to her bookshelves and scanned the titles. Where was that old ballad book?

Heart clenching, she pulled books out and piled them in

haphazard stacks. There - *English and Scottish Popular Ballads*. Relief made her fingers tremble as she traced the faded green lettering on the cover. She opened it, wrinkling her nose at the faint musty odor clinging to the pages, and scanned the table of contents.

The ballads were listed by number, not title. She flipped to the section where the songs about the faeries were, and started reading. The Elfin Knight, The Wee Wee Man....

An hour later her head was full of images. Silver bells braided into a horse's mane, jewel-studded goblets made of red gold, faeries leading humans astray. Humans tricking faeries in return. But nothing, so far, about escaping from the Realm of Faerie.

She turned the page, read the title of the next ballad, and froze. Then reaction set in - a punch to the gut that left her gasping. She blinked, but the words remained, the script indelible on the page.

### *Tam Lin*

Heart thudding, Jennet read the song.

A mortal girl named Janet must rescue her true love from the Faerie Queen. Oh god, how could this ballad be here? How could a song hundreds of years old be about her and Tam? Her hands shook as she turned the page, her mind hazed with disbelief.

*THE NIGHT IS HALLOWEEN, lady,*
    *The morn is Hallowday,*
    *And for to win me, win me well*

*Take heed to what I say.*


JUST AT THE *mirk and midnight hour*
*The faerie folk will ride,*
*And they that would their true-love win*
*At Miles Cross must bide.*


JENNET SWALLOWED, the flavor of fear sharp in her mouth. Halloween was tomorrow. And even though she had no idea where it was, she had to be someplace called Miles Cross at midnight. There was enough time for her to go in-game and find it. Except that she couldn't let Dad catch her - and he'd probably told HANA, and... damn. All right, she'd figure that out later.

Taking a deep breath, she bent over the book and read.

When she finished the ballad, a shiver ran through her. Did the Dark Queen really have that kind of power?

"Jennet?" It was Dad, knocking on her door. "Are you feeling any better?"

She shut the book and slipped it under of one of the stacks around her. "Yes. Come in if you want."

Dad opened the door, but stayed at the threshold. "It's getting late. I know it has been a... a hard day, but try and get some sleep. It will help."

Finding the ballad helped more, but she nodded. "All right. You too, Dad - you look tired."

He did, tired and sad and old. Pushing the books aside,

Jennet stood and went to the door to give him a hug. Even at her age, it was comforting. Probably for both of them.

"Ok, honey." Dad let her go with a weary smile. "Have a good day at school tomorrow. I'll get off work early, and we can go see how Tam is doing."

Even though her mind was clamoring for her to turn on the sim and go in-game, to find Miles Cross, to get ready, she knew she couldn't risk it. If Dad found her playing tonight, there would be no way she could get back into Feyland. No. She'd have to wait until late tomorrow. If she still had a system to play on, that was.

"Um, Dad? Maybe you should wait to pull out the Full-D systems. So that everything is still there, in place. Just in case..."

She wasn't even sure what she was trying to argue. If Tam didn't make it, would the police, or anyone, care if they had removed the system?

Dad frowned. "I see your point. We'll leave the systems intact for now - though it probably won't be an issue. Tam is getting the best of care."

It sounded like he was trying to convince himself, too, that everything was going to be all right. Still, her dad was a stickler for the rules. If he said the Full-D was staying, then it would.

One obstacle down. At least she'd *have* a system to sneak onto. She had the feeling she had to do it exactly as the ballad said - which meant waiting until tomorrow, Halloween, at the 'mirk and midnight hour.'

All she had to do was make it through the next twenty-four hours. All she had to do was act normally while despair and hope and eerie ballads collided inside her head, so hard that she felt she was about to implode.

"Goodnight, Jennet. I love you."

"You too, Dad. 'Night." She shut her door. Sleep felt a thousand miles away.

Somewhere, in the dark, Tam's body lay quietly, kept alive by the hum of machines. Somewhere, in the dark, the Wild Hunt slipped free, fey hounds baying through the desperate night.

# CHAPTER 40

TAM STOOD UTTERLY STILL AS TWO FAERIE MAIDENS swirled about him. One fixed gilded oak leaves to the front of his tunic while the other wove a cloak of cobwebs about his shoulders. The faerie glade was glittering with excitement, but none of it touched him. He felt as if there were a layer of fog between him and the world. Between his thoughts and his heart.

In the shadows, Bard Thomas strummed his guitar. Silvery riffs of music blended with the laughter and motion of the fey-folk, and the words of Thomas's song lilted to Tam.

*"Tonight so mirk and deep we ride,*
*Depart unseelie from the glade,*
*This Hallow's Eve the Hunt will bide,*
*To pay the tiend the Faerie Rade."*

Half of it sounded like gibberish, but it was clear the faeries were getting ready to go somewhere. And taking him with them.

"Brave Tamlin." The Dark Queen's voice slid over his senses like midnight silk.

He turned his head to see her standing beside him. Her dress was layers of moon-dappled cloud, with pale glimpses of her skin beneath. The scent of night-blooming flowers perfumed the air with their secrets. He felt dizzy.

"My lady," he said.

She moved to stand before him, her slim body so close it made his skin vibrate. Her slender fingers caressed his cheek. Then she leaned forward and brushed her lips against his. Stars exploded through his body, a rush of painful sensation like blood returning to a frozen limb. She tasted of spices and wild honey. Like everything perfect, and forbidden.

An instant later, the kiss ended. Tam clenched his hands. If he reached for her, she would slip through his grasp like smoke, laughing.

"You are strong and fair, my knight."

"I..." Someone else had called him her knight. For a bare second Tam remembered pale hair, a soft smile - and then the memory was gone. Lost to the dusky magic of the faerie realm.

A hint of sorrow touched the queen's voice. "A bonny offering you make. Would that I could keep you."

"What's going on?" Vague curiosity uncurled inside him.

"You fulfill your destiny, brave knight. And ours. Now - to the final preparations."

The queen held a mask in her hands. Tam caught a glimpse of gold and crimson laid in opulent patterns. She lifted it to his face, and his vision narrowed. Directly in front of him stood a hairy brown figure holding the bridle of a white horse. Gold and crimson caparisons draped the steed, and tiny silver bells were braided into its mane. They chimed, high and delicate, as he mounted.

Before him, the Black Knight handed the queen up onto a chestnut brown horse. Then the knight mounted his own dark steed and held up one black-gloved hand.

The clearing grew still, the air hushed and expectant.

"Now, my court," the queen said, her words falling, clear as frozen crystal, into the silence. "Now the gateway lies within our grasp. Now we ride!"

It was late - way late. Jennet lay in her bed, watching the numbers glow on her clock while her body grew cold and tight with fear. Ten. Ten-thirty. Light still shone from the crack under her door. What was Dad doing? Why didn't he go to bed?

Every nerve in her body was screaming for her to go, go, go! Jump out of bed and get in-game. Save Tam, before it was too late.

But she couldn't risk it, even though her stomach churned with fear. Not until Dad turned off the lights.

Finally, at eleven-oh-five, the house darkened. Jennet forced herself to wait another few minutes before silently slipping out of bed. The thick carpeting made her feet noise-less as she tiptoed down the hall. There was a game she used to play - moving so slowly and silently that she wouldn't trigger HANA's sensors. She held her breath and hoped she hadn't forgotten the knack. She trailed one hand along the wall, careful to avoid the table at the corner. There was no way she could explain her way out of this if she were caught.

She closed and locked the game room door behind her, wincing as the lock made a quiet metallic noise. Still feeling her way, she fumbled for the jamming field switch. It hummed to life, and she let out a breath. Her lungs felt like they were made of metal, impervious to air.

The sim chair powered on smoothly, and Jennet pulled on the helmet, the gloves. Time to go.

Feyland unfurled, and she plunged into the swirl of golden light.

She landed, as usual, in a grassy circle, then fell to her knees while sick shudders racked her. Gasping, she fought back the sensation. Tam. She couldn't waste time vomiting in a faerie ring. She had to find Miles Cross.

As soon as she stepped over the mushrooms, a thin hand tugged at her robes. "Quickly, quickly," a high voice said.

"Puck?" She held up her staff. The blue glow illuminated the figure of the sprite. His usual grin was gone, and he danced back and forth with impatience.

"Of course it is I. Follow!" He dashed down the path.

Jennet gathered her skirts in one hand and ran after him. It was bad, if the sprite wasn't even giving her cryptic hints and riddles. They must be nearly out of time.

They burst out of the forest of pale trees into a midnight landscape. Shadows lay heavy on the land, and there was no moon.

"Puck - where are you?" The blackness pressed against Jennet. She swallowed the sourness of her own fear.

"Here!" The sprite grabbed her robes again and towed her forward, at a speed that made her stumble.

Up one hill, then down. Up another, pressing forward through brambles that raked at her skin. Breath rasped through her throat.

Puck was grimly silent. Only the constant pull on her robes let her know he was still there.

Up ahead, a faint light shone through the dark. She squinted and made out a single lantern hanging from a post, illuminating the pale dust of two roads crossing. A crossroads.

"Miles Cross?" she gasped.

"Hurry!" Abruptly, Puck's grip on her eased.

She whirled, but the sprite had disappeared. With his last command ringing in her ears, Jennet sprinted forward.

# CHAPTER 41

JENNET RAN INTO THE PALE CIRCLE OF LIGHT AT THE crossroads. The silence of the night was marred by her great, gasping breaths.

Nobody here yet. She had made it in time. She wrapped both hands around her staff and tried to get her breathing back under control.

She could make out a circle of standing stones in the darkness across the road. The trembling rush of her blood steadied as she looked at the stones, faintly illuminated by the lantern. Wait. She blinked and looked again. The stones themselves were softly lit, as though they were glowing with centuries of absorbed starlight.

A noise pulled her attention back to the road. Something was coming, something still distant - barely felt in the vibration of hooves, the faint drift of chiming bells.

Her heartbeat slammed through her chest. She had to hide - but where? Not the stone circle, it was too far. Her gaze darted around the shadowed edges of the light. There, a bit of leaves with a darker mass behind. A thorny bush, just big enough for her to crouch behind. She hurried behind it and knelt down. The soil was cool beneath her knees and a prickle grazed the back of one hand, but it was the best she could do.

There were lights moving along the road, some twinkling, some steady. The sound of bells was stronger. A soft wind swirled around her, carrying the scent of spice and frost. The Dark Queen's court was approaching. And with them, Tam Linn.

The words of the ballad ran through her head. She had read them over and over all day, until she felt the shape of them burned into her brain.

OH FIRST LET PASS *the black horse,*
>   *And then let pass the brown,*
>   *But quickly run to the milk-white steed*
>   *And pull the rider down.*

TAM WOULD BE RIDING the white horse. She'd grab on to him - and then the transformations she'd read about would begin. No matter what, she had to hold on.

Something tickled the back of her mind. Something essential she had forgotten. Come on, what was it. Think! She covered her ears with her hands, trying to block out the sound of the imminent faeries. Trying to block out the fear that rose in a dark, suffocating wave. The ballad said... it said...

*AT LAST THEY'LL turn me in your arms*
    *Into a naked knight,*
    *Then cloak me in your mantle green*
    *And cover me from sight.*

THAT WAS IT; the green cloak. Oh god, she'd nearly lost before she'd even begun. She drew in a ragged breath, trying to imagine it in perfect detail. Long green cloak. With a hood.

"A mantle green." She whispered the words.

It appeared, lying soft and heavy in her arms. She pulled it on, awkwardly, since she was kneeling on the ground, and tied it around her neck. Now she was ready. Barely.

The Dark Court slowed as they reached the crossroads. From her hiding place, she scanned the ranks of creatures. The very front of the company was led by a row of figures in pale armor, lances prickling up, faces covered by their helms. Behind them cavorted redcap goblins, their faces grotesque, their teeth glinting and sharp.

Other creatures, half-animal in form, trailed them. Was that walking clump of brown hair Fynnod? Before she could tell, a faerie with the head of a bird and feathery wings blocked her view. A delicate bevy of maidens followed, their hair like spun moonlight, silver bells edging their gossamer robes.

And behind them.... she shivered. The Black Knight riding his black charger, forbidding in his midnight armor. Then came the Dark Queen, beautiful as an eclipse, on a chestnut mare. Jennet's mouth went dry and she shrank down behind her bush, which suddenly felt far too small to conceal her. The black horse, and the brown. Where was the white horse?

The company halted and the queen spoke. Her voice was the edge of twilight, full of mystery and dark promise.

"My court, long have we waited. Long have we languished while our strength waned, deprived of the essence that sustains us. But on this eve we renew the land. On this eve we reclaim our ancient birthright. On this eve we open a gateway to the mortal realm!"

A clamor of fey and feral voices greeted her words. The queen raised one hand, and the noise subsided.

"Honor our sacrifice," she said, "for he is a brave knight, and true. And now, we shall pay the tiend. Onward - the stones await!"

The faeries surged forward, and Jennet bolted to her feet. Fear sliced through her, sharp and unstoppable. Where was Tam?

The Black Knight thundered past. Next came the queen, her gaze fixed on the stones ahead, her face lit with unearthly beauty. Finally, finally, a white horse. The rider was garbed in gold and crimson glory, an ornate mask covering his face. It had to be Tam. Had to be. Jennet flung herself forward.

The horse was tall, but she was desperate. She managed to get her arms around Tam's waist, even though he didn't stop. Her shoulders burned as she was dragged forward. There was no traction, no way to pull him down.

"Tam!" she yelled. "Get off the horse! Tam, do you hear me?"

He didn't even glance at her - it was like she didn't exist. Jennet swallowed the desperate sob building in her throat. She couldn't hold on much longer.

From the corner of her eye, she saw a figure overtaking them. Some fey creature, ready to strike her down. Fingers numb, she ignored it and kept holding onto Tam. The figure drew up on the other side of the white horse.

"Get ready," a voice called, and Jennet jerked her gaze up to see an achingly familiar face. Thomas. Here to help.

She nodded, and Thomas set his hands to Tam's unresponsive shoulder. He gave a shove. Tam teetered a moment in the saddle then, finally, fell. Jennet's arms were locked around his waist as together they tumbled backward to land in a bone-jarring tangle on the ground. Her side burned and she couldn't grab a breath. The mask slid off to reveal Tam's face, his eyes wide and confused.

"Tam!" Air whooshed into her lungs. She leaned forward and kissed him, a quick, relieved press of her lips to his. They would get through this. "Can you stand up?"

It would be easier to hold on to him that way. Her right arm was twisted uncomfortably underneath his waist, but she didn't want to tug it free. Hold on - no matter what. Hold on.

"Jennet?" Tam shook his head, sending a swatch of brown hair across one eye. He sat up, and she shifted her grip, both hands tight around his arm. "I—"

A blast of thunder shook the sky, the sound so deep Jennet felt more than heard it. Her whole body vibrated, and she nearly lost her grasp on Tam again. The air brightened, as though the sun had leaped into the sky. She looked up, then wished she hadn't. The night sky was now a tattered cloth, the stars blazing white-hot behind the scrim of dark, shedding an eerie, furious glow.

Around them, the fey-folk were crying out and covering their heads. The orderly procession was now a panicked jumble, the sound of bells clashing and discordant.

"HALT!" The queen's command filled the air, like an echo of thunder.

Silence followed - an awful, frozen silence. The only movement was the Dark Queen, her face filled with a terrifying wrath as she rode to where Jennet knelt beside Tam.

"Brave knight," she said, turning the force of her midnight beauty on Tam. "Rise, and mount again. The circle lies but nine paces on, and you shall be safe therein."

Jennet bit her lip, hard. If Tam wanted to pull free, she didn't know if she could fight him. "Tam," she breathed.

He gave no sign that he'd heard her.

The queen's face softened and she held out one delicate hand. "Come."

"No," he said. "I'm safe right here."

Jennet swayed with relief. Then she saw the queen's expression and stiffened again. It wasn't going to be that easy. Of course not. There were all the transformations to get through. She tightened her hands around Tam's arm.

"No?" The queen's voice was a killing frost. "If you will

not take leave of this mortal, then I shall make *her* take leave of you." She raised an arm and cast her voice over the eldritch crowd. "The final price then they will pay, 'ere I cry Tamlin's away!"

Whatever that meant. Jennet looked at Tam, about to urge him to get up again, but the words stilled in her throat. He was changing, his features flattening out grotesquely, his limbs disappearing... she couldn't hold his arm anymore because he had no arm.

The icy laughter of the Dark Queen cut through her panic. Jennet reached forward and grabbed what Tam was turning into. Scales slid under her palms, but she hugged him tight against her. The smell of something dry and ancient assaulted her nose. The body pressed against hers was one long rope of writhing muscle.

*Snake!* the primitive part of her brain shrieked, but she made herself hold on. Even when a sibilant hiss made her look up, right into a fanged mouth. Even when she felt the coiled tension that signaled it was about to strike.

A single whimper crawled out of her throat.

Hold on. No matter what.

The scales under her hand roughened, turned to fur. Another smell, rank and greasy, assaulted her senses. Tam had regained limbs, but they ended in wicked-looking yellow claws. Instead of fangs, she was confronted with a bear's mouth, full of rending teeth.

Oh god. Hold on. It was Tam, under all that coarse black hair. He wouldn't bite her. Please, don't let him bite her.

The bear opened its mouth wider. She threaded her

fingers into the fur and squeezed her eyes closed. The roar, when it came, shook through her. Midway through it changed from a bear's bellowing to the threatening growl of a great cat.

She forced her eyes open, and met the feral gaze of a lion. *Run!* the mouse inside her squeaked. Death and ruin in those yellow eyes.

Don't let go.

From a distance, she heard the Dark Queen's voice, raised in wild chanting. The huge, furry body in her arms began to shrink and darken. It grew heavy and cool, one moment a live thing, the next inert metal in her hands. She looked down and blinked. A bar of iron lay in her palms.

They were almost done.

# CHAPTER 42

THE IRON BAR BEGAN TO GLOW. A SULLEN RED AT FIRST, it started to give off heat, like a stove that had just been turned on. Jennet's palms tingled, then stung, but she didn't dare shift the bar from hand to hand. She couldn't risk dropping it.

The metal got brighter, and with it the heat. She gritted her teeth and held on, despite the scorching in her hands. Despite the pain, the blisters forming on her skin. Her breath came in little pants, dry and shallow. Hold on.

The bar flared crimson. Too. Hot. Each breath carried a sob with it now, a high, keening noise she barely recognized as coming from her. She couldn't... hold on. Dammit. Hold *on*.

It was like clutching a piece of the sun. So bright she couldn't look at it, a pulsing gold-red that seared itself against her eyes. She couldn't take her hands away - it felt as though the molten metal had fused itself to her body.

Agony burned into her bones. Her throat hurt, and it took a moment for her to realize it was because she was screaming. There was nothing left. Only pain.

And then it was over.

She bent, dry-heaving, tasting nothing but sour bile. She couldn't feel her hands.

"Jennet?" It was Tam's voice, shaky and close. "Hey, Jen. Look at me. Right here."

She straightened, met his worried green eyes. All traces of his elaborate costume were gone. He knelt before her, naked.

"The cloak," she gasped, fumbling at the ties. "We have to cover you." Her fingers weren't working - there was something wet and slick getting in her way.

Tam reached out and helped loosen the cloak, and together they spread it over him. When she drew the hood over his face, her hands left dark blotches on the cloth. Blood.

The Dark Queen swept up to them. Her eyes held hurricanes.

"Ill met, Fair Jennet," she said, her voice cold with rage. "You have stolen the fairest knight in all my company."

Jennet scraped in a breath. "You stole him first. I just took him back."

She had, hadn't she? A tremble started, low in the pit of her stomach, the first unbelieving stirrings of triumph. They had won.

"Brave Tamlin." The queen turned to Tam, her voice changing to smoke and sorrow. "If I had seen what would pass this night, I would not have stayed my hand. Your mortal heart betrayed us. Better by far if I had taken it and given you one of stone."

"I'd rather be mortal," Tam said, "than sacrificed so the faeries could rampage through the human realm. You lost."

The air grew chill. Frost sparkled in the Dark Queen's hair. "The gateway remains closed, 'tis true. For now."

"Forever," Jennet said.

God, she hoped so. She couldn't go through this again. Her hands felt like lumps of wood attached to her wrists. If she looked at them, she knew she'd be sick.

The queen lifted her fingers and traced a silvery symbol in the air. "Begone from here, mortals. Be gone!"

The eerie starlight brightened to gold, and a wind began to whirl about Jennet and Tam. The edges of the cloak he was wearing lifted and spun.

"Wait!" Jennet reached for him. "Tam—"

Too late. Her words were lost in a flare of swirling light as she was hurtled back into her own world.

She fell into the sim chair with a whimper. Somehow her helmet and gloves had come off - and the chair next to her was empty. Where was Tam?

The door to the game room banged open.

"Jennet!" her dad yelled, running to the chair and thumbing off the jammer. "What the hell are you doing? I told you the system was dangerous and - oh my god." He was staring at her hands. "What happened to you? HANA! Call George - and get me an emergency kit, right away."

"*Of course. Here you are, sir.*" A cupboard door popped

open from the wall. Dad pulled a medi-pack out and ripped it open.

"Jennet, your hands..."

Finally, she looked down. Bile rose in her throat, and she wished she hadn't. Her hands looked like raw meat. The skin was gone, and blood oozed to the surface. They had hurt before, but seeing the damage made the pain blaze up. Hot tears pricked her eyes.

"Sorry, Dad," she whispered, then tried not to cry out as he laid plas-skin bandages over her palms. "I had to save Tam."

Face set, Dad just shook his head. "I'm taking you to the ER."

"Central Hospital?" She had to find out if Tam was all right. What had happened to him when the Dark Queen flung them back into the mortal world?

She was probably grounded for life. But as long as Tam was all right, she didn't care.

## CHAPTER 43

"WE HAVE TO ASK ABOUT TAM, DAD." JENNET KEPT HER voice low, though it didn't seem like anyone else in the ER waiting room was remotely interested. The pain in her hands was a distant, fuzzy thing, numbed by the plas-skin Dad had slathered on and the pills he'd made her swallow.

"Not until we get your hands looked at."

She knew better than to push it, though hope and worry knocked through her with every breath. At least she was in the same hospital as Tam.

It didn't take long for the med techs to get to her. They peeled off the plas-skin, making worried, interested noises.

"How'd this happen?" one of the techs asked.

"I, um, touched something hot." She couldn't meet Dad's eyes. It was true, just not in any way he could understand.

"More than touched it, I'd say." The tech shook his head. "Luckily, it looks like you got the plas-skin on in time to stop any permanent nerve damage. You're not going to be able to use your hands for a while, though."

"Ok." As long as Tam was all right, it was worth it. Was he all right? The question pushed through her, insistent as her own heartbeat.

Finally, they were done. Her hands were numbed and re-wrapped, and Dad finished signing the last of the forms, and then tucked his tablet away. In response to her pleading glance, he gave her a weary nod.

"We'll ask at the main desk," he said. "The techs here have enough to do without checking on a patient already admitted."

"Thanks." Her voice trembled.

The windows in the main corridors showed a pale sky. Dawn. All Hallow's Eve was over.

The woman at the main desk looked up Tam's record. "I don't see any change," she said. "Visiting hours start at seven, if you'd like to go up then."

Jennet peeked at the desk display. "That's only ten minutes from now. Please, could we go up early? He's a good friend." She lifted her bandaged hands and set them carefully on the counter. Playing the sympathy card.

"We're here now, after all," Dad said.

"Well..." The woman shook her head, but she was smiling. "Okay. But don't tell them I sent you."

"Thanks so much." Jennet hurried to the bank of eleva-tors and pushed the button with her elbow. It was strange to have no working hands.

As the elevator doors closed behind them, Dad cleared

his throat. "Jen. I know you think that the game has something to do with Tam's condition. And I know you think you were able to change it. But you should be prepared for the fact that he's still in a coma."

"I know." Worry shivered across the back of her neck. But no matter what the receptionist had said, *something* had to have changed.

They got off on the fourth floor. Nobody was at the nurse's station. Ignoring Dad's cautionary look, Jennet marched down the hall to Tam's room and peeked in the half-open door.

Three med-techs crowded around Tam's bed. His mom was there, too, and his little brother. She slipped inside, holding her breath until she could catch a glimpse of him.

Tam. He was awake, hair falling across his face, green eyes open as he nodded at something a med-tech had said. Her heart opened like the sun breaking free.

Tam's little brother looked up, and caught sight of her. He gave her a big smile. "Hey, Jennet! Tam waked up."

Tears itched the back of her eyes. "Yes."

She stepped forward, and one of the techs made room for her at the side of the bed. Behind her, she felt Dad's solid presence. He put a hand on her shoulder, apology and forgiveness in that touch.

"Jennet," Tam said.

Just her name, but it was enough. Their gazes locked. He was pale, and his eyes held shadows. Shadows she knew lurked in her own - memories of Feyland and their battles against the Dark Queen.

"Hi." She wanted to touch him, but her hands were unwieldy lumps of gauze.

He reached for her, instead, and set one hand on her wrist, just above the bandages. His fingers were warm and alive, and her skin tingled at the touch.

They had won.

THAT NIGHT, Jennet dreamed she was in Feyland. She stood in a meadow of pale flowers. Above her the sky was pink with approaching dawn, and the air tasted of magic and possibility. There was a peaceful hush on the land, as though at any moment birds would break into full-throated song.

"Jennet?"

She turned to find Tam standing beside her. The light breeze ruffled his hair and pulled at his T-shirt. It was strange to see him without his armor. He smiled at her, something tentative and tender in his eyes.

"Hi," she said.

A thousand other words danced on her tongue, things like thanks and sacrifice, fear and joy, hope and longing. Love. She didn't know where to begin.

"Are you ok?" he asked. "I mean... it was a little confusing there for a while."

"I'm all right. But how could you sacrifice yourself like that, Tam? I nearly lost you."

Her heart clenched at the memory. She wanted to shake

him. She wanted to throw her arms tight around him and never let go.

"I had to." His eyes held hers, their expression unguarded. "Trading myself for you was the only way. But I'm glad you figured out how to free me."

"Me, too." She had to look away from him, or she'd start crying. "Puck helped, though. And Thomas."

"Thomas. Do you think we'll ever see him again?"

"At least once." The quiet answer came from behind them.

Jennet whirled, to see the bard. The first sunlight lay on his cheek and glinted in his wise and weary eyes.

"Thomas!" She hugged him, hard. "I was so afraid...but your book of ballads had the answer, and then you helped..." The tears she'd tried to hide from Tam tipped over onto her cheeks.

"Hush." Thomas stroked her hair. "Your battle with the Dark Queen is over now. The gate remains closed. You and your champion both sacrificed much, but you have won."

"What about you?" she asked. "Can you come back to the real world now?"

He shook his head, and she pulled away. She should have known better than to hope. Her voice trembled. "Will I see you again?"

"Perchance. I have an inkling that the magic of Faerie is not yet done with the two of you." He looked at Tam. "Guard your lady well, bold knight."

Tam stepped up beside her and slid his arm around her

shoulders. He felt warm and solid - a strength she could lean into.

"I will," Tam said. "And she's watching out for me too, you know."

Thomas nodded. "Then I bid you both farewell. And good luck."

He began to fade as though he were made of mist. Jennet could see the pale bells of the meadow flowers through him, the transparent half-smile on his face.

"Goodbye, Thomas," she whispered as he disappeared.

Then there was only empty air, and birds singing. And Tam beside her, holding her, strong and true.

He looked at her, his green eyes so serious. Slowly, he dipped his head, bringing their faces close. His hair brushed over her cheek and she tilted her mouth up to meet his. Their lips touched in a perfect kiss.

Jennet closed her eyes. Light spread through her, like she'd sipped the sunrise.

No matter what happened next, she and Tam would face it. Together.

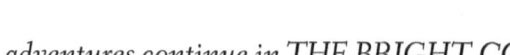

*The adventures continue in THE BRIGHT COURT*
*Discover what's next for Tam and Jennet...*

## THE BALLAD OF TAM LIN

*I forbid you maidens all*
*That wear gold in your hair*
*To come or go by Carter Hall*
*For young Tam Lin is there.*

*Janet has kilted her kirtle green*
*A little about her knee,*
*And she has braided her yellow hair*
*A little above her bree,*
*And she's away to Carter Hall,*
*As fast as she can hie.*

*When she came to Carter Hall*
*Tam Lin was at the well,*
*And there she found his steed standing,*
*But away was himself.*

*The steed that my true-love rides on*
*Is lighter than the wind,*
*With silver he is shod before,*
*With burning gold behind.*

*She had not pulled a double rose,*
*A rose but only two,*
*Till up then started young Tam Lin,*
*Says, 'Lady, pick no more.*

*And once it fell upon a day,*
*A cold day and a snell,*
*When we were from the hunting come,*
*That from my horse I fell;*
*The Queen o Fairies she caught me,*
*In yon green hill to dwell.'*

*'And pleasant is the fairy land,*
*But an eerie tale to tell,*
*Aye at the end of seven years*
*We pay a tiend to hell;*
*I am so fair and full o flesh,*
*I'm feared it be myself.*

*The night is Halloween, lady,*
*The morn is Hallowday,*
*And for to win me, win me well*
*Take heed to what I say.*

*Just at the mirk and midnight hour*
*The faerie folk will ride,*
*And they that would their true-love win,*
*At Miles Cross must bide.*

*Oh first let pass the black horse,*
*And then let pass the brown,*
*But quickly run to the milk-white steed*
*And pull the rider down.*

*'They'll turn me in your arms, lady,*
*An adder and a snake;*
*But hold me fast, let me not go,*
*To be your worldly mate.*

*'They'll turn me to a bear*
*And then a lion bold;*
*But hold me fast, and fear me not,*
*As ye shall love your child.*

*'Again they'll turn me in your arms*
*To a red hot bar of iron;*
*But hold me fast, and fear me not,*
*I'll do to you no harm.*

*At last they'll turn me in your arms*
*Into a naked knight,*
*Then cloak me in your mantle green,*
*And cover me from sight.'*

*Gloomy, gloomy was the night,*
*And eerie was the way,*
*As fair Janet in her mantle green*
*To Miles Cross she did go.*

*About the middle of the night*
*She heard the bridles ring;*
*This lady was as glad at that*
*As any earthly thing.*

*First she let the black pass by,*
*And then she let the brown;*
*But quickly she ran to the milk-white steed,*
*And pulled the rider down.*

*So well she minded what he did say,*
*And young Tam Lin did win;*
*Then covered him with her mantle green,*
*As blithe's a bird in spring.*

*Out then spoke the Queen o Fairies,*
*Out of a bush of broom;*
*'She that has gotten young Tam Lin*
*Has got a stately groom.'*

*Out then spoke the Queen o Fairies,*
*Out of a bush of rye:*
*'She that has gotten young Tam Lin*
*Has the best knight in my company.*

*Had I but known, Tam Lin,' she says,*
*'Before I came from home,*
*I'd taken out that heart of flesh,*
*Put in a heart of stone.'*

Collected by Francis James Child, *English and Scottish Popular Ballads,* published in 1882, though the actual ballad dates several hundred years earlier.

## ACKNOWLEDGMENTS

Thank you to the many people who made this book possible: the encouragement of my terrific CP Peggy, fabulous proof and beta-readers Colin, Sean (aka Captain Grammar Pants), Chassily, Marissa, Nicole, Kaitlynn, and Brynn. My patient and supportive in-house editor, Lawson, and keen-eyed reader Ginger. Thanks also to Annette Nishimoto for copy-editing.

For great design work, Ravven, and for the inspiration to move forward, gratitude to Kris, Dean, and PG.

Finally, for all the adventures in-game, epic thanks to Sylven, Dom, and Fates Legion that was.

For other wonderful YA retellings of the ballad of Tam Lin, Anthea recommends Elizabeth Pope's *The Perilous Gard* and Diana Wynne Jones's *Fire and Hemlock*.

## Want the Prequel for FREE?

Only available to newsletter members ~
Experience Jennet's *FIRST ADVENTURE*

Join today to get your free copy!

https://www.subscribepage.com/AntheaSharp

## ~ THE FEYLAND SERIES ~

*What if a high-tech game was a gateway to the treacherous Realm of Faerie?*

THE FIRST ADVENTURE (Newsletter only)

THE DARK REALM

THE BRIGHT COURT

THE TWILIGHT KINGDOM

FAERIE SWAP

SPARK

BREA'S TALE

ROYAL

MARNY

## ~ THE DARKWOOD CHRONICLES ~

*The hidden world of the Dark Elves is discovered by a mortal girl... romance and adventure ensue~*

ELFHAME

HAWTHORNE

RAINE

**~THE DARKWOOD TRILOGY ~**

WHITE AS FROST

BLACK AS NIGHT

RED AS FLAME

**~ VICTORIA ETERNAL ~**

STAR COMPASS

STARS & STEAM

COMETS & CORSETS

**~ STORY COLLECTIONS ~**

TALES OF FEYLAND & FAERIE

TALES OF MUSIC & MAGIC

THE FAERIE GIRL & OTHER TALES

THE PERFECT PERFUME & OTHER TALES

MERMAID SONG

# ABOUT THE AUTHOR

*~USA Today* bestselling, award-winning author of Fantasy-flavored fiction ~

Growing up on fairy tales and computer games, Anthea Sharp has melded the two in her award-winning, bestselling Feyland series, which has sold over 150k copies worldwide.

In addition to the fae fantasy/cyberpunk mashup of Feyland, she also writes Victorian Spacepunk, and fantasy romance. Her books have won awards and topped bestseller lists, and garnered over a million reads at Wattpad. Her short fiction has appeared in Fiction River, DAW anthologies, The Future Chronicles, and Beyond The Stars: At Galaxy's edge, as well as many other publications.

Anthea lives in Southern California, where she writes, hangs out in virtual worlds, plays the fiddle with her Celtic band Fiddlehead, and spends time with her small-but-good family.

Anthea also writes historical romance under the pen name Anthea Lawson. Find out about her acclaimed Victorian romantic adventure novels at

www.anthealawson.com

Be the first to hear about new releases and reader perks by subscribing to Anthea's newsletter, Sharp Tales.

www.antheasharp.com